Mr Harris Makes It Up

Also by Francis Prendiville
(co-authored with Nigel Toye)

'Drama and Traditional Story for the early years'
published by Routledge/Falmer 2000

'Speaking and Listening through Drama 7-11'
published by Paul Chapman Publishing 2007

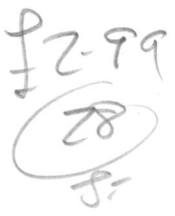

Mr Harris Makes It Up

F X Prendiville

Matador
Unit E2 Airfield Business Park,
Harrison Road, Market Harborough,
Leicestershire. LE16 7UL
Tel: 0116 2792299
Email: books@troubador.co.uk
Web: www.troubador.co.uk/matador
Twitter: @matadorbooks

Paperback ISBN 978 1803137 407
Hardback ISBN 978 1803137 414

British Library Cataloguing in Publication Data.
A catalogue record for this book is available from the British Library.

Printed and bound in Great Britain by 4edge Limited
Typeset in 12pt Adobe Garamond Pro by Troubador Publishing Ltd, Leicester, UK

Matador is an imprint of Troubador Publishing Ltd

For Vivien
With Love

Author's Note

This story is set in the years 1977 and 1978 when the far-right fascist party, the National Front, was at the height of its electoral success in the U.K. Alarmingly, there were at this time teachers who shared this party's toxic world view. So, the challenge in writing this tale was how do you reflect the reality of a fascist teacher in the staffroom? In chapter five there is a racist slur, also in chapter thirteen, both spoken by a racist character. I wanted to convey how awful these people were and I hope I got the balance right.

Francis Prendiville

But if I imagine myself as a sort of jovial carnival barker, trying to usher you into my magical black box, the workings of which even I don't fully understand – that, I can do.

"What's going to happen to me in there?" you ask.

"I really don't know," I say, "but I promise I've done my best to make it thrilling and non-trivial."

"Will there be any joy in there?" you ask.

"Well, I hope so," I say. I mean that's what I was trying to feel as I made it so..."

George Saunders
A Swim in A Pond in the Rain

Contents

Summer Term 1978

AUTUMN TERM

⸻ ⦵⦵⦵ ⸻

1977

One

The Unsavoury Kidney

Union Street Junior School, Manchester

A voice, deep from within the Welsh dragon's lair.

— Come in, boyo.

Graham swallows hard, takes a breath and pushes the polished brass fingerplate. The hefty door creeps open.

— Not late, am I, Mr Jenkins?

— No, lad. Twenty minutes 'til I ring the school bell. Sit you down, bach.

That's a 'boyo', a 'lad' and a 'bach' in two sentences. Graham Harris, 27 when he stepped into the head's office, is now sitting on his hands like a nine-year-old.

— Mr Harris, I'm sure you can guess why I've asked you to pop your 'ead round the door.

He can. He swallows hard once more.

— Yesterday's assembly, Mr Jenkins?

Jenkins moves behind his captain's chair, grasps the back and leans into Graham.

— Yesterday's disaster, boy.

Graham shifts nervously.

— I've 'ad Mr Formby accusing me of presiding over a 'Whitehall farce' while Aiden Wright's dad is demanding replacement tracksuit bottoms, what with the old ones 'avin melted with friction burns.

Graham studies his platform shoes. No point arguing. You try something different, something exciting for the bottom stream untouchables. Something that will grab their attention and... it's not appreciated.

— Look, bach, you've only been with us six weeks. I know your heart's in the right place but an assembly about the functions of the kidney, well... it's different. You'd obviously gone to a lot of trouble.

He had. Shoeboxes marked 'Urea' and 'Glucose'. A slide into a children's paddling pool labelled 'The Bladder'. Two hours cutting out the fluorescent yellow lettering.

— But, like Miss Broadstairs said, 'Where was Jesus?'

Miss Broadstairs. Graham had watched her, massaging her temples, pulling faces as if she was sucking a lemon. He knew what kind of class assembly she'd do. A dollop of the Good Samaritan followed by meaningless mumblings of Our Father, Harold be thy name. Meanwhile, her henchman, Syd Formby, would patrol the class lines checking whether lips were moving, ready to drag any mutes to the front for ritual humiliation.

In Graham's 'Kidney' assembly, children were having fun, swaying and clapping to the sounds of Tomita's Moog synthesiser blasting from a tape recorder, faces a crop of smiles in full bloom. If Syd hadn't taken umbrage, climbed onto the stage just as Aiden shot along the urinary tract, a collision might have been avoided. You can't blame Aiden. Syd, of all people, is familiar with the defence, 'I was just obeying orders'.

Graham registers a protest.

— He shouldn't have called Aiden a scruffy little mongrel. He can't help being poor, Mr Jenkins.

Taffy's tone mellows.

— OK. He went too far. But you 'aven't 'elped yourself by bringing that Anti Nasty League mug into the staff room.

— Anti Nazi League, Mr Jenkins. And Neil Kinnock is a supporter.

— Well, whatever. It upset old Syd.

The headteacher returns to his chair and does a quarter swivel to face the latest recruit to his teaching staff.

— I'll support you all the way. But your next assembly, try to make it a bit more traditional, eh? From the Bible?

— So something about Jesus, Mr Jenkins?

— Or Moses, boy.

Graham realises he's being dismissed and shuffles backwards, bowing to Emperor Jenkins as he exits. Pulling the door closed, the handle feels as cold as Miss Broadstairs' heart. Once he's in the corridor, he squeezes his eyes closed, cringing at his pathetic self-defence. An opportunity to put the case for his class, to show his support for the underdog... and he's blown it.

— You might well pull a face, Mr Harris.

It's her. Hands on hips, full double teapot with added scowl.

Her dyed-black Jackie Kennedy flick-ups are stiff with hair lacquer. She's a walking fire hazard.

— I take it he's spoken to you about yesterday's debacle.

— He had words.

— Good. I'm glad to hear it.

There's a smirk in her voice. Graham knows he should walk away but he can't stop himself.

— What you and Syd Formby can't abide is an assembly where the children actually enjoy themselves.

— Enjoy themselves! Your bottom stream hasn't got time to enjoy themselves. They'll be in secondary school next September. No time for fun and kidneys there, young man.

Her raised voice is sharpened by the acoustics of the glass-roofed corridor. School's early arrivals scurry past, not daring to lift their eyes from the concrete floor. Graham blows out his cheeks.

— OK. You can tell your mate Formby I'll do a Bible story next time. I'll need lots of ketchup, though.

— What are you talking about?

— Gospel according to Matthew. Massacre of the Innocents. Heavy on ketchup, that one.

— Blasphemer!

Miss Broadstairs forearms Graham aside and sweeps into the office.

— Headmaster. A word.

Jenkins clears his throat.

— Leave the door open, if you don't mind, Miss Broadstairs.

Indignation quickening his pace, Graham seeks sanctuary in his classroom. He tramps out into Manchester's waterlogged landscape. Crossing the girls' playground, dark clouds have ganged up to hand out a meteorological lashing. Soaked, he makes a pit stop at the staff toilet. He grips the wash basin and stares into the plug hole. A spider's leg strokes the pitted chrome, seeking purchase. Spidey has a choice: life in the dark drain or a dash to freedom across the cracked, grimy porcelain. Just pray no one turns the tap on. Graham lets it run on to the back of his hand.

— Don't worry, Spidey, I won't wash your dreams away

He gently deposits it on the windowsill.

In the mirror, Graham's Kevin Keegan curly perm is damp and bedraggled. He dries the lenses of his black Buddy Holly glasses with a crumpled handkerchief.

Addressing his reflection, he rewrites his argument with Taffy.

— I'll make the next assembly biblical if that's what they

want, Mr Jenkins. Moses, you say? Well, how about Moses and the burning tobacco bush? An anti-smoking theme. My star player, little Andrew Wiseman, can be the gangster, Al Veoli.

There's a hoot of laughter from one of the cubicles behind him. It's the caretaker, Don Middleton, Graham's one and only ally at Union Street Junior. He's an old acquaintance of Graham's dad, a fellow caretaker, and he's kept an eye out for Graham since he arrived. Caretakers' brotherhood. Don wheezes a smoker's laugh as he drags a mop and bucket noisily from the cubicle. His brown overalls are frayed at the cuffs; half a dozen biros and fountain pens fill his breast pocket like medals crowding a veteran's blazer.

— Al Veoli! S'pose young Miriam's gonna play the part of a gangster's moll, Bron Keyhole, eh, Bomber?

Don's sharp, terse, upper-class voice bounces off the green tiled walls. His accent belies his appearance. Close your eyes, you imagine an RAF wing commander, fat handlebar moustache, blue uniform with glinting brass buttons, pointing his swagger stick and issuing orders. Instead, emerging from the stall is a stubby, 60 something with a cannonball of a head. His moustache is limp, his grey-flecked brown hair combed over. From fighter pilot to school caretaker in a few alcohol-fuelled slips down the stepladder of life. There are stories, rumours — a crashed jet, a dishonourable discharge. Who knows? He doesn't talk about it and no one asks. The closest he ever got to a confession was a rueful, 'I was a fool to meself. A fool to meself, Bomber'.

The kids love Don. They greet him with smiles and waves, unperturbed even when he's barking orders at them.

— Andrew Wiseman, get off the milk trolley before you break your neck, lad!

— Sorry, Mr Miggleton.

Don leans on his mop.

— How long have you been talking to yourself, old boy?

Graham points a finger at him.

— You'd talk to yourself if the boss had hauled you over the coals for someone else's cock-up. Syd Formby climbed on that stage and hijacked my assembly because the kids were enjoying it so much. He just had to bring it to an end.

— Yah, I heard. Little Aiden told me all. Said Formby shouted at him in front of the whole school. Out of order in my book.

— Syd's a nasty piece of work, Don. But I won't give up. I refuse to be one of those teachers who bores everyone rigid with Bible-bashing tedium. Kids like doing little plays and so do I. Even if it gets up the nose of the old guard.

— Man on a mission, eh?

Graham raises his eyebrows non-committedly.

—Anyway, Mr Missionary Man, there's a posse of lost sheep waiting for you in the classroom.

— Right-oh, Don.

As Graham marches away, Don calls after him.

— Don't worry, Bomber, I won't tell anyone you talk to yourself.

His words dissolve into another phlegm-filled cough.

Consigned to a prefab, built as a 'temporary' measure 30 years ago, the bottom stream class of Four Harris, aka 4H, lies away from the school buildings, just inside the perimeter railings. A paint peeling, dirty white, forgotten outhouse.

Sally-Anne, Miriam and Andrew are sitting on desks, their legs swinging out of sync. They look up in unison as Graham walks in. Andrew appears pensive.

— You ask him.

— Ask me what, Andrew?

Sally-Anne purses her lips, brushes her pleated navy skirt, clasps her hands together as if she is about to say grace.

— We want to know if you're OK. After yesterday, sir.

— I'm fine.

She frowns. Miriam has her Bay City Rollers scarf slung around her neck and signals to speak by jiggling the tassel.

— Yes, Miriam?

— We was worried. You in trouble 'cos of Mr Formby?

She replaces words ending in 'y' with an 'eh' sound. 'Form-beh'.

— Sally-Anne heard Mr Jenkins say he wanted a word with you. She clocked yer looking miffed.

Sally-Anne misses nothing. Miss Marple in embryo. She slips off the desk and speaks precisely.

— I was worried, Mr Harris, because last time I heard Mr Jenkins ask a teacher if he could have a word, I never saw him again.

She's referring to the time Mr Clarke was caught *in flagrante* with a dinner lady in his stockroom. Miss Broadstairs claimed she'd heard animal noises and had gone in to investigate. Taffy sent Mr Clarke home that very day. According to Don, Clarkey and his lover moved to Norfolk and set up a petting zoo.

Mr Harris tries to reassure the posse.

— I know the assembly didn't end well, but it wasn't your fault. And we've got another chance next week...

Andrew beams.

— Oh, top for that, sir. We loved the kidney thingy.

The girls grin. Miriam twirls her scarf.

— What we gonna do, sir?

— Well, I'm thinking of something on the dangers of smoking. Moses and the burning tobacco bush.

— Sir! Sir! Sir! Can I be Alexander Fleming? That man who collected spit. I saw a programme on telly about him. And I can talk dead good Scotch, sir.

Miriam's eyes enlarge.

— Sir, me and Lorraine and Alyson and Anna, we could do the music.

Graham is infected with their enthusiasm.

— Of course. A musical. How about Bay City Roll-Ups, Miriam?

She frowns, not impressed, but Andrew is.

— Like it, sir! What d'yer think, Sal?

— It's Sally-Anne, Andrew, not Sal.

Sally-Anne turns back to Mr Harris.

— My daddy says, 'It's not the cough that carries you off, it's the coffin they carry you off in.'

Andrew mouths 'What?' at her.

The bell rings.

— OK. Mr Jenkins insists we must do something from the Bible this time. Think Moses and his Technicolor Tobacco Pipe.

The posse exchange bemused frowns. Mr Harris gestures for them to exit.

— We'll do more planning with the rest of the class. Now, off you go to line up. You've got hymn practice this morning.

A collective moan goes up before the girls, laughing, grab each other's hands and bound out of the building. Andrew hangs back.

— Sir, Karl's the best smoker in our class. He does smoke rings *and* blows out of his nose, like that Smaug you was reading to us about. Bonfire night he won a comp to flick fag butts over the boys' toilets. Marlon's brother Ant'nee was well impressed and he rolls 'is own.

— Careful, Andy, we don't want smoking to look cool, do we?

He winks.

— I get you, sir. Wait 'til I tell the lads.

He breaks into a run.

Two

Soldier, Soldier

Leaning back in his chair, Graham wedges his knees against his desk and surveys the class who are quietly submerged in Tuesday morning arithmetic. The only sounds are Lorraine's liquid sniffles and the tick–clunk of the Manchester Education Committee wall clock.

Lorraine,

Sniff-slurp.

Clock,

Tick-clunk.

Rows of wooden desks of light brown beech, carved, defaced, Quink-spattered, each with a redundant inkwell stuffed with sweetie papers. The walls lined with dark oak cupboards, dusted and smudged with primary colours and crammed with sugar paper, crayons, tins of powder paint; heaps of newspapers and rows of jam jars; tobacco tins chock-full of cracked wax crayons, flaking chalks and brittle charcoal sticks, bunches of fat filbert paint brushes with nothing fine in sight. The furniture is as tall as a top junior and three times as old.

Sniff–slurp.

Tick–clunk.

Four desks to a row, two pupils to a desk. Four by four and two by two. A carpenter's shopping list. In his head, Graham can hear Syd Formby as he delivers another of his pronouncements in the staffroom.

— There's plenty of wood in Harris's class. That lot, thick as two short ones. Enough timber to build an ark.

Syd Formby is Noah and Philomena Broadstairs, Mrs Noah. Old Testament, both of them. Angry, harsh and vengeful. Syd is building an ark at Union Street Juniors, the upper deck for Formby's toffs, with Harris's lot in steerage. Top stream and the untouchables. Mrs Noah has devised a home-spun selection test. Sort the sheep from the goats.

Can yer speak proper? Does yer talk dead good? Is yer scrawl top scribble?

Sniff–slurp.

Tick–clunk.

And so it is written, 'They shall not *all* enter the kingdom of Formby'.

Sniff–slurp.

Tick–clunk.

Graham squints through the poorly lit room. There's not much light in steerage. But here they are, doing 'maffs'.

Tick–clunk.

Sniff–slurp.

Sally-Anne sighs. She can't concentrate: Lorraine's sniffles are just too distracting so she pulls a handkerchief from the waistband of her navy blue school skirt, leans across the aisle and drops it on Lorraine's desk. Graham surveys his charges. A nest of baby cuckoos.

Tick–clunk followed by a handkerchief-filling trumpet.

Slumping down, Andrew nestles his head in the crook of his arm, squashing a prominent ear. He sucks the end of his pencil, a comforter. A sour glance from Sally-Anne signals her disapproval. He turns the page of his textbook, a slim, green, tired paperback, *Mathematics, More Practice*. Sally-Anne has a version with a darker cover, *Even More Practice*.

The sound of Mr Formby's class on the move seeps in from the playground. Their talk and laughter are like the smell of fresh doughnuts, an irresistible distraction. Whispered alerts break the silence. Andrew voices the concerns of others.

— What they doing? It's not playtime.

Sally-Anne flicks through her pocket size diary.

— Nope, they're not timetabled for the baths today.

— Mr Harris! cries Andrew. Mr Formby's class are goin' out!

Graham shares his puzzlement.

— They are, Andrew. They are.

Andrew eases himself up, chin raised, head swivelling, peeping over the edge of the nest. His blonde hair curtains his big, flat-pan face. He can see Mr Formby, immaculate in his midnight blue barathea sports jacket and beige cavalry twill trousers, striding ahead of his elite troops who skip and run to keep up. Andrew wonders aloud.

— Why? he says. It's not their swimming. Or PE.

His blue, doe-like eyes dart in search of clues as to why 'maffs' has been so unexpectedly and mysteriously disrupted. Others bob up and down to catch a glimpse of the manoeuvres outside. Mr Harris reminds them of the task in hand.

— Back to *More Practice*, 4H.

— *Even More Practice*, says Sally-Anne.

Formby's top-stream intelligentsia file into the school's main building while Mr Harris's class return to the clock ticking, occasional nose blowing mathematical monotony.

Suddenly there's a noise; the sound of a side drum beating somewhere in the distance. Heads rise. Bewildered glances are exchanged. Outside, marching across the netball court, a soldier, a Redcoat. His long, pillar box red tailcoat has white lapels, glinting brass buttons. Gold silk piping edges the coat and the cuffs of his sleeves. His red trousers tuck into white leather gaiters that stretch from the ankle to above the knee, crumpled and loose fitting with black buttons down each side.

As he marches, he strikes the drum which swings in time with each step. The barrel of his musket, slung over his right shoulder, rocks back and forth like a metronome. Two white straps across his chest; one attached to the drum, the other clipped to a white canvas bag for the shot. His features are sharp, his hair cropped and a stern expression signals the seriousness of his task.

A scramble as everyone pushes back their chairs and heads for the window. Andrew's there first. All around him there's pushing, shoving. An Aintree racecourse, Becher's Brook jostle. A David Cassidy fan club grapple to get a better view. Some leap onto their chairs. Only one remains at his desk. Chintagan has too-recent memories of Sri Lanka and knows you don't rush to the window when you hear the crack of a drum; it might be a gun. He blinks hard behind his gold-rimmed wire spectacles.

The soldier stops and marks time in the centre of the playground. He looks confused. Seeing 4H's faces at the classroom window, he resumes his advance, keeping time with his drum. Thump. Thump. Rat-a-tat thump. Thump. Thump. Rat-a-tat thump. His coat tails sway to the rhythm of his gait.

Mr Harris is as confused as the rest of the room and attempts to restore order.

— Whoa! Back to your desks, please.

— It's a soldier, Andrew shouts. He's got a gun. Whoa, yis!

Chintagan's forehead wrinkles underneath his black basin cut fringe. Graham catches his eye with a reassuring, don't worry shake of the head. Chinti ducks down once more. Graham's voice moves up an octave.

— Will you please get away from the window? *Immediately.*

Ghazala puts her arm around Chinti.

— Not a prob, Chint. It's just a teacher dressed up.

Chinti, his eyes squeezed shut, allows her to steer him towards their classmates who, deaf to their teacher's pleading, have formed a mob at the window. Karl, tall for 11 with a greasy quiff that adds to his height, strikes a casual pose at the back. Hands flat in his pockets, he wiggles his thumbs.

— It's not a gun, Wiseyman. It's a rifle, right?

Sally-Anne chimes in.

— Actually, it's a musket.

With a swish of her blue-bobbled ponytail, Lorraine emerges from the scrummage.

— Sir! Who is he?

— Whoever he is, could you please return to your seats? You're supposed to be doing maths.

Marlon is defiant.

— C'mon, sir, this is top.

— Well, we'll have a little look. Then back to maths, OK?

Marlon's thumb springs up.

— Nice one, sir.

Lorraine, her eyes huge, grabs Miriam's arm.

— I'm scared, she squeals.

Robert's gruff voice is woven with the coarse hessian of a Manchester accent.

— He looks well smart, sir. That Serena Fullerton in Mr Formby's said they was 'avin another visitor. From a theatre group or summat.

His voice takes on a pleading tone.

— Sir, how come them gets treats, and we have to do boring maffs?

Graham feels nettled. An actor! His class would love a visit from an actor. But no, it's another privilege for the select few. Privilege heaped upon privilege. There's something rotten in the state of Union Street Juniors. But then Graham has an idea and suddenly he sniffs the scent of sweet revenge in the air. Syd Formby is about to be stood up.

— Back to your desks. Quick, before he comes in.

Miriam shouts out.

— In here?

She tenses every muscle as if she's expecting to be drenched by a bucket of freezing water.

Andrew bellows.

— Whoa!

As the soldier vanishes around the corner of the prefab, Graham rushes to the fire door at the back of the classroom to ambush him as he passes. He pushes the door open, startling the soldier who comes to an abrupt halt.

— Mr Formby?

— No. Mr Harris. A change of plan. We're in here now, not in the hall.

— Are they ready?

— They can't wait. The door's around the corner.

Glancing at his three gold stripes, he adds,

— Sergeant?

— Sergeant Hughes.

— Welcome to our world.

— Good. On with the motley!

In the classroom, the boiling liquid response to the first sighting has fast chilled to an ice sculpture of seated pupils staring at the classroom door.

Marching feet move around to the prefab entrance, every other step accompanied by a thump on the side drum. Graham grabs a piece of paper and scribbles a note.

'Redcoat confused. Missed the Highlands ended up in the Lowlands. Shame to stop him in full flow. Best tell your lot to stand down. G.H.'

He hands it to Sally-Anne.

— Take this to Mr Formby in the hall. Fast as you can. Don't wait for a reply. Use the fire door, it'll be quicker.

— Yes, Mr Harris.

Three
Hijack!

Military boots clack along the corridor. Andrew scrambles to open the classroom door. He pulls it back to reveal the soldier and salutes. The soldier, splendid in his red and white uniform, holds a pose for a moment, framed in the paint peeling door casing.

Janine is aghast.

— Look at Wiseyman! Plonker.

Graham intervenes.

— Well done, Andrew Wiseman. Just what our guest is looking for: keen recruits. Isn't that right Sergeant Hughes?

— It is, Mr Form... er... Mr Harris.

Andrew stands rigidly to attention, his fingers pressed hard against his forehead. He's up for it. He's not sure what: maybe that's part of the attraction? In the playground, he's the writer, director, lead, stuntman and, of course, if only briefly, a dead body. 'Pretending' has stepped into the classroom, and he's comfortable with it.

The Redcoat soaks in the scene before him, eyeing each pupil. Unsmiling, his tone is solemn.

— A word with these loyal citizens of good King George, Mr Harris.

Andrew remains statue-still, maintaining his salute.

— At ease, soldier. You can sit down now.

— Yes, sir! Andrew shouts, throwing back his head before dropping obediently onto his chair.

Miriam stifles her laughter.

The Redcoat unhooks the drum from his belt and places it on the floor. Dipping his shoulder, he unhitches his musket and leans on it, clasping the end of the barrel with both hands, like a shepherd resting on a crook.

— My name is Sergeant Hughes of the 20th Foot Regiment. I've come to ask for your help. Our good King George needs volunteers. Honest English men and women to fight these troublemaking Scots. I have good news. The battle against this rabble has been a great success. We thumped the Scottish rebels.

Andrew clenches his fists and exclaims as if a ball has burst the back of the net at the Stretford End.

— Yis!

The Redcoat stares at him.

— You're right, soldier, it was a great victory, but we need to finish the job. We need to round up those wild Highland heathens and civilise them. That's where you come in.

— Yes, sir, Mr soldier man.

— Sergeant Hughes, if you don't mind.

— Sorry, Sarge... I mean, Sergeant Hughes, sir!

There is more laughter, but Andrew is immune to the mockery.

The Redcoat carefully places his musket against the frame of the blackboard. Digging into his pocket, he pulls out a parchment map and pins it to the frame of the blackboard as the children gather round. Graham notices Sally-Anne slip back into the classroom through the fire door, her mission to Formby's class complete. She gives a quick thumbs up. Graham squeezes between Chintagan and Aiden. They stand at the back, as far away from the soldier as they can get.

Timid little Aiden seems destined to spend his whole life at the back of the crowd, never able to see what's happening. He's happiest as Don Middleton's helper. He follows Don everywhere. They stare into dark, smelly drains together. Aiden fetches and carries buckets, rags and mops. He'd much rather be with Don than play with the other children. If Don isn't in, he hangs around in the playground, hands in his pockets, at a loss. If he is ever allowed to join in a game of football, it's as a ball fetcher. Graham lifts him up and stands him on a chair. Aiden turns and smiles at his teacher.

— It's good, dis, intit, sir?

The soldier's gaze meanders over the group. His tone is grave.

— It's a long march to Culloden Fields. It won't be easy.

Janine is worried.

— Mr Sergeant, sir?

— Yes, soldier.

— When do we leave?

— Today. After playtime. There's no time to lose.

Aiden looks uneasily at Mr Harris.

— Sir, I can't go. Me dad will shout if I don't get straight home and polish his work boots.

Graham places his hand gently on the child's shoulder.

— Don't worry, Aiden. It's a play. We won't really be going anywhere.

The boy balloons his cheeks and lets the air out slowly.

— Phew, sir. Thought I was in dead trouble then.

The Redcoat pushes his thumbs into his belt.

— An army needs to be fed. There are tents to be erected, horses to graze, a thousand jobs to do.

Ghazala whispers to Miriam.

— I wanna look after the 'orses.

To reassure her, Miriam links arms with her friend. She admires Ghazala's mustard-coloured silk kurta and strokes the gold and chocolate brown embroidery on the sleeve. She angles her head to Ghazala's ear.

— I'll do the 'orses wiv yer.

Ghazala tightens their looped arms, an affectionate smile on her lips.

The soldier continues.

— Miss Sellars is the boss, and she pays well. You'll get one and sixpence a day and your keep.

Sally-Anne puts her hand up.

— Does Miss Sellars fight for King George? What's in it for her?

— What's your name, soldier?

— Sally-Anne, Sergeant.

— I'll remember you. You'll go far. Miss Sellars needs the Highlands to graze *her* livestock, not waste it on crofters with their scraggy sheep and meatless cattle.

— Sergeant, what are crofters? asks Pauline.

— Small-time Scottish farmers. Troublemakers. No use to anyone.

Pauline frowns and whispers, 'Troublemakers' to Aaron.

— One final thing. Discipline. Remember, the officers will stand for no nonsense. Soldiers out of line will face the lash. But don't worry, you'll be fine with me.

Again, Aiden turns anxiously to Mr Harris.

— It's OK, Aiden. The sergeant and I will look out for you.

His hunched shoulders fall; he relaxes. The Redcoat stretches to his full height.

— So, be careful what you say to Miss Sellars. Have I made myself clear, troops?

There's a weak, mumbled response of 'Yes, Sergeant'.

Drawing his musket to his side, he addresses his battalion fiercely.

— I can't hear you, soldiers! Do I make myself clear!?

— *Yes, Sergeant!*

He shouts again.

— Yes, Sergeant HUGHES!

The children call back once more, delighting in the chance to shout in the classroom.

— Yes, Sergeant HUGHES!

The fictional world of soldiers, Highlanders and battles has dropped like a silk parachute to cover them all. The 23 individuals who were doin' maffs a few minutes ago are now a loyal, tightknit fighting force. Only Karl looks sceptical and doesn't shout out. He's reserving judgement on all this play-acting.

Sergeant Hughes shifts to the at-ease position. Surveying the class, he nods his approval.

— Now, I'll rejoin the 20th Foot Regiment, and I'll see you all in the hall after you've had your playtime. Good day to you all.

He gathers his side drum, swings his musket over his shoulder and does a sharp about-turn. Andrew rushes to open the door. Chin forward, his neck muscles rigid, he salutes as the sergeant leaves. The sergeant throws Graham the briefest glance. It says, 'I'm looking forward to this, Mr Harris'.

The playtime bell rings. Fizzing with excitement, 4H stream out of the classroom. Graham sits at his desk to take stock. OK, he's hijacked Syd's visitor but, in his own defence, he could reasonably argue that visitors make mistakes when they're in unfamiliar surroundings, don't they? Nevertheless, there will be consequences. Worth it, though. A slice of history marches into the classroom, fires up the class. Their faces! Engrossed. Rapt. Anyway, Syd destroyed Graham's assembly; now, in return, Graham has hijacked Syd's visitor. A sweet revenge.

Outside, children are running, screaming, squawking, skipping, laughing. A girl in a green puffa jacket and red bobble hat leans against the railings. She's been left out. She frowns at everyone around her. Then suddenly, her face brightens and she dances back to the play, throwing away her unnoticed sulk.

In the brief time Graham has been a teacher, he's watched children play, usually while on playground duty, a steaming mug of tea in his hand. This morning, his classroom had been illuminated by the joy of playtime. Unlike out there, it wasn't chaotic: it was managed, focused. How was that done? Oh, to hijack that skill!

The third-year bottom stream teacher, Dennis Oldham, pushes the door open and angles into the room like a figurehead on the bow of a ship. His Zapata moustache widens as he grins.

— I've just heard what happened. It was supposed to be *The Highland Clearances* not *Kidnapped*.

Graham rests his hand on his chin in mock thinking mode. Dennis continues.

— Well, be warned: Syd the Staffordshire bull terrier is looking for you.

He raises a mug decorated with blue and orange flowers.

— I've brought your tea over. One sugar, lots of milk. Better go: I'm on whistle.

He dumps the cup on the windowsill. Through the window, Graham watches Dennis make his way back to the playground, turning up his collar against the chilly wind. As he passes Lorraine, she salutes Karen who, in turn, stands to attention. Ghazala and Miriam feed and groom a horse. Janine is the horse.

Four
Guilty as Hell

Syd Formby strides across the girls' playground. He makes no allowance for hopscotch, jacks and lines of girls awaiting their turn in skipping games. Children retreat to avoid being trampled on or pushed to one side out of Syd's way. As Graham watches through the classroom window he feels a prickle of unease. A blazing row with Syd would risk a premature end to the Redcoat's visit. It'd be the kidney assembly all over again. The class would be deeply disappointed, and so would their teacher. No, he decides, better to lie low. This is guerrilla warfare and tactics need to be considered carefully. Choose your battleground, Graham tells himself. Take the rap after the event. Let the class have their drama, then deal with the consequences.

As Syd advances Graham is puzzled by the look on his face. It's not anger. A sneer? A smirk? Disdain? No time to hang around. Graham grabs the stockroom key and darts down the prefab corridor, ignoring the steaming mug of tea that Dennis had left for him on the windowsill. He unlocks the stockroom door but then drops the key. No time to pick it up, though. He slips inside and flicks off the light before grabbing the handle and leaning against the door to keep it shut. The snick–clack of Syd's steel-tipped heels announces his approach. Graham holds his breath until it seems Syd has marched past the stockroom. Phew! Graham relaxes while endeavouring not to retch as he takes in the pungent, damp smell of dirt-smeared footballs, the musty, mouldy stench of netball bibs, the stale aroma of unwashed football kits, all laced with the odour of dank shinty sticks, smudged with dog faeces. Public park perfume. If it were a perfume, it would be called 'Scent from Hell' by Formby. Graham's heart thumps inside his ribcage as a booming posh voice shouts,

— Trotsky! Are you in there?

Oh, how Graham despises the nickname Syd bestowed on him the day he brought in his Anti-Nazi League mug.

Without warning, Graham's sweaty hands slip on the door handle. He falls backwards into a metal dustbin that holds 12 shinty sticks. There's an almighty crash. The door opens and Syd flicks on the light. He stands over Graham, a key dangling from the fingers of his outstretched hand.

— Lost something?

Graham clambers out of the bin and smooths his trousers, trying to look nonchalant. As he reaches for the key, Syd drops it to the floor.

Graham stoops to pick it up, muttering.

— Just doing some stocktaking.

— In the dark? Of course, you were. You'll be disappointed to hear your pathetic attempt at hijacking our visitor backfired. In fact, you've just done me a favour, Trotsky. Saved me from wasting a morning playing soldiers with a limp wristed thesp. I got your note from your little pet oddity, Silly-Anne, or whatever you call her, and took my lot straight back to the classroom to do some *real* work. I told them the lesson was intended for the remedials.

— I feel sorry for your class, Syd. They're the ones missing out.

Syd jerks his upper body towards Graham. Graham pulls back. Syd's Friends of the Hallé silk tie dangles in front of him.

— Far from it, Trotsky. Mine are the crème de la crème. The elite. They know visits by theatricals are for the thickies.

And, with that, he clicks the heels of his highly polished black brogues and marches off.

Part two of the drama is safe. Graham clenches his fist, the way Andy Wiseyman does in moments of triumph.

— Yis and double Yis!

***

Graham watches Sergeant Hughes drill the new recruits in the hall. They form two rigid lines, save for Andrew and Robert who are demonstrating their marching skills. They mimic the Redcoat's every move, swinging one stiff arm as they march while shouldering a flat plywood musket with the other hand. They're grinning, unlike Sergeant Hughes who's wearing a severely impassive expression. He stamps to an abrupt halt. The boys stumble to a stop but recover before he turns around. He barks.

— Right then. Much better, lads. You're looking a bit more like King George's army now. Wiseman, Jones, return to the ranks.

Andrew beams as he joins the others. Rob, ungainly and more self-aware, clumps back.

The sergeant places his musket on the floor and beckons the class to gather around. He slips a hand into his jacket and pulls out a silver milk jug.

— Feast yer eyes on this, soldiers!

He clouds the surface with his warm breath, polishes it with his sleeve and holds it aloft.

Aaron approves.

— Wow, that's well expensive.

There follow soft whistles of admiration.

— This, squad, is what's known as booty.

He gestures for the class to move even closer and lowers his voice to a whisper.

— In this job, we get orders to search enemy houses. There's plenty of rich pickings if you keeps yer eyes peeled. But take care, me lads – if you get caught it's a hundred lashes.

A woman's voice, raucous, menacing, rings through the hall.

— Sergeant Hughes! What in heaven's name have you got there?

Dressed in a long black skirt, white blouse and black, funnel shaped hat, the woman marches towards the class, demonstrating her irritation by snapping a riding crop against her boot. A startled Sergeant Hughes tries to stuff the jug back into his jacket but it falls to the floor with a clunk. There's an audible intake of breath from the class. He springs to attention and exchanges a look of terror with the class. The woman in the tall hat picks up the silver jug and holds it under his nose as he stares into the distance. Her voice is raspy. She spits the words out.

— Sergeant Hughes.

He bellows his reply.

— Miss Sellars!

— You know the punishment for being caught with booty?

— Ma'am!

— Strapped to a cannon for one hundred lashes.

His eyes bulge with fear.

— When your troops have locked up the Scottish horde, I want to see you. Then, and only then, will I decide your fate.

— Yes, ma'am!

His posture is taut, head back, chest out. His spine and long legs form the convex profile of an English longbow.

Miss Sellars glowers at the class.

— Let this be a warning to you. Anyone found with booty will get a lashing.

She stuffs the silver jug into a satchel hanging from her shoulder.

— Sergeant, show me what this lot can do.

***

It's the end of the school day and Graham takes a break from outlining a mural that runs along the back wall of the classroom. He picks up Sally-Anne's written record of the morning's events. In her neat, rounded script she has written:

When we arrived in Scotland (the hall) we met Sergeant Hughes again. He drilled us. I stood by Katherine Smith so I didn't have to be next to Andrew Wiseman. I sit next to him every day and he's a pain. We did 'attention', 'at ease', 'aim' and 'fire'. We were given our 20th Foot Regiment badges. I felt like a proper Redcoat. Andrew, Sean and Rob sneaked out. Rob told me they were after some rich pickings from the trophy cabinet outside Mr Jenkins'. They were caught red-handed. They told Mr Jenkins it was allowed because it was booty and they were soldiers and it was a play. Mr Jenkins gave me a note for Mr Harris. When sir read it I thought he was going to say a rude word, instead he said 'sugar' but with a long shush. His face was red and he had to talk to Mr Oldham, quick.

Sally-Anne. Aged 11. Class 4 Harris.

✢✢✢

Little Aiden's writing is crabbed and hard to read. He has composed eight lines, four more than he's ever managed before:

it was dead good doing drama the redcoat got into bother because he nicked a silver jug I think the boss lady was cross because she didn't have a musket like what the soldier did Sean said stuff and got into trouble Mr Jenkins asked me if I had seen anyone with the football cups I said I think Robbo was taking them to be cleaned he said thank you Aidey that's a great help. I am going to tell my best friend Mr Miggleton that Mr Jenkins speaked to me.

Aiden Wright. Aged 10. Class 4H

÷÷÷

Sean Caldwell made me laugh. He cheeked Miss Sellars. 'It's not fair. He's got nowt and you're dead rich!' Miss Sellars told Hughesy to keep his troops in order or they'll be two for a lashing. She gave Sean a mega stare. Sean put his hands in his pockets and whistled. Which is wot he always does when he's told off.

Lorraine O'Hara. Aged 10. Class 4H

÷÷÷

The sarge was holding up the silver jug that he'd nicked. This big voice shouted, "Sergeant Hughes!" Me and Andy jumped like we was caught with ciggies. Miss Sellars went mad with Hughesy. Me and Sean thought she was dead mean so we made a plan to help the sarge.

Robert Jones. Aged 10. Class 4H

÷÷÷

That Miss Sellars said Hughesy was getting a hundred lashes. I was right mad because it was her what stuffed the silver mug in her satchel. I said to Robbo, Hughesy is in for a right leathering. We done a job what helped Hughesy. We got caught. I told Mr Jenkins it wasn't real. It were a play. We still got in bother.

Andrew Wiseman. Aged 11. Class 4H

Having read the children's work, Graham sits at his desk beaming contentedly. The rattle of keys as Don Middleton makes his end-of-the-day 'locking-up tour' brings him back to reality. He decides tomorrow will be dedicated to painting the class mural and pasting today's pieces of creative writing on it. Copies of *More Practice* and *Even More Practice* will be put to one side to make room for art and history. And next week the tables will be turned, the actors are to return and this time the class will be the Highlanders. Graham Harris is the Young Pretender. Long live pretending!

Five

An Inspector Calls

Graham stands outside the Head's open door, looking around self-consciously. He takes his hands out of his trouser pockets and tucks them under his armpits. Finally, he clasps them behind his back in the style of Prince Charles on a walkabout. Taffy Jenkins has his back to him. He picks his way across the second shelf of the bookcase that fills one wall of his study. A figure wearing an expensive looking grey suit is sitting at Taffy's desk, his long legs stretched and crossed. He taps together his polished black Church's impatiently and screws up his eyes to examine the young teacher still awaiting an invitation to enter.

It's the school inspector Dennis had warned him about as they passed on the corridor.

—Watch out, Graham, he'd said, tapping his nose and raising an eyebrow, the Pink Panther's about.

— Come in, boy! shouts Jenkins, sounding chipper.

Graham is a 'boy' once more. A good sign.

— Before you sit down, lad, meet Mr Earnshaw, our very own drama inspector.

— English and dwama, Headmaster. English and dwama.

He makes drama sound like an unwanted younger sibling; one who tags along. Graham shakes the inspector's hand. It's cold and moist, like a leather glove retrieved from a puddle.

— How do you do, Mr Earnshaw?

— Call me John, dear boy.

There's that 'boy' again.

A loud knock on the connecting door to the school secretary's office is followed by the entry of Mrs Groom. She has the air of a housekeeper who has served many years in a stately home. Joan Groom is in her early fifties, old enough to have wiped Graham's nose when he was an infant. Her voice and manner are poised; her heart-shaped face and fading film-star glamour belie her sensible navy cardigan and A-line skirt. She fixes her boss with her hazel, almond-shaped eyes. She knows how to manage Taffy as she has managed the last four head teachers, all male and in the twilight of their careers. She turns to the inspector, addressing him in a business-like tone.

— Mr Earnshaw, there's a call from head office. They said it was important.

— I'll take it in your office, Mrs Gwoom.

Taffy, now at the top of a ladder, is still scanning the shelves. He's chuntering.

— Joan, you 'aven't seen the sherry, 'av you, bach?

— No, I have not, Mr Jenkins.

Her tone suggests she does not appreciate his impertinence. Shaking her head and setting her shoulder-length hair swaying, she leaves, shutting the door gently as if she were exiting a sleeping baby's nursery. Taffy continues his search for the elusive secret sherry bottle.

— Bloody Mrs Topham! She 'ad it last, I'm sure! Promised me she'd refill it.

Mrs Topham is the staff authority on all matters concerning alcohol, including its consumption. Mr Earnshaw returns from his phone call and adopts a new pose. He leans against the edge of the desk, puts one hand into his jacket, Lord Nelson like. He cocks his head, glances at his watch and frowns towards Taffy at the top of the ladder.

— Whenever you're ready, Mr Jenkins.

His tone is clipped, confident, and Graham feels intimidated by his easy self-importance. The grey suit wraps Mr Earnshaw's tall, slim frame snugly, elegantly. His hair is short at the back and sides, a long triangular fringe flopping over his forehead. Graham imagines him standing precariously on a chair in his art deco apartment in Didsbury wearing a striped kitchen apron and conducting Mahler's Ninth with a meat skewer. His sharp angular nose and pointed jaw suggest he was designed by an architect not an impressionist.

There's a voice from above.

— Ah, here it is, bach. At bloody last. It's OK, Joan. I've found it!

Ignoring her reply of, 'found what?', he descends to floor level, in his hand a large grey tome with the words *Secrets of the Edwardian Bee Keeper* emblazoned on the spine in gold Gothic font. He lays it on the desk and opens it to reveal, slotted into a red velvet box, a miniature cut glass decanter and two small sherry glasses. The drinks cabinet of a convivial headteacher.

— Now, how about a sherry, John? Celebrate your move to higher things, eh?

— Most kind, headmaster. Most kind.

— I'll bet you're looking forward to joining the ranks of Her Majesty's Inspectorate. Well deserved, bach. Have you a replacement, may I ask?

— Indeed, I have. A young, enthusiastic advisowee teacher from the Inner London Education Authority. Degwee from the Central School. Abbi Tomkins, she's called. A gal with a lot of new ideas.

Mr Earnshaw takes out a small black diary and flicks through it, dabbing his tongue with his index finger. Taffy, once more upon his throne, glass of sherry in hand, nods discreetly at Graham.

— Graham, says Mr Earnshaw, the headmaster tells me you have an interest in child dwama?

— I do, sir. Mr Earnshaw… er… John. This term we did a drama about the Highland Clearances. First week we were the Redcoats, second week the Highlanders. The kids loved it. Loads of great work from them.

The inspector, still engrossed in his diary, isn't listening. Then he stops, taps a page and raises his eyes.

— Graham, my boy, I'm on the look-out for new weecruits. Each year I run a Woyal Society for the Arts, Dwama Diploma. Would you be interested?

— I would be. Very much so. What would I have to do?

— Straightforward enough. Keep a portfolio of your dwama work. This term you'll need to oversee a couple of class assemblies and at the end of term a whole class performance for staff and parents. Chance to showcase your charges' talents. I'll be there. Maybe invite a couple of councillors, headmaster?

Taffy nods gravely.

— Give the evening some kudos, as 'twere. Then, spring and summer term, you'll be mentored by Miss Tomkins, or rather, *Ms* Tomkins.

He emphasises the 'zzz', and throws Taffy a knowing glance.

— *Ms* Tomkins will introduce you to classroom dwama. Dwama in education, I think they call it. Not my sort of thing. Much pwefer theatre, dear boy. But she's top-dwawer. End of the year, a practical exam and, *if* you cut the mustard, a feather in your cap. A diploma on your study wall.

Graham imagines proudly hanging the diploma on the wall of his one-room bedsit in Whalley Range.

— Headmaster will sign off each stage of your development. Make sure you stay on twack, as 'twere.

Taffy grins at his appointment as overseer. The inspector stands up.

— So, what say ye, me boy? Make an excellent climax to your pwobationary year. Might even tempt headmaster to make you permanent. Eh, Gwillam?

Taffy's eyes grow wide. He hesitates, doesn't say yes.

— Well, er, won't do no 'arm, that's for sure. Keep the boy busy, John.

With a nod, he signals to Graham that a response to the offer is due.

— I'm up for it, Mr Earnshaw.

Taffy begins to show a greater level of interest in the scheme.

— End-of-term play, you say? Finish off the term nice, like.

Mr Earnshaw eyes the top shelf of the bookcase.

— It's so lovely to see younger staff members showcasing their talents. Don't you agwee, Headmaster?

— It's what the lad needs, John. Bit of structure to his ambitions.

— Pencil in Thursday the 15th of December, Headmaster. I'll be here. And I'll bring Ms Tomkins.

Graham sees an opportunity to show what his class can really do.

— Great. I'd love to be involved, Mr Earnshaw... er... sir, John.

Taffy throws his head back.

— Steady, Graham, they've not knighted 'im yet, boy.

The inspector leans over to Graham and offers a clammy hand to seal the deal. He then raises his glass, throws the sherry down his gullet and plonks the glass down on the desk.

— Onward and upward, gentlemen.

Graham opens the door for the inspector who strides past,

tossing his fringe with a flick of his head as he departs. Once he's gone, Graham smiles and feels a warm glow of excitement as he considers what he's agreed to. His class are putting on an end of term play. Taffy is beaming too.

— Well, that'll do you no 'arm, Graham. Get this right and who knows… Put on a little play for the great and good. Bang! Union Street Juniors is on the drama map.

The headteacher regards the lawn beyond the bay window, making an audible adjustment to his false teeth with his tongue. He adopts a more serious tone.

— Couple of things, Graham, bach. First of all, find a suitable published script. Save your own writing talents for the Cheadle Hulme Players, eh? Leave your tales of the bladder, the kidneys and the urinary tract locked in the cellar of your creative mind, boy.

Graham nods. Taffy's expression darkens.

— Second thing is, given your rather underhand intervention regarding our theatre visit the other day…

He makes another realignment of his dentures while searching the ceiling for his next line.

—… your, if I might put it this way, misguided seizure of an actor bound for Mr Formby's class…

Graham shakes his head, faking ignorance. Taffy's eyes narrow.

— Don't look as if you don't know what I'm talking about, lad. I've seen the note you scribbled to Syd Formby.

Graham avoids eye contact and senses his cheeks reddening.

— Syd and his flock missed out… missed out on something *I* had arranged. So, I propose you use *his* class and not your own for the play. What you failed to realise when you snaffled that soldier was: I had a plan, boy. That visit was to have given Syd's class and, more importantly, Syd, an injection of the arts into their daily diet of maths, comprehension and astrophysics. You scuppered it, boy.

He begins to tidy up the sherry glasses and decanter, wiping each glass with his pillar box red handkerchief. Graham tries to make light of the accusation.

— But Mr Formby wasn't bothered, Mr Jenkins. He told me as much. And his class like being little boffins.

Taffy shuts *Secrets of the Edwardian Bee Keeper* with more force than necessary.

— I am well aware he was 'not bothered', boy. But *I* bloody was. You blocked my plan!

He takes a deep breath.

— Anyway, his crew will be more reliable than your bunch. No offence, like, but we can't take a chance with this one. Public performance and all.

Graham's flustered. Jenkins can't do that? Can he?

— But... Mr Jenkins... my class will be good. They love drama.

Taffy is back up the library ladder sliding The Bee Keeper's tipple tome into place.

— If we're going to showcase Union Street, a performance in front of dignitaries, no less, we need to be sure we use the ablest and most confident children. Your future at Union Street is at stake here, lad. Let's not take any chances. Anyway, Syd can take your class for music while you rehearse his class for the show. Build some bridges after recent events, boy.

— But, Mr Jenkins, I already do music with them. *Singing Together*, BBC School Radio. We record it every week. Admittedly it's the tone deaf leading the tone deaf...

The joke misfires.

— Exactly, boy. They'll have the chance to make some proper music with Maestro Formby. Parents will be delighted. No matter what you think of him, Mr Formby has status. He's seen as top drawer, lad. A degree, Royal Northern College and all that.

He steps off the ladder and opens the door, cueing Graham's exit.

— Not another word. And anyway, well done you, as the inspector said. I'll tell Mr Formby to drop in to see you, talk through the arrangements.

Crestfallen, the young teacher leaves. With each step back to his classroom, the implications of having to work with Formby's class become starker. Graham is deserting his own little brood. He has colluded with the elitist system he despises. Worse, he didn't have the guts to stand up for 4H. He should have insisted they were reliable enough to do it. How is he going to explain it to them? They can't stand Formby. They can smell his snobbery, his condescension. Syd in return will be bad-tempered, resentful. Worse still, he'll be free with his hands. Crossing the girls' playground, he imagines one of Formby's top-stream whizz kids bouncing up to Miriam at playtime.

— We're going to do a play for some top people with Mr Harris. Our teacher says you lot are too dumb to remember your lines. Sir will be taking you lot for singing. He says he'll have to dig out some nursery rhymes.

His class will blame him. He's sold them short; he needs to think of an exciting project to make up for his betrayal. Something cooler than a play for posh visitors. Something with bragging rights. But what?

Still mulling this over, Graham enters the classroom. Samantha Greenwood, who's been covering his absence, is stuffing exercise books into a big red and black holdall, her peripatetic kitbag. She smiles.

— Can I just say, your class have been wonderful while you were out. Sally-Anne showed me where everything was, reminded me it's swimming tomorrow and where you were up to in *The Hobbit*. Oh, and Andrew was a sweetie. He helped me get into your locked book cabinet to get Paula's inhaler. I don't know how he did it, but it involved my hair clips.

Graham appreciates her enthusiasm but he's feeling increasingly gloomy.

— You'll have to excuse me, Sam. I need to get the kids' work onto the mural at the back before I leave tonight.

— Would you like me to help you? I'm in no rush home tonight.

She pauses and licks her upper lip.

— So, I could give you a hand.

The door opens. Dennis Oldham pushes his head inside, twitching his luxuriant David Crosby moustache. He sees Samantha and gives Graham a knowing wink.

— Sorry to interrupt. Catch you tomorrow.

Samantha, looking uncomfortable and suddenly anxious to leave, grabs her jacket and holdall. She pauses at the door and addresses Graham.

— Another time, perhaps?

Then sniffs the air and is gone.

Graham returns to putting up the children's work. The mural is almost complete. Thinking about the drama lifts his spirits. It was a revelation. The class discussion crammed with their ideas and enthusiasm. The whole project has been unlike anything he's done before. Far from being a bunch of 'thickies', as Noah and his wife would have it, this class are capable of great work.

Graham picks up and admires a piece of writing titled 'GHAZALA, CLASS 4H, THE HIGHLAND CLEARANCES'. She has illuminated the margins tastefully with yellow and red shadows. He pastes it carefully on to the mural, smoothing the edges away from the centre of the paper with the fleshy part of his hand. The classroom door flies open. It's Syd. Six foot of bulk, hands on hips. He clicks his heels and extends a straightened right arm, hand flat, palm down. Graham freezes in horror.

— I hope that wasn't what I thought it was, Mr Formby.

— If you mean the salute of a Roman centurion, yes, it was *actually*, Trotsky.

He titters, smiles to himself then strides towards Graham. His eyes fixed upon the class mural and Ghazala's writing.

— You're not putting a wog's work up, are you?

Graham's lips part. He gapes. This monster is going to be let loose on his class. Formby angles his head, closes his eyes and puts the back of his hand to his forehead in a mock-tragic pose.

— Oops, forgot you were a fully paid-up Trot.

— What the fuck are you on about? You've just walked into my classroom, given a Nazi salute and called one of my kids a w...

He can't finish the word.

— Just a bit of banter, Trotsky. You'll get over it. Anyway, to business.

— Er, no. Not to business. I could report you for that.

— Report away, new boy. Do you think anyone would listen?

He scans the room.

— I don't see any witnesses. Do you?

Syd jabs a finger in Graham's face.

— So try it, sonny. See how far you get. You've already upset our leader bringing politics into the staffroom with your commie mug. And, while we're on the subject of the feeble-minded Bardic priest, he requires me to take your crew for music lessons. God help us. Apparently, you're to work with the talented children. My class. Something you won't have experienced before. So that's the deal: I knock some sense into your lot; you learn about real teaching.

Graham's face is burning. He mirrors the finger pointing.

— You lay a hand on any of my kids…

Syd smiles.

—Yeah, yeah. What you going to do, Trotsky?

He pushes Graham's raised hand to one side, lowers his voice, enunciating each word precisely.

— They won't mess with me.

Syd fastens the top silver button of his jacket and moves towards the door. He stops, turns and grins.

— Careful when you rock Taffy's coracle, sonny. You're in your probationary year. He who shall be obeyed doesn't like troublemakers on the Good Ship Union Street.

He slams the door behind him.

Graham slumps into his chair, lays his arms on his desk, lowers his head to rest like a traitor on the execution block. He feels sick at the thought of a numpty like Formby taking charge of his class. But what can he do? The RSA drama diploma would be a ticket out of this place, but Taffy has to sign him off.

He's trapped.

Worse still, God only knows the damage Formby will do once he has power over Graham's kids.

— You all right, Bomber?

Don Middleton is framed in the doorway, a milk crate in his hands, the late afternoon sunlight forming a halo around his big head.

— Don't ask.

Graham rises from his chair.

— Anyway, gotta go. I'm off to Mum and Dad's for the weekend. Get some time to think, hopefully.

Don backs off.

— Right-ho! Regards to your pa, old boy. Tell him, North West T&G wish him all the best. Retirement and all that.

— Will do, Don.

Graham pauses at the classroom door.

— Don, the T&G don't have a Sicilian branch, do they?

— What?

— You know – a hit squad? For hire?

— Sorry?

— Don't worry. I'll explain next week.

He raises a hand in nonchalant farewell. Defeated by the day, he heads for his bedsit and the consolations of a fish finger butty for tea.

Six

No Hiding Place

The railway carriage rattles to a halt at Liverpool Lime Street. The 10.45 from Manchester Victoria sounds as tired as the interior looks. Blue and grey rectangular patterned seats are spattered and streaked with stains of dubious origin. Graham is fleeing the isolation of his bedsit for the weekend, heading home to the warmth of Mum and Dad. The memory of Formby's Nazi salute is a constant aggravation. He needs a distraction.

As he steps onto the platform, a British Rail porter, his red-badged cap perched on the back of his head, points at the former sewing machine case that carries Graham's washing.

— Who sold you that, pal? You was stitched up there.

He's back home. The comforting pulse of a Scouser's gift wrapped joke. Everyone's a comedian here.

A cat's cradle of metal girders hangs from the roof, and the autumn sun bullies its way through the immense, muck-encrusted glass ceiling. The Victorians had a talent for architectural showpieces.

Across the platform, an attractive young woman in a floppy-brimmed hat and brightly patterned blue and orange dress leans out of the train window. Her hands hold her lover's cheeks as she kisses him goodbye. A whistle blows. He starts walking alongside the slow moving train, breaks into a trot, then runs. She laughs and gives a metronomic wave.

Graham's stomach lurches. Here is where he said goodbye to Cheryl as she departed for her final term at Edinburgh University. He can see her in the long musquash fur coat she inherited from her granny. Holding back her long blonde hair, she'd leaned out of the window to kiss him goodbye.

As the train moved off, Graham watched through the window as a smart businessman, helping to lift her case, chatted her up. Her head at a flirtatious angle, smiling, she let the man take her coat off. A viper of jealousy uncoiled in Graham's guts. She finished with him three weeks later. Dumped him for a student vet. It still hurts, but he's home now and must try to forget, consign the memories to a corner at the back of his mind until a new love renders them irrelevant and he can dismiss them for ever.

Graham makes his way onto a bustling, rowdy Lime Street as the Saturday morning traffic creeps towards the Adelphi Hotel. On his right is the vast dirty-grey, once white Lewis's department store. Jacob Epstein's huge 'exceedingly bare' statue, Resurgent, looms over the shop's entrance. It's known locally as Dickie Lewis.

Graham lugs his case towards the Mersey underground. A flock of Terry Mac and Kevin Keegan hairdos bounce past, heading for St John's market and a football bus to Anfield. He passes the Art Deco Futurist cinema, catching his reflection in the big glass and polished brass doors, he stops. Opening his bulky, Army and Navy store civil defence coat, he admires his beige bell-bottom trousers, the jacket's wide lapels, all topped off with a fat, brown and orange paisley-patterned silk tie fronting a yellow shirt. Hands on hips, he decides he's the image of a successful young teacher. Even if he doesn't feel it, he might as well look it. Anyway, it'll please Mum.

His reverie is disturbed by a voice from behind.

— Very dandy, lad.

The voice's owner holds up his bottle of cider.

— Yer looks like one of dem Bee Gees.

— Which one?

— The fuckin' ugly one. Which d'yer think?

Having rock-and-railed under the River Mersey, Graham stands at Birkenhead Woodside bus station, waiting for the 36A to Bromborough. His thoughts drift to ghosts of a past life before teacher training opened an escape hatch. Above the rows of bus shelters and overlooking the Mersey is perched the Woodside Hotel. There he'd meet Cheryl, at the midpoint between their homes in Bromborough and Wallasey. She'd sit on a barstool, her long, slim legs crossed, regarding a glass of whisky and Coke. Ice? Of course. The finger and thumb of her left hand pressing the base of the glass, she would dip a long, elegant, pale pink pearlised nail-varnished finger into the liquid before circling around and around the rim of the glass. An eerie pitch of melancholy. Graham still aches for her. Brown shift dress with delicate yellow and white flowers, puff sleeves, Peter Pan collar. Chic, sophisticated. Breathing in deeply, arching her back, unintentionally sensual. She lifted her aquamarine eyelids, Cleopatra fishtails drawn in black eyeliner at the corners of her velvet-brown eyes, and pouted.

— So that's it? she said. Vauxhall Motors. On the production line for the rest of your life? Is that what you really want?

Graham chewed his bottom lip.

— Money's good.

She closed her eyes in exasperation. Wrong answer.

— Graham, where's your ambition? Don't you want something more than chucking toolkits and spare wheels in the back of bloody Vauxhall Vivas? Jesus!

So, he did it. Studied part-time, re-took O and A levels, worked in a pub in the evenings and got a place at teacher training college.

Later, there was the fateful phone call. His muffled sobs inside the phone box attracted sympathetic glances from the queue waiting outside. A little old lady put her hand on his arm.

— Never mind, luvvie. Plenty more fish in the sea.

Cue for Graham to begin blubbing again.

The present rescues him from the uncomfortable past as the blue and white bus clatters in. A new driver clambers into the cab; the retiring one squeezes his lunchbox under his elbow, slings his mac over his arm, throws back his head and addresses his colleague,

— Who's your clippy, Joe?

Joe gives him a crusty glance.

— Only fuckin' Pink Mittens, John.

— Bet yer wouldn't say it to his face?

— Maybe not. Fuckin' law unto himself, that one.

Graham steps onto the open platform at the back of the bus, dumps the sewing machine case in the luggage space under the stairs and, hauling himself up to the top deck, heads for the back seat. He removes his coat to show off his gear.

A familiar voice, followed by a thumping sprint up the stairs. A figure freezes, the autumn sunlight transforming him into a backlit silhouette. His voice booms.

— Well, fuck me, it's Bomber. All right, Bomber!

Pete Corlett. Tug, to Graham. Biggest, best-est friend of his teenage years. He moves down the aisle, six foot and the rest, in full Birkenhead Corpy-clippy regalia, pulling himself along with each seat back like a canoeist travelling upstream. He's wearing bright pink washing-up gloves and a conductor's cap set at a rakish tilt on his large, oblong head. It barely covers his long brown locks. He clutches a ticket machine as if it's a grenade. Graham gives him the thumbs up and echoes his scouse surprise,

— All right, Tug, la.

Tug wraps his arm around a polished, stainless-steel pole. A grin stretches his jaw and his eyes laugh.

— The Prodigal Son returns.

Graham dips his head in response.

— Ah, well, you know…

Tug shifts to his best, Rex Harrison posh.

— Home to see Mummy and Daddy?

— Ah, well, you know…

— 'Ah, well, you know?' Is that it? Years of taxpayers' money thrown at your education and all you can say is 'Ah, well, you know'?

— Ah, well…

— Stop it!

The bus engine coughs into life. Tug raises a hand.

— Let me sort this knobhead of a driver out. Won't be a min.

He spins around and clomps down the stairs. Graham can clearly hear him berating the driver.

— We're not going to Chester Zoo, you pillock. We're going to the Mill Park Estate. Although, in your case, Chester Zoo might be better; they're short of wombats.

Graham moves up the aisle to watch his friend's antics. Tug jumps off the bus, clambers on to the wheel arch. The driver is perplexed.

What you doing, Peter?

The clanks and squeaks filling the bus indicate that Tug is changing the destination board. When he's finished, he shouts into the driver's cab.

— Right. I've put up 'Driver in Training – No Service'. So, no stopping. I wanna talk to me mate upstairs.

— No, Peter! You can't do that. You'll get us the sack. What about them that's waiting for Chester Zoo?

— Buses come in fuckin' threes, don't they? Now, gerra move on, or we'll be late picking no fucker up.

The driver is sounding increasingly desperate.

— And if there's an inspector?

— I'll blame you, won't I?

Tug returns to the top deck and sits beside his old mate. The bus pulls out. He's still grinning, scanning Graham up and down. Graham questions him to avoid interrogation. He doesn't want to discuss recent events.

— What's with the pink rubber gloves, Tug?

— They don't leave bruises when you smack the naughty ones. Anyway, pink matches me eyes.

His big laugh fills the top deck. Graham pulls a bemused faced. Tug becomes serious.

— Between you and me, it's psoriasis. Not pretty. It was either cover up or wear a fuckin' bell round me neck. I thought another bell might confuse soft arse up front.

— Psoriasis? What's that?

— Skin trouble. Flares up. Doc says it's stress related. It's been worse, though. I'm getting meself fit. Knocked the booze on the 'ead. Taken up martial arts.

He slices the air with a sequence of karate chops then, laughing to himself, pushes back along the seat to get a better look at his old mate.

— But never mind me. Worrabout yous? How's the college boy?

Graham shakes his head.

— Teacher mate! Qualified in the summer. Got a job in a junior school in Manchester.

Tug forms a silent 'Ooh' with his lips.

— Fuck me. Bomber a teacher. It's hard to imagine you as

a *hintellectual*, buddy. Given you were as thick as me at school.

Graham pulls back, screws up his face.

— We weren't thick. We just weren't posh enough. Wrong accent. Grammar school bottom stream. Sink set.

Tug shrugs and looks out of the window. The bus labours up the Chester Road.

Graham flicks Tug's shoulder.

— You don't really think we were thick, do you?

Tug inverts a smile and wobbles his head.

— It was a class thing. C'mon, our faces didn't fit. Haven't you forgotten? The mock general election at school when you stood as a communist. You got three votes – me, you and that lad Forshaw, the one who followed you around.

Tug smiles.

— I blame your dad. Remember he lent me that book, 'The Ragged Trousered Philanthropists'? Never looked back. I've still got it.

He shifts to get square on to Graham.

— So, come on, tell us what it's like, Mr Schoolteacher?

— The kids are great. Good fun. Staff, mixed bunch. There's one complete knobhead of a teacher. Nasty piece of work. NF sympathiser. Hits the kids as well.

— I thought they was little'uns? Primary school, isn't it?

— Junior school, 10 and 11-year-olds.

—He hits 'em? Ffffuck.

— I know. Teaching's not like Vauxhall's. You can't take 'em behind the lockers and sort 'em out. You have to put on this polite face.

— Since when did you take anyone behind the lockers, soft arse? It was always me what had words on your behalf, if you remember.

— Well, you're not there, so I have to sort this one out myself, don't I?

Tug screws up his face and looks doubtful. Graham presses on.

— So, how come you're not at Vauxhall's anymore?

— Well, unlike you, surrounded by comfy carpets and cosy cushions in the soft trim department, I was on the spot welding line. It wasn't called the Burma railway for nothing. Don't you remember the first day? I wore a Bri-Nylon shirt and got showered with sparks. When I went home it looked like a string vest. Talking of which, just look at you.

Tug leans over and rubs the lapel of Graham's jacket between his index finger and thumb.

— Nice piece of schmutter. Finished paying for it yet?

— Ha ha.

— And what's with the curly perm? Did your sister tell you to stick your finger in your dad's shaver socket again?

— Never mind that, how come you never came to see us? Did you not get me letter? I invited you up to a folk night at the college.

— I hate folk music. And I hate fucking students. Anyway, I was too involved with the union at Vauxhall's. Well, I was, that is... until I got the sack. Had a bit of a disagreement with a bloke in the club bar.

— What about?

— You know, usual stuff. Politics. He'd lived in South Africa and he was blabbering on about how thick his black gardener was. The usual shite. Anyway, it got heated. He took a swing. I decked him. Goodnight Vienna. I wasn't bothered. I hated nights, anyway. Time to move on. On the upside, I've saved up a load of dosh *and* I'm looking to start me own business.

— Oh yeah?

— So, on me days off from this bag of laughs, I've started working with Jimmy Carroll. You know, Carroll Brothers, the roofing outfit? Anyway, Jimmy's doing damp coursing. They inject this damp proofing liquid into bricks. Twenty five year guarantee. Piece of piss.

— Taking the piss, more like.

— No, I'm serious, Bomber. There's grants, housing improvement grants. Loads of work in Birkenhead, Wallasey, New Ferry. All old housing stock. Jimmy's going to take me on after Christmas. Once I've got me head round how it works, I'll start on me own. Buy some drills, damp coursing liquid. Get a van. Corlett Damp Coursing.

— Corlett Damp Coursing! Call it what you like. Sounds like a scam to me.

— Very funny. Just 'cos you're sorted, Mr Schoolteacher.

Tug looks out of the window again. There's an uncomfortable pause before Tug asks,

— So what happened to the witch Cheryl?

He breaks into *'I put a spell on you'*.

Graham's retort is sharp.

— She wasn't a witch.

— Bewitched you, mate. You didn't really think your mohair flares, silk shirt and Fiat 500 would be enough did you? I told you, once she went off to uni, she'd be on the hunt.

— She got me to go to night school. So, it worked out. OK?

— Fair enough.

Tug stands and bends his back to see where they are.

— Your stop next, buddy. Tell you what, teachers get loads of holidays, don't they? So, when I'm set up, you can come and give me a lift. Bit of extra cash won't go amiss, eh? Be good to work together again. What do you think?

— Yeh. OK, I'm up for it. Could do with the money.

***

Tug stands on the platform at the back of the bus. He hangs on to the stainless-steel pole one-handed and swings out, like a fairground chancer showing off to the girls on the waltzer.

— Tell your dad I'll drop the book in. Good to see you.

— Ta-rah, Tug.

The bus jolts, then moves off. He bellows,

— Ta-rah, Bomber, lad.

Tug shakes his ticket machine like a cocktail mixer, and it winks in the sunlight.

Seven

Not So Sweet Home

Graham stands facing a small, grey, pebble-dashed council house. The modest wooden slatted gate has been recently painted. Black gloss. He opens it. It still creaks. That sound used to alert his mother whenever he got home from the pub, pissed. Each time he'd vow to oil it but never did. He looks up at his parents' bedroom, half expecting the light to go on and his mother's voice to ring out.

— Is that you, Graham? What time do you call this? You treat this place like a hotel.

Looking around, he can tell things are different. The once neatly manicured lawn is overgrown, the grass a foot high, wilting in places under its own weight. The privet hedge no longer boxed but straggly. The jumble of plants in a vibrant medley of colours is no more. The gardener, Graham's dad, is on the sick, has been ever since the breakdown.

After 27 years of stacking crates of milk, tending the coke boiler, fixing, mending and keeping Canon Heaney Memorial School spick, span and shipshape, Jack Harris is finished.

He was happy serving Sister Imelda until breast cancer took her and robbed the school of her gentle spirit and caring leadership. In swept the harridan in a wimple, aka Sister Dominic, a reject from a school reorganisation. Father Fiscal Expediency seizes the opportunity to save a salary and divert it into the diocesan coffers. When her reign of terror began, the school caretaker was first in line for a kicking. Before taking the milk crates into the classrooms, he was required to sponge down the statues of Our Lady. On Mondays, he had to wash her car. There was no more sitting with the children at lunchtime; he had his school dinner in the cellar. She made him sharpen her pencils on Friday afternoons. Humiliation heaped upon ridicule. Finally, she screamed at him to get out of her office.

— Can't you see I'm in conference with Monsignor Gibbons?

Followed by an aside to her visitor,

— Sorry, Father, he's useless.

Jack hasn't talked to Graham about it. Kitty Harris told her son how she came home early from work and found his dad in front of the fireplace, staring at the empty grate, sobbing. It all came out. The bullying, the anxiety attacks. In June he was off for a month and when he finally went back, he found Sister Dominic had sent his box of woodworking tools to a bring and buy sale. Tools he had used all his working life, sold off cheap. Like his career.

Graham takes a deep breath and walks up to the front door. He slides his key into the lock and pauses, uneasy at what he's about to find inside. A broken dad.

The front door is yanked open. His dad's as grey as an old dishcloth. His voice as frayed as the cuffs of his off-white shirt.

— Thought it was you.

Jack hitches up his sagging trousers.

— Good to see you, Dad.

Graham dumps the case and puts his arms around his father.

Jack stiffens. His shirt is damp under his arms. It's a moment of awkwardness. Jack steps away from his son.

— Steady on, lad.

— How are you, Dad?

— Ah, well, you know.

— Don was asking after you. Sends his best…

— Good man, Don Middleton. Always good for a pint and a story. You know I wrote to him, asked him to keep an eye open for you. Caretakers' union. Not that I'm a part of…

His voice trails off, then he shouts towards the kitchen.

— Kitty. The boy's here.

Graham's mum emerges, adjusting a loose strand of hair before wiping her floured hands on the Paddington Bear pinny bought for her two Christmases ago. She clasps her son's cheeks, then grips his shoulders and makes a visual assessment. Her north Dublin modulation is at its softest in moments of affection.

— Jack, will you look at this boy? Isn't he the grand one? All spruced up for his mammy.

But Graham's dad has picked up the sewing machine suitcase and is heading towards the stairs.

Graham frowns, tipping his head towards him.

Kitty pulls her son towards her.

— Give your old mammy a big hug, will you?

As she squeezes Graham, she whispers into his ear.

— Come into the dining room. We can talk while he's upstairs.

Graham leads the way. There's an old staff portrait of Jack that sits on the small glass-topped hall stand. He's laughing. This was before Sister Dominic's cultural revolution. Kitty runs her fingers through Graham's hair.

— It's getting too long, you know.

She grabs a handful and massages it.

— Mum! Geroff, will you!

— Jesus, Mary and Joseph. You've had one of those perms the boys are getting, haven't you? And sideburns and all, like Kevin Klingon.

— Keegan, Mummy. Keegan.

— And him an Irish boy.

— He's from Doncaster, Mum.

The dining room has shrunk. A crisp white cloth covers the table, half made up, laid for three, not five as it used to be before the girls left home. Jack has filled the shelves with his books. The well-read caretaker. One of that 1930s generation who couldn't afford to take up a place at grammar school. There was no money for books or uniform. Graham's mum glances behind her and lowers her voice once more.

— He's not great, Graham. Taken it poorly. Anyway, Dr Bennion's seen him, put him on long-term sick. He'll not be going back to school. The union's on to it. A nice young man came round. Tried to reassure Dad but... that bloody Dominic... Sisters of Mercy, indeed... She'll need a bucketful of mercy when she meets her maker, I know that. I'd swing for her.

She breaks off at the sound of footsteps on the stairs. Her voice is now a whisper.

— Don't say nothing to him, son. He's not ready. Doesn't want to get upset in front of you. Feels he's let us all down.

She puts a finger to her lips.

Graham's dad shuffles into the room, and his mum brightens.

— Now, son, did you bring some washing?

— Only a few bits. In my case, Mum.

— Let me give 'em a good boil.

His dad almost smiles as Graham raises his eyes to heaven. He's been trying to wean his mum off doing his washing. It's four years since he left home for college, but she still asks. Refuses to hear his protestations.

— Mum, I'm 27. I can wash my gear, you know.

Graham's trying a managed withdrawal programme, reduction by a garment per visit. He likes doing his washing. There's a communal laundry in the basement of the flats where he enjoys chatting with the other residents. Like June with the bubbly hair from the top floor. She's kind. One Sunday night, at about 9pm, Graham knocked on her door and told her he hadn't spoken to anyone since he'd dismissed the kids at half three on Friday. They had a cup of cocoa. She told him all about her course at the poly. She was doing theatre studies; wanted to be an actress. She kicked Graham out at 10 o'clock. She'd been a nurse on a men's medical ward so she was used to telling blokes when it was time for them to shut up and go to sleep.

Kitty shouts from the kitchen.

— Graham, go and give your hands a good scrub for dinner and bring down your dirty washing.

She's operating a time machine, taking them back to when Graham was 14 years old. He lets her. Doesn't mind. Jack calls out.

— I'll light the fire, Kitty. There's a chill in here.

— Not ready for central heating yet, Dad?

Before Dad can speak, Mum answers.

— Oh, we've got plans, Graham. We've got plans.

Jack kneels at the grate and begins twisting sheets of newspaper into branch-thick U shapes.

— She's got plans for us all, lad. Plans for us all.

Graham makes his way to the bathroom. Mum's singing. Her sweet voice drifts up the stairs. An Irish ballad about walking in springtime, down old country lanes. About travellers, birdsong and blossom and isn't life grand. Oh and Jesus, of course. Unlike Graham, she hasn't forgotten Jesus.

He stops at his safe place at the top of the stairs to listen. If she's singing, she's happy. He learned that early on. There was a period when the songbird stopped singing. The teenage war years when Graham's older sister went astray. A sexual and emotional maelstrom of slammed doors and plates, cups, cutlery thrown across the room. Catholicism clashing with 1960s teenagehood. The Pope pushed puberty into a darkened room and locked the door. From Graham's safe place, peeping through the rails, he'd witnessed the bloody combat downstairs. The adolescent after-school skirmishes that climaxed in Armageddon on Saturdays. It would begin with an opening shot of disobedience from a 15-year-old who was going on 21. Mummy calls for back up.

— Will you tell her, Jack? She's not going to Liverpool… to the Cabin Club. She's 15; God help us. A child! And with that strumpet Anne Delaney. Her, with a skirt no more than a belt and her mascara as thick as the muck under the devil's fingernails. Will you tell her, Jack?

The reply has muted conviction.

— Bernadette, you're not going. You'll do what your mother tells you.

— Bloody am going. You'll not stop me.

Jack's voice cracks in a fury.

— Don't 'bloody' me, my girl.

Mummy chucks in a grenade.

— She's laughing at yus, Jack. The bare-faced insolence of it.

Jack would stride across the hall, rolling up one of his sleeves. Graham squeezed the stair post. He knew what was coming. The other sister, the peacemaker, scurried after their father, her hands reaching to pull him back.

— Don't hit her, Dad.

Too late. From bullets to fixed bayonets and now hand-to-hand combat. The smack, the scream. The trenches filled with yelps and howls.

— You bastard!

— What did you say?

Another scuffle and plates hit the floor. Pans collided, cutlery flew. The other sister would be sobbing now as Mummy declared,

— Dear God in heaven, what have we brought into this world, Jack?

Squeals and shrieks and scuffling as the beating continued. Graham would close his eyes and squeeze the stair posts tighter. The accused stumbled into the hall and tore up the stairs, her face red, eyes bulging with rage. She'd see Graham and, grabbing the banister, stab a kick to his ribs.

— Who you looking at, you creep?

Young Graham would slump to the floor and cover his head.

Grown up Graham opens his eyes and moves to the bathroom. Full-lipped blue fish stare at him from a garish green roller blind, like mutants escaped from a Disney laboratory. Graham raises the blind, exposing a crack in the window. A reminder of the day he tried to hit a cricket ball out of Old Trafford. Except he wasn't in Old Trafford; he was in the back garden. A smack round the back of the head was his reward when he went back into the house.

Mummy's voice returns. She's singing along in perfect harmony with her treasured cassette of Irish folksong. She's happy.

— Dinner's ready! Sausage, beans and mash. Your favourite, darlin'.

***

Jack squeezes mustard along the length of his sausages like yellow acrylic on a painter's palette. Graham knows this ritual.

As a child, he witnessed it every Saturday lunchtime. He'll start shaping his mashed potato into a conical mountain, flatten the top and scoop out a small well. Then he'll place a knob of butter in it. Graham used to think of Mount Etna as he watched the pool of yellow lava form, imagining it gurgling, boiling and erupting in a fountain of butter high enough to hit the ceiling.

— Graham, get on; it'll be going cold.

— So, any news of the girls, Dad?

Head down, Jack draws in a heavy breath and pumps it out through his nose. He seems unable to speak. Kitty comes to his aid.

— Well, of course, your father and I won't have anything to do with Bernadette. As far as I know, she and the baby are fine. As for him, we don't ask. Teresa's looking after three little ones for a family in Hampstead. She doesn't get much time off. We'd like to see more of her.

Intermittently, Graham's mum checks out his dad, filling his silences when she can.

— So, I was telling yer da about the theatricals yer doin', son. Wasn't I, Jack?

He grunts. Graham wills her not to talk about school. He's here to forget about it for a while. She smiles as she saws into her sausages.

— Sounds like a whizz, Graham. All those little tinkers dancing around being blood cells. Them remedials like drama stuff, don't they?

— Don't call them remedials, Mum. They've been dumped in the bottom stream, so they think they can't do things, but they can. I just haven't found the right... vehicle to show off their talents. Yet.

Kitty puts her knife and fork on her plate, places her elbows on the table and knits her fingers together. His dad has put his knife and fork down. He has his head in his hands. Graham looks at Mum. She looks frightened.

— We had streaming at school, didn't we, Da? Your dad was in the top stream. But his mammy couldn't afford the uniform for grammar school.

Dad says nothing. Mum leaps in to fill the conversational gap.

— Anyways. I'm so glad you've got yourself a proper job, after all the tomfoolery of labouring and factory work, an' all. I bless the day you met lovely Cheryl. It was a shame you couldn't hang on to her. Still, I suppose she had her sights set on grander things.

— Thanks, Mum.

— All I'm saying... it was a shame you didn't get hitched.

— Yeah, Mum. I thought it was a shame, if you remember. I cried me bleeding eyes out for three days. Or have you forgotten?

Graham tries to eject Cheryl from the conversation.

— You'll never guess who I saw on the bus from Woodside, Dad.

Jack presses mashed potato on to a forked slice of sausage without looking up. Or saying anything.

— Only Tug. He's a clippy on the corpy buses. Wears his hat like that bloke in *On the Buses*. What was his name? Jack something. Harper?

— Jack the Lad, more like. I thank the Lord you left him behind, that Tug.

— I didn't leave him behind, Mum. We went different ways. Anyway, he's starting his own business. Damp coursing.

Undeterred she ploughs on.

— Whatever. You've got yourself a decent career. Good prospects and nice long holidays. Ask your father about the importance of long holidays.

Dad stops eating and does another dragon exhalation. Mum realises what she's saying.

— I'm sorry, Jack love. I wasn't thinking. I...

Finally, she's speechless. Graham needs to say something, to lighten the atmosphere. To make a joke. To be the jester. Like he'd had to when he was a child.

— Imagine, Dad, if I'd ended up a bus conductor like Tug? It would've made a good book. The best of times, the worst of times. A tale of two clippies.

At last, his dad smiles.

***

Graham's enduring a jolting, bum-bruising ride on the 108 from Piccadilly, last leg of the journey back to his Whalley Range bedsit. The plastic moulded seats can't be ripped but they make a perfect canvas for the travelling graffiti artist. The felt pen is mightier than the penknife.

He can't escape thoughts of his beaten and bruised dad, a man tormented into submission in the workplace. He's not going to let that happen to him. Taffy is no Sister Dominic, but Syd Formby? A bully who gets away with it. Graham squirms at the thought of what Monday morning will bring. He'll have to tell 4H that Mr Formby, Formby the racist bully, will be taking them once a week for music. While their teacher, champion of their rights, deserts them to play the great director. He covers his face with his hands. He knows he is complicit. His diffidence and desire to please Inspector Earnshaw have put his class at risk. He has betrayed them. He massages his forehead with his fingertips, squeezes his temples. What will they say when he tells them?

A Manc voice shouts up the stairs.

— Alex Park, Demesne Road, the Foo King chippy.

Another clippy comedian. Graham's not laughing.

Eight

The Piano

It's gone 10am. Mr Harris still hasn't found the courage to break the bad news to the class yet when Sally-Anne asks for a word in the corridor.

— Mr Harris, Serena Fullerton said you're going to do a play with *her* class?

He swallows hard. Her eyes narrow. She continues.

— Mr Formby's going to be taking us for singing?

He makes a low groaning noise.

— Do the rest of the class know, Sally-Anne?

— I haven't told anyone.

— Thank you. Let's go in. I'll explain to everyone.

She purses her lips and scrutinises her teacher.

— They won't like it, sir.

Back in the classroom, Mr Harris takes a deep breath, switches on a beaming good news expression and a sunshiny voice.

— Pens down and look at me. When I can see your faces, I'll know you are listening.

Aaron has his back to him, hands below the desk. His head's bowed because he's sorting Football Action cards, getting ready for swaps at playtime.

— Aaron? Are you tuned into Radio Harris?

Aaron grabs his right ear, twists it and starts making electronic noises.

— *Buzzniap – mmmcrik – niap*. This is Radio Harris with an important announcement. Are you sitting comfortably? Then he'll begin.

Sean laughs.

— He's a card, eh, sir?

Sally-Anne's hand shoots up.

— Sir, you have only four minutes to make your announcement before the bell goes, and we haven't given the milk out yet.

— Thanks, Sally-Anne. OK, Class 4H, you're to have a special treat. I'll be taking Mr Formby's class every Tuesday afternoon.

Heads turn, chins are raised, like a family of meerkats sensing danger.

— You're going to have a *proper* music teacher. Tuesday will be...

Pause. Mr Harris plays a drum roll on his desk.

— singing with Mr Formby.

A stunned silence.

The light-hearted banter leaves the room like an embarrassed guest sensing a family row. He tries rewrapping the package.

— Mr Formby is going to move his piano into our classroom! You don't even have to swap classes. *He'll* come *here*.

The silence persists. All he can see is a sea of frowning, disappointed faces. Aiden squeaks up.

— He smacks, sir.

Aiden rarely makes his voice heard. His little face is lined with worry. His unevenly spiked hair sticks up like a pot of scissored chives.

— No, Aiden. Only Mr Jenkins is allowed to give the strap. Teachers can't hit children any more. It's the law.

— He does though, sir. Jimmy Ridgethorn said he smacked him on his legs in the cloakroom. When no one was around. He told me.

Lorraine twists in her chair to address the class.

— Yeah, me mam said Mrs Ridgethorn's goin' to give Formby a right mouthful if she sees him in the Spar shop.

Sally-Anne corrects her.

— Mr Formby doesn't go to the Spar shop; he goes to Sainsbury's. Mum and I've seen him in there.

Lorraine rolls her eyes at Sally-Anne's punctiliousness. Andrew takes up the baton.

— He doesn't like us, sir. He thinks we're thick.

— That's not true, Andrew. You are *not* thick. You were brilliant in the Highland drama.

— That's *you* talking, sir. He likes the top-stream toffs. Not us kind.

Mr Harris presses on but he can hear the desperation in his own voice.

— C'mon, team, Mr Formby knows some great songs and you'll have a proper piano player. No more BBC School Radio's *Singing Together*. You'll get *live* music. In your very own classroom. Wow!

This is met with a dull echo from Andrew.

— Wow.

But suddenly his tone changes.

— Anyway, sir, I love *Singing Together*. All those daft songs about pixies and dancing.

With his elbows pointing out, he pumps his arms, clenches his fists and starts to sing. Mr Harris lifts his eyes to the sky. He knows what's coming: Andrew's Andy Stewart Hogmanay impersonation.

— *I love a lassie, a bonnie, bonnie lassie. She's as poor as the lily in the dell.*

— It's pure, Andrew. *Pure* as the lily in the dell.

Ignoring Mr Harris, he faces the class.

— It's just daft. *I love a Lassie?* Why would you fall in love with a dog?

Everyone laughs. Aiden brings the hilarity to a stop as he shouts in frustration.

— He *does* do smacking, sir.

The smallest, quietest and most inarticulate member of the class holds up a mirror to Mr Harris's deceit.

Ghazala's plaintive voice breaks the silence.

— We'd rather have you doing *Singing Together*, sir.

Mr Harris doesn't know what to say. It's decided. He can't change it now.

Lorraine is next to interrupt the uncomfortable hush.

— So what are you going to do with Formby's class, sir?

— *Mr* Formby, Lorraine.

— What are you going to do with *Mr* Formby's class, *sir?*

— We're going to do a play, Lorraine.

— A play!

Robert is outraged.

— *We'll* do a play, sir! We're top play doers. We did the Redcoat thingy. You said we were ace.

— This is different, Robert.

Andrew leans forward, speaking in a confidential tone.

— You don't wanna do a play with Formby's lot, sir. Some of them are dead posh kids. They'll find out your spelling isn't good, sir. We don't mind, but they'll go home and tell their mams and dads.

Spelling has always been Mr Harris's weak spot.

Sally-Anne rescues him.

— It *really is* time for milk, Mr Harris. Mr Oldham's class are starting to go out to play.

Mr Harris sees his chance.

— OK. Khalid and Susan, can you give the milk out?

He makes his exit and slinks down the corridor to Dennis's classroom. Dennis is leaning over his desk, counting calculators before stacking them in a cardboard box.

— 26. Remember 26, Graham.

He stops, stares out of the window and ruminates.

— I'm one short.

But he has a theory.

— It's Simon Bosherston, I'm bloody sure it is. Since he's found out how to write words on the calculator screen…

Theory becomes hypothesis.

— I know what he's at. He's half-inched one to show off to the others at play.

Dennis digs into his jacket pocket and pulls out a scrap of paper. Holding it out at arm's length, he flutters it at Graham.

— Look. Gaynor Law wrote down what he'd showed her.

Graham studies the list of words all in numerals: inverted sevens, zeros, upside-down fives. Numerals whose shape could also be seen as letters. hELLo, BooBS, BooBIES, BIgBooBIES, go2hELL and LESBo

— Of course, she asked me what a lesbo was. I told her to speak to Mr Jenkins.

Dennis looks hard at Graham.

— What's up? You've gorra face on yer like a bursted welly.

— I've just broken the bad news to my lot. You know, about Formby.

Dennis waves his hand dismissively.

— They'll be all right. So long as they're wearing a head protector and shin pads and paint their faces white…

— Not funny, Dennis. I've agreed to a racist bully teaching my class. What was I doing?

Dennis signals Graham to sit. There's concern in his voice.

— Who are you worried about?

— Well, Ghazala, of course. Then there's Aiden. He's got history with Formby after the assembly debacle. If I'm honest, all of them.

Dennis is pensive, moving his tongue and lips as if removing all traces of toffee from his teeth before a dental inspection. He brightens.

— Why don't you take Ghazala with you? Tell Formby she's your special assistant. You need a gofer while you're doing the play. He won't care. It's one less for him to teach.

— Brilliant. That's something. Thanks.

***

Don Middleton is transferring Formby's piano to Graham's classroom, assisted by members of 4H. They pause at the door of the prefab. He addresses the team, his voice deep and resonant.

— OK, sprogs, stand easy. Get yer breath back.

Don leans on the piano. His cotton boiler suit is covered in oil stains and coal dust smudges, his partially exposed vest hammocking a sagging beer belly. Don is always available to move pianos and clean drains, but large black blotches on his knees hint at his main occupation: kneeling down to feed shovelfuls of coke into the school's voracious central heating dragon. The boiler house, deep beneath the school hall, is Don's lair, his domain, his sett. The winter cold will soon be here and he'll have to rouse the dragon once more. Boiler room duties will dominate his working day until spring.

— Careful now, sprogs. I'll lift this end.

There's a collective groan.

— Sally-Anne! Pull the trolley out... now, put it on the step. Here gal! Behind my feet.

He moans, his voice a strangulated falsetto.

— Sprogs, LIFT!

The piano lands on the trolley. Don roars triumphantly.

— Well done, sprogs.

Taffy had asked Graham to supply four strapping lads to help Don move the piano. Instead, he sent the biggest girls in the class, Katherine, Lorraine, Miriam and Sally-Anne. Sally-Anne can be heard above the chatter of the rest of the crew. She's flight lieutenant to Don's squadron leader.

— Mr Middleton, sir, do you want us to push or pull?

— You lot push and I'll pull.

Don takes a deep, wheezing breath and rasps out,

— OK, arfter three: *un*, *deux*, *trois*, PUSH.

There are more groans, squeaks and wheel scraping as the trolley starts to trundle towards the classroom. Don's large backside nudges open the classroom door, followed by a light oak upright piano and the girls, backs bent into shoving it. Graham suspects they might be breaking the 1833 Child Labour Act, or even the new Health and Safety at Work legislation, which Dennis had found a copy of in Taffy's bin.

Don commands his troops.

— STOP!

Twisting one end of his moustache then the other, he rests an elbow on the piano.

— Where do you want the old joanna, Bomber?

— In the corner by my desk, please.

Sally-Anne, perplexed at the name 'Bomber', mouths the word, attempting to make sense of it.

As he grasps one end of the piano, he directs the girls.

— Right-ho, sprogs. Bear left and... *push*.

Graham clears the desks to make room for this new piece of furniture.

— Planning a mess room knees-up, Bomber?

— I wish. Mr Formby's going to take the class for music. Isn't he, girls?

Lorraine doesn't hide her disappointment.

— Yeah. Worse luck.

Don pulls a face.

— Sprogs don't seem happy, Bomber.

Graham says nothing but opens his palms and shrugs his shoulders. Don gives him an I-get-it nod.

Sally-Anne salutes.

— Can we go now, sir?

Graham gives a thumbs up and they head for the door.

— He called sir 'Bomber'! cries Sally-Anne as they scurry out of the room.

A burst of laughter.

Graham tries to open the piano lid but it's locked.

— Formby always locks joannas, Bomber. Doesn't trust sprogs, methinks. Or the teachers. Well, I'd better skedaddle before the old man finds me and asks me to unblock his khazi again. By the way, little Aiden Wright, can you remind him he's meeting me at the boiler room after school.

— What's he done?

— Nothing. He's helping me paint the drainpipes. Funny little chap. He loves it when I call him Leading Airman Aiden. He's a good little helper. Passes the brushes, holds the pot. Doesn't go home until his dad's gone off to work. Nights at McVitie's. Pa's a bit free with his hands. Bad form, Bomber. Shame.

As he waddles out of the classroom, he turns to Graham.

— Tell him to wear the old rugger jersey I gave him. Swamps the poor little chap but stops him getting covered in sticky black goo. Don't forget, will ya?

— Nope, good as done, Don. Good as done.

Don is Aiden's guardian angel. It all started with an absence note.

Mr Harris

Our Aiden won't be in for a couple of weeks. Hurt his eye. Messin about as usual. Doctor said he got to wear a patch. Keepin im at home until it comes off.

Mr Wright

There had been mutterings in the staffroom about Aiden Wright's dad.

— Nasty piece of work. Remember when he picked him up from nursery that time? Flung the little thing over his shoulder like a sack of spuds. Not nice, that one.

And comments from parents at the school gate. Graham's heard them. Snatches of conversation, remarks overheard:

— His dad, apt to give him a clip. Too free with his hands, if you ask me.

Even the children are aware what's happening.

— Aiden's dad told Andy, if his ball hits his door one more time, he'd get it good an' 'ard.

And the worst is from the boy himself:

— Me dad's gorra belt wiv a buckle.

Graham spoke to Don because he knew he looked out for the lad.

Can't say I'm surprised, Bomber. I pick things up. When they do little jobs, they chat. Offload. Confide in you. Hear all sorts.

Graham showed Don the absence note.

— Don't like the sound of him being kept orf, Bomber, lad. Aiden at home for two weeks with his dad on nights? Rules will be imposed. The grumpy dragon in bed all day. 'Do not disturb, OR ELSE.' Tread quietly, little Aidey: the monster's sleeping.

So, Don made a decision and called for the lad on his way into work. Aiden's mum was keen to get him out of the house.

— Yeh, tek 'im in. Gerr'im from under my feet.

The only problem was the eyepatch. As soon as the other children saw Aiden in the playground, the name calling started.

— Aiden Wright's a pirate dwarf. Doo da, doo da.

— Aiden Wright's a pirate dwarf. Doo da, doo da day.

The laughter and the tormenting began, and Aiden retreated to Don's boiler room lair.

Then Don had an idea. He'd wear an eyepatch himself and wondered if Graham would too.

— It might work. Worth a try. Kids won't pick on Aiden if the staff show their support for the lad.

Graham put it to Taffy who couldn't see any harm in it and shared the idea with the rest of the staff.

— You don't have to, of course. Up to you, like.

There was general agreement. As long as Aiden wore a patch, they would as well. And so the eyepatch solidarity movement was born.

Graham's class had an eyepatch playtime day. He handed out patches and the children were keen to join the club. Dennis did an assembly, talking about everything from marauding pirates to mythical cyclopses to the challenges partially sighted folk face. And it worked. And that's Don. Much more than a caretaker. When Graham mentioned it during his weekly phone call home, his dad's words were 'I'm not surprised. The man's a legend. It's the war, you see. People learned how to deal with things. Turn things around'.

There were only two staff members who wouldn't play along, who thought the whole idea was ridiculous: Mr Formby and Miss Broadstairs.

Nine

Sanctuary

From the corridor, bursts of lively chatter signal the arrival of Formby's top-streamers. By the time Graham gets to the hall door, Formby is issuing his final instructions.

— Right, 4F, enjoy your extended playtime with Mr Harris. I'll see you at two-thirty, when we'll get back to our Cecil Rhodes project.

Syd stares at Graham, as if he were a violinist handing over his Stradivarius to one of the Sex Pistols.

He marches away from his elite regiment towards the prefab and its untouchables. His class carry board games – chess, Scrabble, Go, mahjong – and bundles of books, fiction and non-fiction.

— Why have you got all those games? Mr Harris asks.

The tall blonde, Serena Fullerton, picks at the badge on her Union Street royal-blue sweater.

— Mr Formby wants us to occupy ourselves usefully while we're hanging around doing the play.

He swallows hard.

— Listen, 4F, you're *all* involved, *all* of the time.

He leads Formby's troop into the hall and awaits the arrival of Ghazala the Gofer. She's borrowed his script to copy up the sound effect cues; rehearsals can't begin without her. For the performance, Mr Harris has chosen 'The Ants', act three of *The Insect Play* by the Brothers Čapek. There are enough parts for a whole colony. Its central theme is anti-fascism which Graham is certain will annoy Formby. Sound effects are a key element to the production. The sound of guns, tanks and military manoeuvres are all part of the atmosphere he wants to create.

Ghazala opens the hall door and stands on the wheeled metal base stanchion of the cassette player. She scoots along, gliding elegantly towards Graham like a figure skater.

— Don't let Mr Jenkins see you, Ghazala. Where've you been?

She smiles and jumps off, running alongside it as if she is alighting from a moving bus.

— I was showing Sally-Anne how to set up the tape recorder for Singing Together. We had to stop because Mr Formby told Sally-Anne he'd heard she was a busybody and to leave the recorder and get into the class. He sounded cross.

Mr Harris's spirit sinks. Ghazala is a great help, but there's been a backlash to appointing her as gofer. Miriam asked him why Ghazala was his special assistant. He couldn't think of an answer that was both truthful and diplomatic. Some of the girls are giving Ghazala the cold shoulder, excluding her from skipping games and moving away from her when they line up at the end of playtime. To cap it all, Lorraine had whispered to Janine, 'Ghazala Goody Two Shoes is Mr Harris's pet'. When he confronted Lorraine, she refused to make eye contact, pursed her lips and tapped her foot. After a long silence, she asked if she could go and then flounced out of the classroom.

He feels bad, but protecting Ghazala is the priority. He'll keep his ears open and step in if there's any more grumbling.

Rehearsals are in full swing. Ghazala has placed a copy of *The Insect Play* on Mr Harris's chair like a holy book. She's carefully creased it to ensure it stays open at the right page. Ghazala would get top marks for attention to detail. She's watched Sally-Anne closely.

Judith Purdy, who plays the leader of the Yellow Ants, strides across the stage, declaiming her lines and punctuating her delivery with brief freeze frames. She's small with gleaming, dark brown, shoulder-length hair that rests neatly on the shoulders of her bright-white blouse. Through the jam jar lenses of her glasses, her eyes are like those of fish straying too close to the side of the bowl. She oozes confidence. She knew all her lines at the first read-through. He told her he was impressed. She tossed her head.

— Mummy's been testing me. She says I have real talent.

Well, thanks to Mummy there's very little for him to do. Now the moves have been plotted, he drops the starting flag and shouts:

— OK, Judith, off you go.

Ghazala, poised, lifts her index finger from the pause button. She makes fine adjustments to the volume of Dukas's *Sorcerer's Apprentice*, as it accompanies the ants traipsing across the stage. Mr Harris has rigged up an enormous white sheet and two overhead projectors. They cast giant shadows of ant workers toiling away. Carrying a cardboard carpet cylinder on her shoulders, one of them stumbles. A foreman ant raises her whip and mimes a beating.

Judith proclaims:

— We, the Yellow Ants, will prevail!

She stands centre stage, a miniature Miss Mussolini, her fists resting on her hips. The pose reminds Graham of Syd. Judith flings her hands wide to receive the adulation of the crowd as if she were on the balcony of the Piazza Venezia.

— We will annex the land of the Red Ants. We will march into our rightful homeland.

Raising a fist, her feet apart, she welds her other hand to her hip and goosesteps to centre stage.

— The Yellows will drive the killing machines into the land of the Red Ants.

Through the glass inner wall Mr Harris clocks a diminutive figure, his head hanging down, shoulders hunched as he shuffles past. Little Aiden. Dropping his script, Mr Harris hurries towards the hall door to catch him.

— Aiden, where are you going?

He stops, shuddering with sobs.

— I'm… I'm go… going home to me mam, sir.

— Why? What's happened?

He doesn't answer. He stands there, his back to Mr Harris, sniffling. He then makes a break for the cloakrooms and the school exit. Mr Harris is caught in a dilemma. Does he run after Aiden or stay with his 38 charges? The longer he leaves it, the more danger Aiden might be in. He'll have to cross busy roads, unsupervised. He dreads to think what'll happen if he does nothing.

Samantha Greenwood comes out of the staff room. Her hips rock from side to side as she sashays up the corridor like it's the catwalk at the House of Dior. All in slow motion. Graham gulps.

— Samantha, can you do me a favour?

She stops, tosses her blonde hair. Graham shoots her an imploring glance.

— I need to grab Aiden before he does a runner.

He nods towards Syd's class.

— Can you keep an eye on this lot?

Screwing her eyes up, she stares through the glass.

— Syd Formby's Junior Fours? What's the problem?

— Long story. I'll tell you later. You don't have to do anything: they're rehearsing a play and they're on autopilot. Thanks, Samantha. I owe you one.

— Be careful, Graham. I might collect.

She opens the door and enters the hall to the sound of Judith Purdy ranting.

— Death to the Red Ants. We are the master race.

Ghazala, her head bobbing up and down anxiously, tries to make out what's going on.

By the time Mr Harris gets away from Samantha, Aiden has gone. Making his way through the cloakroom, he scans the tarmac desert of the boys' playground. No sign of him.

Aiden lives in a little terraced house on Maude Street, three minutes away. Breaking into a jog, Graham dodges the traffic on Union Street, sprints down a back alley. Weaving his way through beer cans and deceased curry cartons, he sidesteps a mangy dog optimistically sniffing a Tesco bag. Still no sign of a small boy in grey shorts, blue school sweater with frayed cuffs and a large hole in one elbow. Graham turns into Maude Street. He's uncertain of the exact house and is about to try number six when he hears muffled shouting from the house next door.

— Where's me fuckin' sarnie box, eh? C'mon, woman, get off your fat arse, will ya?

It's Aiden's dad. Graham has met him only once, and the memory causes him to hesitate. Mr Wright had burst into the classroom one morning unannounced. Striding towards his son, he'd shouted:

— Eh, you, bugalugs, come with me. Yuv' gorra appointment.

He then grabbed Aiden and left.

Mr Harris is about to knock on the door of a certified headcase. But he needs to find Aiden. He has no choice. Taking a deep breath, he moves next door and gives a quick rat-a-tat.

Aiden's dad opens the door. He squints, frowns a weasel stare. Dressed in smart black trousers, his red braces hanging loosely about his thighs, he's getting ready for work. His open-neck grey shirt has a clip-on black tie hanging loose. He flicks his head back and stares at Graham.

— Mr Wright, I'm…

— Yeah, I know who you are. Soft boy's teacher. Yer bollocked me for comin' in your class.

His nasal tone and refusal to blink are unnerving.

— What d'you want?

He smooths down the front of his shirt and checks his ironed creases are in line. Graham's throat is dry.

— Has Aiden come home?

— Nope. Why? Is 'e waggin' it? Yer want me to give 'im a leatherin' when 'e gets in? Don't worry, I will.

— No. No need, please, Mr Wright. He's not done anything wrong.

Over his breast pocket in black cotton letters on a red background is the word SECURITY. He still hasn't blinked.

— He wasn't feeling well and walked out of school. I thought he was heading here. Must have missed him. I'll check back at school.

— Shouldn't you 'ave checked before yer left? Or are you waggin' it as well?

From the shadows, a small, plump figure emerges. Mrs Wright's striped tent dress is grubby. Her slippers are lopsided and her stubby pink feet overflow like warm soufflés.

— Who is it, Wayne?

— It's soft lad's teacher.

An Elastoplast covers one lens of her pink-rimmed glasses; yellowing skin discolours her cheekbone. She pokes her head forward. Aiden's dad leans against the door frame and blinks for the first time. He twists his head towards his wife:

— You've seen enough. Are me boots clean?

— I were just lookin', Wayne. What's he done?

— He's waggin' it. I'll sort 'im when 'e shows, don't worry.

Graham's stomach lurches.

— Like I said, Mr Wright, no need. He's done nothing wrong.

— We'll see, eh?

Graham knows he should leave. He's making things worse for Aiden.

— I'll check back at school. Sorry to have troub—

The door slams. The shouting recommences, waves of insults, a verbal storm. The soundtrack to Aiden's home life.

Ten

The Class Reunion

Graham returns to school to find Samantha shepherding Syd's children along the corridor. In the hall, Ghazala's taking her time reeling in the extension lead. She's in no hurry to get back to Mr Formby's music lesson. Samantha spots Graham.

— Did you find Aiden?

— Not yet, Sam. How was the rehearsal?

Samantha puts her hands on her hips and purses her lips.

— Mmm. Judith Purdy? A bit full of herself, methinks.

She adopts a posh voice.

— 'Mrs Greenwood, one usually takes notes at the end of the rehearsal'. Cheeky minx. Then she asked whether I thought her performance 'lives'. Assaults, more like.

Graham glances at his watch.

— Anyway, Sam, can't stop. Thanks again for stepping in.

Giving her a thumbs up, he sprints towards the prefabs.

Chinti is standing outside the classroom door. Graham can't believe he's been sent out. He's so well behaved. So polite. He has his hands behind his back, like a squaddie at ease, his large eyes staring ahead, his brow rigid, locked in a frown.

— What are you doing out here, Chinti?

The boy maintains his gaze into nothingness.

— Prime number, Mr Hurries.

It doesn't make sense, but Mark will know.

Graham steps into the classroom. No sign of Syd. Sally-Anne ambushes him.

— Mr Harris, I tried to record *Singing Together* in the cloakroom, like you said. But Mr Formby told me to get inside. I didn't press stop, so it kept on recording.

— It's OK. Ghazala said there was a problem. But don't worry, Mr Middleton will put the machine away at home time. He always checks the tapes. He'll sort it out.

Graham surveys his class. They're milling about in small groups. Kathy's reading intently, a copy of *Goodbye to Mallory Towers* resting against a ruler that she's jammed in the inkwell. Aaron and Sean are swapping footie cards. Mark sits on his own. He looks crestfallen without his best friend. Miriam has drawn a huge heart on the blackboard, within it the words 'Bay City Rollers' are inscribed in a tartan font. Next to the point of a Cupid's arrow, she's written, 'I love Les'. Her assistant, Lorraine, stands by her with a box of coloured chalks while Pauline voices her approval.

— It's top, that, Miriam.

Around the piano, Rob, Marlon and Barry are bent over the lid in a scrum. Andrew is lying on the floor, a screwdriver in hand.

Graham bends down to inquire what he is doing.

Cheeks flushed, Andrew scrambles to his feet, slipping the screwdriver into his pocket. He diverts attention from his activities by raising the topic of Mr Formby's evictions.

— Chinti got sent out, sir.

— So I see.

Graham turns to Chinti's best friend.

— Mark, can you help me? Why's Chinti outside the classroom?

Mark rises to his feet, like a barrister about to address a jury, and slips into his role as Chinti's chief advocate.

— There's no need to stand, Mark.

— I like to stand when I do this kind of stuff, sir.

Graham, bemused, signals for him to continue.

— OK. If you must.

The class gathers round. Mark places both hands on his desk, palms down, giving his stance added gravitas. He lifts his head slowly.

— Well, you know how Chint loves numbers?

— He's the only one in purple group, pipes up Andrew.

— Well, Mr Formby was teaching us the song 'What Shall We Do with the Drunken Sailor?' Chint was counting the bricks on the front wall, to see if any line was a prime number.

— How do you know that? asks Graham.

— He was writing numbers on the back of his hand so I said, dead quiet so Mr Formby wouldn't hear, 'What you doin', Chint?' And he said, 'Count bricks. Look prime number.' And he points to the back of his hand. I thought, he's playing number games. He's always doing it, sir. Then Formby clocked 'im.

— *Mr* Formby, please, Mark.

— Yeah. *Mr* Formby said, 'You! What are you writing?' Dead posh. Like what he does. Chinti didn't know he was talking to him. Then *Mr* Formby got louder. Real cross, like. 'I'm talking to you. The coloured one with glasses'. So I nudged Chint and said...

Mark lowers his voice.

— 'He wants to know what you're doing.' Chint looks up at Formby and says 'count'. But, 'cos of his funny accent, Formby thinks it was a rude word and he starts shouting at him, 'What did you say?' Very angry, like. So Chinti says it again. Formby goes red and says, 'WHAT DID YOU CALL ME?' Chint sees he's mad, so this time he shouts it, 'cos he thinks if he shouts it, Formby'll understand.

Mark pauses for dramatic effect but Graham urges him on.

— So Formby charges at him. He's right up dead close screaming, 'GET OUT, YOU RUDE BOY!' His spit is going everywhere. It was 'orrible. And he sends him out and tells him he's insolvent.

— You mean 'insolent'.

— Yeah, 'insolent'. Thing is, Mr Harris, Chinti is on purple book *three* in maths. Nobody's on purple book three. Not even Adam Whitehorn in Formby's, and he's the cleverest kid in the school. It was Chint's accent what done 'im.

— Thanks, Mark. OK, the Chinti mystery is solved. Tell him to come back in and explain to him he's done nothing wrong.

As Mark bounds towards the classroom door, Graham moves the inquiry on.

— Next question: what happened to Aiden?

There are cries of 'He's gone' and 'He got sent out as well'.

Closing his eyes, Graham hears the peevishness in his own voice.

— Why was Aiden sent out?

They all start talking at once.

— Whoa, discussion rules, please. Discussion rules. Remember: I point, you talk. Sean, you start.

Sean takes the floor and pinches his school jersey, another barrister clasping his lapels.

— This is how it was, sir. We were singing 'What Shall We Do with the Drunken Sailor', but Aiden's lips weren't moving. He couldn't follow the words. 'Cos he's last at reading out loud. Mr Formby told him he had to come out to the front and sing on his own. Aiden just stood there, saying nowt 'cos, like I said he's in Mrs Day's poor readers, 'cos he can't read good.

— You mean 'read very well'.

— Yeah, read very well. Aiden were scared stiff; he were moving from one leg t'other. Like he wanted a wee.

Some of the class start giggling, infuriating Sean.

— Don't laugh! Weren't funny, right?

The class stops immediately. Sean composes himself.

— Formby grabbed him by his jumper and Aidey said, 'Don't smack me. You're not allowed'. Then Formby pulled him outside and we heard Aidey cryin'.

Lorraine shoots her hand up. Mr Harris points to her.

— He smacked his legs. I heard it. And he called 'im an insect.

— So Chinti saw all this?

— No, this was *before* Chinti got sent out. By the time Chinti got sent out, Aidey had done a runner.

Miriam puts in her three penn'orth.

— I said 'E's done a runner, sir' and he said, 'That's *his* problem'. If you ask me, 'e were gettin' 'is own back on Aiden after he got bladdered in the kidney assembly. Which Aidey never meant 'cos it was Karl what set it up by pushing Aidey down the slide.

Karl pulls a 'So what?' face. Chinti and Mark return to the classroom. Mark has his arm round his friend's shoulder.

Graham scribbles a short note to Joan Groom.

Joan,

Aiden Wright has gone AWOL. Can you ring his home to see if he has turned up yet? Also, can you check with Don? Aiden might seek sanctuary with him in the cellar.

Thanks,

Graham.

— Sally-Anne, will you take this note to Mrs Groom?

Graham folds the note and hands it to Sally-Anne. She takes a felt tip from Mr Harris's pencil case and a sheet of blank paper from the desk and writes in large letters:

DON'T FORGET
SWIMMING KIT TOMORROW.
TELL THE CLASS AT HOME TIME.
S.-A.

— In case I'm not back in time to remind you, Mr Harris.

Eleven

The Revenge Tragedy

Aiden is found sitting on the steps outside Don's boiler room, his sobs mingled with juddering intakes of breath. Don let Joan Groom know he was safe. Graham could barely contain his fury. Syd Formby has it coming to him, but a conviction won't be easy: he's sly and always covers his tracks.

At lunchtime, Graham goes to see Don who is sitting in a battered, oil-stained armchair. The springs have gone, as has one of the castors. It leans at an awkward angle, jolting him awake if he shifts his weight during a nap. Above, children's shoes clomp over the coke delivery grill. Hauling himself onto the workbench, Graham gets straight to the point.

— Don, about Aiden Wright. Did he tell you what happened?

Don's growling voice is an echo from a black and white British war movie… Jack Hawkins with whiskers.

— Certainly did. Life's hard enough for the little man, and Oberschutze Formby's too free with his bloody hands.

— You heard about his Nazi salute?

— Hitler bloody salute! He needs pulling through with the school Christmas tree, Bomber. Didn't spend five years fighting

Jerry for that malarkey to start up again. No. Aidey came down here crying his little socks off. Red marks on his legs. Took three Werther's Originals and a visit to feed the terrapins to get him back on track. Formby needs a bit of his own medicine, if you ask me.

— But what can we do? He gets away with this stuff all the time. There are never any witnesses. Even the marks on Aidey's legs prove nothing because his dad smacks him, and Formby will say that's where he got them. He's a racist bully.

Don presses more tobacco into a short, stubby pipe. He angles his lighter, then sucks and puffs aggressively. He pulls the pipe away, and from the depths of the fug he fulminates.

— We need a plan. We need hard evidence. We need to nail the bastard.

He takes another drag and the tobacco crackles. He blows the smoke towards the light of the delivery grill, then nods towards Graham. He's made a decision.

— I'm going undercover, Bomber.

— Undercover? As what?

— A school caretaker.

— But that's what you are.

— Ah, but a caretaker on red alert. Keep me eyes peeled. Nose to the ground. Ears pricked.

Disturbing as this image is, Flight Lieutenant Middleton is emerging from the bombed out rubble of his life. Special Operations Executive. One of the Jeds. Swapping his RAF blue for oily overalls. The Battle of Britain spirit is reawakened.

He stands creakily to attention, knees clicking like castanets. Laying down his pipe, he twiddles his crumb-laden handlebar moustache. He flattens a piece of paper with the fleshy part of his right hand, then fishes a fat black marker pen from his top pocket and writes:

OPERATION TRAP THE RAT.
Stage 1
Collection of Evidence.

He waddles over to his notice board and pins it next to a fading Giles cartoon. He's ready for a scrap. Organised with RAF-style precision.

— I'll keep you posted, Bomber. Now you get on with your *Cockroach* play.

— It's called 'The Ants', Don.

By the end of the day, there's a brown envelope lying on the big portable tape recorder. It's sealed and marked PRIVATE FAO MR HARRIS. Graham opens it. Wrapped around a C90 red cassette tape is a note headed 'TRAP THE RAT' and below:

Found this in the tape player. Have a listen. Can only think the internal mike must have been left on. Think you'll find it interesting.
Don.

The tape's label is marked 'Singing Together Week 7' in Sally-Anne's precise script. Graham puts on headphones, slides the cassette into the tape machine and listens. It's dynamite. Don's done well. The question is: what to do with it? Take it to Taffy? He'll just bury it, too afraid of scandal staining the name of Union Street Juniors. He paces up and down, thinking, thinking. Eventually, an idea germinates. *Hamlet*, a play within a play. It'll take careful planning. Precision audio tape editing. Graham has seen how it's done at Cheadle Hulme Players when he's helped Robbie Myers with the sound effects. Nobody must know. Not even Ghazala, operator of the sound effects tape. It has to be a bombshell. Graham will watch Syd's face, his horrified reaction. He's excited just thinking about it. A trap to catch a rat.

***

It's the night of the performance in the school hall. Pianos stand either side of the stage area; one draped in a red cloth, the other in yellow. A metre square picture depicting a conical mound with the words 'The Red Ant Hill' is stapled to the first piano. The other is similarly decorated with a mirror image that proclaims 'The Yellow Ant Hill'.

A voluminous white dust sheet drapes the back of the stage, a backcloth on which huge shadows of ants labouring underground will be projected. Honoured guests occupy the centre of the front row. Graham can see a young woman with auburn hair sitting next to John Earnshaw. Is that the new drama advisor, Abbi Tomkins? Graham's only spoken to her on the phone; she looks younger than he'd imagined. Bit of a stunner, in fact. Seated behind the top brass are Dennis and Graham's bottom streamers.

The dull murmurings of the adults mingle with the soprano chatter of children. Sporadic outbreaks of giggles and laughter. The kids wave and call to their parents who are seated separately; lost lambs bleating across a field. Teachers patrol the perimeter in their smarter-than-daytime dress. The female staff wear their deluxe face: heavier eyeliner, deeper blusher, risqué lipstick. The men have cast off corduroy and denim for sports jackets, smart trousers, white shirts and kipper ties.

Taffy climbs onto the stage. Graham feels both nervous and excited.

— Right-ho, ladies and gentlemen. Now, before the highlight of the evening, performed by Mr Formby's top class, we have a special treat. Miss Broadstairs will conduct the senior choir. I don't have to remind you – they're the current holders of the South Manchester Lesley Gratton Bowl for choir of the year. So, without further ado, I'll leave you in the capable hands of our choir mistress, Miss Broadstairs, assisted by Maestro Formby.

Syd's nostrils flare. He casts a resentful glance towards Taffy. Miss Broadstairs strides to the conductor's platform. Her usual twinset replaced by glad rags: a blue and white flared polka dot dress. Its décolleté neckline reveals a white metal snake choker which is eyeing the mole on her neck. Her hair is sculptured to a heavily lacquered beehive. For a moment, Graham imagines it catching fire under the hot stage lights and, fearful that such a conflagration would scupper his plans, places one hand on the fire extinguisher he's standing next to.

Whenever she's conducting, Miss Broadstairs's expression is either a cadaverous grin or ossified scowl. The grin would transform a viper into a jellied eel. This is how she mesmerises the children. She raises her hands in a giant crab-like pincer movement; the choir SHUT UP and FREEZE. The grin is to remind them of HOW MUCH THEY ARE ENJOYING THEMSELVES. If they look as if THEY ARE ENJOYING THEMSELVES, the audience will mistakenly believe THEY ARE ENJOYING THEMSELVES. Should any member of the choir forget THEY ARE ENJOYING THEMSELVES, she will lasso their attention with the BROAD STARE. The audience, who can't see her face, are oblivious to this intimidation. Her ability to terrify goes beyond the school choir. Even Taffy is nervous about being left alone with her. Whenever she crosses his threshold, he fumbles for his Celtic warrior letter opener and insists she leaves the door ajar.

The choir sing 'Nymphs and Shepherds'. Syd accompanies them in the manner of a cruise liner pianist on a rough sea, rolling around on the stool, his eyes half closed.

As the final words fall from the choir's cherubic lips, Miss Broadstairs swings round to the audience and BROAD STARES. THEY CLAP.

Taffy returns to the lectern.

— Now it's your turn to join in the community singing. A medley of children's favourites accompanied by our own, our *very* own, Mr Formby on the pianoforte. Take it away, Sydney.

He waves an arm towards Syd, who pouts and furrows his brow. A medley of Uncle Mac's favourites is anathema to Syd, the humiliation compounded by the manner of Taffy's introduction. The years of practising Chopin, Liszt and Debussy études were not supposed to lead to this. Beside him, Miss Broadstairs stands ready to flick the pages of the music at each upward jerk of his chin. He pulls up his jacket sleeves, casts a resigned glance at his assistant.

Miss Broadstairs turns her head to the audience and switches on THE GRIN. At the opening chords of 'Nellie the Elephant', her upper body begins jolting from side to side, as if she is receiving small electric shocks. GRIN OFF when leaning in to turn the pages of the music, GRIN ON when regarding the audience. Everyone in the hall joins in. Sing-along with Syd, available for old people's homes and children's parties (but not Rock Against Racism gigs). As he arpeggios into 'How Much Is That Doggie in the Window', the audience follow obediently. Sean shouts 'Ruff! Ruff!', to the delight of his classmates. The audience choruses 'Ruff! Ruff!' and Sean smirks with pride.

As the enthusiastic applause dies down, Taffy mounts the stage.

— Thank you, Miss Broadstairs. Thank you, children. Not quite the Treorchy Male Voice Choir but nevertheless a bit of fun!

Miss Broadstairs shoots a venomous glance Taffy's way.

— Now, the highlight of the evening.

He consults a scrap of paper, holding it at arm's length to get the text into focus.

— The third act of the *Insect Play*, 'The Ants', by the

Brothers Čapek. Performed by a troupe of top stream thespians from Mr Formby's class. And directed by the latest recruit to our staff, Mr Harris.

Graham's stomach churns.

***

The play is going down a treat. Dame Judith Purdy's mini-Mussolini struts and frets like a semaphore signaller who's lost her flags. The shadows of worker ants on the sheet at the back of the stage stretch and distort. Ugly outlines are cast as they bend their backs to the pulsating bassoons of the *Sorcerer's Apprentice*. The smallest ant crawls and falls under the weight of a log (carpet tube from Withington Carpet Emporium). The menacing shape of the foreman ant raises a whip (skipping rope tied to a shinty stick). Ghazala, arched over the tape player, readies the next cue. Graham concentrates on Syd's facial expression as the splice on the tape hurtles towards the tape head. To Ghazala's surprise and frowning disbelief, the music fades. Syd's rasping voice roars from the speaker.

— When I tell you to do something, you do it!

Aiden's high-pitched pleading echoes through the hall. Another slap and another cry for help. Syd swivels on his piano stool and looks towards Graham, blanching at the public exposure. The sound of Syd beating Aiden fills the hall until the music fades in again. Syd's eyes bulge like a frog with a goitre. Guilty as hell. Ghazala scowls at the tape player, simultaneously flicking back and forth through the script. Graham looks down the line of his seated class. Sally-Anne has her arm round Aiden. He's pulling away, trying to leave.

The faces of his class are frozen in horror at what they've just heard, but the audience are wreathed in appreciative smiles, enthralled by Syd's powerful performance. To them, this is not evidence of a bully at work. No, the willing suspension of disbelief has twisted the real-life actions of a real-life monster into the magic of theatre. Gripping drama. To them, it's not real; it's Mr Formby's muscular contribution to the play. Bravo, Mr Formby!

Graham's class turn to face him. They *know* this is not fiction and want an explanation. All they get is a cowardly shrug. A big, fat tear slides down Chinti's cheek. Instead of bodies littering the stage and a guilt-ridden Claudius breaking down and confessing, a row of children sit, incredulous at what they've heard. A tableau of shock and disbelief.

Graham is numb with sorrow and regret. It was Syd he'd wanted to expose, not his victims, Aiden and Chinti. He's made a huge blunder. He's used and abused the children in his battle with Syd. Aiden pulls away from Sally-Anne's embrace. He clambers over feet, legs, bodies and school bags, towards the exit. There's a straw-coloured puddle of shame under the seat where he'd been sitting.

The show draws to a close. Rapturous applause follows but it holds no delight for Graham. He can't wait to get away. Inspector Earnshaw rises to make a speech.

Weally, weally lovely, Headmaster. Super. The joy in those moon-penny eyes. Childwen – such a delight!

Taffy asks for a special round of applause for multi-talented Syd, pianist and special effects actor, and for his star performer, Judith Purdy.

As 4H file out, they avoid eye contact with Mr Harris. No farewells, no goodnights, no 'See yer tomozz, sir'. The hall empties. As Graham retrieves the tape from the cassette player, he looks up to see a stubby figure with a mop and bucket heading for the pool beneath Aiden's seat.

— Don, I...

Don raises his head and glowers.

— Don't say anything. I'm seething, Bomber. What in God's name were you trying to do? Whose side are you on? It's not enough that Formby dishes out the physical; you have to dish out a psychological second helping. In public! You prat.

Graham stuffs the cassette tape into his jacket pocket. He moves towards Don, his palms up, signalling contrition.

— I thought I'd expose him. Make the evidence public. Let the whole school hear him at work so it was obvious what he'd done. I never thought people would think it was part of the play.

— So, what did you think would happen? That Formby would throw himself on the floor? Wash little Aiden's feet? Resign? If you thought less about personal revenge and more about the kids you teach, how to act on *their* behalf…

Don lifts his eyes to the heavens as he dips his mop into the bucket.

— Now leave me to clear up the aftermath of your stupidity.

As Graham skulks away, Don says,

— You could begin by telling little Aiden to meet me at the cellar door after he's had his dinner tomorrow. He can help me flush the playground drains. Might help a bit. *If* he comes into school, that is.

Graham slinks off to catch the 152. When he reaches the bus stop, he decides he'll walk instead. Three and a half miles to curse, to confess, to accept responsibility. To cry. Passers-by give him a wide berth. Cross the road. Avoid eye contact. They're thinking he's on something. Booze, drugs, whatever. They're thinking he needs help. They're right.

***

Graham stands at his desk. He can hear the subdued talk of the children waiting outside to come into the classroom. He opens up his RSA portfolio and reads again Taffy's glowing comments about the play. Oh, what a fraud he is. He's about to face those who know this, those who've not been fooled, deceived, conned. They traipse into the classroom with none of their usual enthusiasm.

— Good morning, 4H.

— Good morning, Mr Harris. Good morning, everybody.

During registration, silence fills the room when he reads out Chinti's name, then Aiden's. He looks up.

— Has anyone seen Aiden and Chinti since last night?

— Didn't look very well, sir.

— They've probably gone to Mrs Turnbull.

— Mrs Turnbull?

Miriam explains.

— She's the dinner lady you go to when you're feeling really sad, sir.

Sally-Anne chimes in.

— They'll be a bit late this morning, sir.

Another long silence. Mr Harris stands in front of his desk.

— There's something I want to say. Could you all look at me, and I'll know you're listening.

No one looks up.

— I'm sorry about what happened last night. I made a mistake and upset some very important people in our class. I gave Ghazala the wrong tape. It wasn't her fault. It was mine, and I'm really sorry.

Embarrassed coughs puncture the silence. Miriam puts up her hand.

— My dad says it takes a big man to say sorry. He should know; he's always telling me mum how sorry he is. Usually on a Sunday morning.

Marlon chips in.

— Learn from your mistakes is what my mam says.

Andrew the Opportunist takes a punt.

— Can *we* do a play? Like what Mr Formby's did. Maybe Chinti and Aiden can be the stars. It'd make up for you making them cry.

Graham quickly welcomes the idea.

— Good thinking, Andy. I'm seeing Manchester's new drama lady at the beginning of next term.

Mark puts up his hand.

— *She* doesn't smack, does she, sir?

Before Graham can respond, the door opens and Chinti and Aiden enter, each holding the handle of a Co-op carrier bag.

— Am I glad to see you two. We were worried.

They stand for a moment in front of their teacher's desk before lifting up the bag.

— It's for you, sir, says Aiden.

— For me?

Graham looks inside. There's a packet of McVitie's Jaffa Cakes, a bag of rice and a sachet of chopped coconut.

Graham swallows hard.

— Why, boys?

— It were Sally-Anne's idea, sir. Remember, we did that assembly on Jean Valjean nickin' dem candles and the priest saying it were all right and don't worry. Sally-Anne said why don't me and 'im be like the priest and say s'all right, like. Chint said yeh, so I did, an' all.

Graham is unable to speak. He nods rapidly, leaves the classroom. Once outside, he holds the door shut so none of them can see the tears of shame sliding down his cheeks.

Spring Term

—◇◇◇—

1978

Twelve

The Battle of the Bulge

Graham sits at his desk. Stares into his sandwich box. On a bed of lettuce rests a pilchard sandwich. The salad looks tired; the corners of Mother's Pride are turned up like warped lino. It's all part of his campaign to eat more healthily. He's stopped going to Doyle's bakery at the back of the school. Two sausage rolls and a chocolate eclair every day have produced a slim wallet and an expanded waistline.

Outside, children play. Like a flock of birds released from captivity, they are delighting in their freedom. Whoops, screams, barks, laughter. Somewhere in the orchestration a skipping motif emerges, fades and then returns.

The ship goes out
The ship comes in
When I go out
Sally comes in.
The ship goes out
The ship comes in
When I go out
Ghazala comes in.

Graham lifts the top slice of the sandwich and sniffs the contents. Doesn't smell quite right.

The ship goes out
The ship comes in
When I go out
Amanda comes in.

The classroom door opens and Lorraine dances in. Her shoulder-length brown hair bounces,

her hands hang straight by her side. Behind her, stands a woman who looks familiar.

— Mr Harris, Mrs Groom said I was to tell you it's the drama lady.

Graham gawps, transfixed mid-bite, the sandwich frozen in time and the space between his teeth. He retracts it, unbitten. Lorraine rocks from one foot to the other, unable to suppress her curiosity.

— Miss, are you doing drama with us?

The drama lady gives a small, enchanting smile as she follows Lorraine into the classroom.

— Will you, miss? We love drama, miss. We do assemblies, but we haven't done a play yet. We will, though, miss, when Mr Harris thinks we're ready.

Graham chips in.

— My class is very keen on drama.

Lorraine soft-shoe shuffles as she speaks.

— Sir said we are going to have a big treat. He's talking to someone very important about it. Are you the important one?

The drama lady looks at Graham and inclines her head.

— I'll have to ask your teacher that question.

Her lips have a gentle fullness. She runs her fingers through her wavy auburn hair. It contrasts with her big, yellow, owl-framed spectacles. She's probably in her late twenties, about five foot three. Turning back to Lorraine, she unhooks her fawn rope bag from her shoulder. Graham's memories of Cheryl begin to morph into the present and the woman in front of him. He hasn't felt a surge of excitement like this since before the break up.

— I'm going to have a chat with Mr Harris. And what's your name?

— Lorraine, miss. My last teacher called me Lorraine the Pain. But Mr Harris said he won't do that. And he hasn't. I didn't like it.

— I should think not. Anyway, I'll talk with your teacher about doing drama.

— Oh, thanks, miss. We love drama. Wait 'til I tell the girls.

Lorraine continues her fancy footwork, like a dancer who doesn't want to leave the audition. Graham notices Ghazala's bobbing up and down outside the window.

— Lorraine, Ghazala's waiting for you.

— Ta, sir. See you, miss.

Lorraine twirls, waves and jigs her way out of the room. Watching her exit, Graham's visitor throws another warm smile. Her tan, flared trousers fit snugly. She scrabbles in her bag and pulls out a diary, pen and notebook.

— I'm sorry. We haven't met before, have we? Abbi Tomkins.

Her loose chunky belt falls at an angle across her flat stomach. She slips off her jacket, revealing a tight polo neck sweater. Graham's thoughts are racing. Concentrate, Graham. Look at her face. She glances down at Graham's tracksuit bottoms. Her brow furrows. He follows her gaze.

— Ah, yes. I boiled them with my red football socks. They went pink. They were grey. Sorry, I'm Graham Harris.

— How do you do?

He wipes his fish-perfumed palm under his arm before shaking hands. Miss Tomkins has the firm, confident grip of a meeting-and-greeting regular. Graham realises he is holding on to her for slightly too long, a couple of seconds too long. She sits on a child's seat. He feels uncomfortable. She's the expert;

shouldn't he be at her knee? Or resting his head in her lap as she caresses his curly locks? Graham, stop! Look at her face. She pushes back her flowing hair and reveals a large, bright red loop earring with a multi-coloured parrot perched inside. It rocks back and forth, kissing her neck. Lucky old bird.

She wraps her hands around her crossed legs.

— There's a couple of things I want to talk about…

She pauses and sniffs the air.

— What's that smell?

— Oh, it'll be this.

Graham raises the pilchard sandwich like a communion host over a Tupperware chalice. She winces as if he's shown her a dead mouse. Embarrassed, he picks it up and stuffs it into his mouth, grinning dumbly. He's now unable to speak. Abbi frowns. Graham swallows hard. There's an uncomfortable pause.

— Right, let's get on, she says.

Graham grunts and struggles to swallow a complete pilchard. His head and neck are going back and forward, like a pelican at a fish party.

— You don't mind if I talk while you eat your lunch? It's just that I don't have much time.

Graham nods. The pilchard is edging its way slowly and painfully down his throat. He's praying she knows the Heimlich manoeuvre. She would have to stand behind him, wrap her arms around his waist and pull his torso into her warm, firm… Get a grip, listen to her.

She spots his RSA folder on the desk.

— Ah! Good. Are you keeping up with the course portfolio?

Graham is afraid if he opens his mouth to speak, he'll send a pilchard straight into her lap.

All he can muster is a strangulated 'Mmm'.

She grimaces.

— I'll take that as a yes. Let me outline what I've planned for you this term. Then we'll take a closer look at your folder.

Graham nods rapidly.

She purses her lips.

— Dorothy Heathcote is coming to Manchester for a demonstration lesson. Now, she's an inspiring drama practitioner. It would be good for you to watch her at work.

Graham suspects this demo lesson may clash with his funeral. She carries on, despite the shifting spectrum in his cheeks. Pink to red, now edging towards purple.

— The next stage is for you and me to work together. I need a class to take to a conference of HM Inspectorate in York and, thinking about what Lorraine said, that could be the big treat you promised them — and a chance for you to experience classroom drama from the inside.

The pilchard refuses to sink any further into his gullet. In desperation, he grabs his mug and takes a hurried swig of cold tea, which proceeds to leak from the corners of his mouth. He bangs the mug back on to the desk. Abbi's brow furrows.

— Are you all right?

Repeatedly jabbing his index finger at his throat, Graham slurs,

— Wallowed an ilchard.

He gives another gormless grin. Surely doubts about his suitability to appear in front of Her Majesty's Inspectorate are growing in Abbi's mind. He tries to reassure her, but sounds like a castrato.

— The class will love it.

In a last ditch attempt to avoid choking to death, he executes an enormous neck-stretching gulp.

— Can I do anything? asks Abbi.

She slides the mug towards him. He takes another swig. The pain subsides. Relieved not to be having this conversation in an ambulance, he regains his composure, closes his eyes and blows out his cheeks.

— Sorry about that.

Abbi picks up the RSA folder and reads aloud.

— Performance Drama Part One. Assemblies. 'I Kid You Knot – How the human kidney works'. Equipment: Slide, bladder, shoe boxes, fluorescent paint.

She seems puzzled and looks up at him.

— It was my first attempt at an assembly, he explains.

She puts her head to one side, nodding encouragement. He continues,

— I had the class stomping about the hall carrying shoeboxes marked "Urea" and "Urine". A paddling pool was the bladder.

She reads from his comments.

— Kids loved it but unfortunately a premature ending. Mr Formby not happy about it. "Something from the Bible next time, please." G. JENKINS

She turns the page.

— Moses and the Burning Tobacco Bush.

Graham interjects,

— It was an anti-smoking assembly.

— That doesn't sound biblical.

— Hang on, wait 'til you hear what we did! We used a fold-up Christmas tree as a burning bush – biblical – a giant-size packet of Camel cigarettes – sort of biblical. And the class all wore tea towels on their heads. Which was very biblical. We had three speaking parts: Moses – top biblical – a tobacco baron called Al Veoli and a gangster's moll, Bron Keyhole. Admittedly not biblical, but they were dressed as shepherds. And finally we had Dr Alexander Fleming. Dressed as Father Christmas.

— Can I stop you there?

Abbi wears the expression of someone watching pandas copulate. Fascinated but incredulous.

— Did it go down well? she asks.

— Ah! Like the first one, the kids thought it was great. The staff... as before, mixed.

She turns the page and reads.

— Performance Drama Part Two. The Ants. Third Act of the Insect Play by the Brothers Čapek. Ah, now I saw this one. But it wasn't with your class was it? Why was that? I couldn't get a straight answer out of your headteacher.

— Mr Jenkins insisted I use the top stream class. He didn't think my bottom streamers could pull it off.

— Oh dear. How did you feel about that?

— Not good, if I'm honest. I know my class are more than capable. Given the chance.

Abbi resolutely slams the folder closed.

— I agree, Graham. So how about we give them the chance to show what they can do?

He smiles. He's found an ally. An impassioned ally.

— I'm sorry, but I can't stand streaming in primary schools. Bottom stream indeed! Tell me this, they can all speak, can't they? They like pretending, making up stories, don't they? They all took part willingly, in your class assemblies?

— Of course! They loved them.

— Well, then. They can do drama. It doesn't have to be big performance drama. From now on, we'll do classroom drama. No audience. No rehearsals. No sound effects, lights, scenery. No more little plays, but drama we can do in here. Push the desks back, create a space. They have ideas, don't they?

— Certainly do!

— And they have imaginations, don't they? They can make things up. You can make things up. You can make things up together and learn at the same time.

— Oh yes, says Graham. I like it!

— Then all we have to do is 'manage' those ideas and

connect them to learning. Graham doesn't understand what she means but is nodding his head vigorously. She continues, her tone now confidential.

— Can I ask you something? And I want you to be honest. She fixes him with her steady gaze.

— Are you a risk taker, Graham?

— In what way?

— Are you the kind of teacher who'll try new ways of working? Be prepared to fail but to learn from it?

— My failure has been quite spectacular so far, so when do we start?

She doesn't smile.

— I'm serious. If you are, we'll begin next week, with Dorothy. Once you've seen Dorothy, you'll understand. You'll see her adopt a role. Play alongside the children. Inside the learning. You understand what I'm saying?

He doesn't.

— Oh yes, of course, he says, not little plays.

— Then we'll plan a lesson together. As I said before, I need a class for a demo lesson in York. HMI conference on creativity in the classroom. I need a class; you and your kids need some drama. They need to feel special. A day out doing some drama!

— My boss may not see it that way.

— Mr Jenkins won't dare refuse. Believe me, HMI is powerful. They are the Greek gods of our education system. Headteachers mere mortals. Do not upset the gods!

— Brilliant. Can't wait. Abbi gets up. Draping her jacket over her arm and hanging her bag from her shoulder, she pauses to peer into the still open sandwich box.

— I won't shake hands.

She walks briskly, hips swaying. Graham sprints past her to open the classroom door. She regards his pink tracksuit bottoms, shakes her head and leaves.

Wow! Graham flops into his chair and closes his eyes. He's at the seaside, about to step into the unknown waters of teaching through drama. He's a trainee lifeguard, Abbi, a confident, beautiful mentor.

They stride towards the rough sea of innovation. Graham is tempted to run back to the beach hut. Abbi grabs his hand and pulls him towards the breakers. They look more daunting with every step, but Graham feels safe with his new-found tutor.

Through the window Graham watches Abbi making her way back to the main school building. A gaggle of girls, led by Lorraine, gathers around her like dress pins drawn to a magnet. The only things missing are autograph books.

Graham feels re-energised by her visit, emboldened. He's looking forward to seeing her again. She's sure to be at the Dorothy demo lesson. Will she recognise him? Well, she's hardly likely to forget his impression of a choking pelican, is she? But he desperately wants her to see his creative side, preferably without the distraction of his shrunken pink tracksuit bottoms. Perhaps he'll don his rust-red paisley shirt, a matching silk tie and his blue velvet jacket. Mustn't overdo it, though. Just a hint of his artistic sensibilities backed up with incisive questions at the post lesson Q&A. Such as what? He'll make a list. If the discussion turns to asphyxiation, smelly fish and pink pants, he'll make a joke out of it.

— Hi, Abbi. Remember me? I'm the one who smells like a fish and wears salmon pink. Do you like my kipper tie?

Maybe not.

The shrill voices of boys having a kickabout on the back field floats into the classroom. It's time for football practice.

He grabs his boots, his whistle and a sack of balls.

***

After practice, Graham's route from the back field is a hazardous one. Two insane geese, Liz and Richard, share a home with a malevolent duck called Laurence. Their living quarters are euphemistically referred to as the school farm. Special Unit, Broadmoor, more like. Liz, Richard and Laurence have serious anger management issues. The 'farm' is supposed to be a resource for children's learning, the pet project of Junior One teacher, Betty Topham. In truth, the birds are defenders of her secret stockpile of Bristol Cream sherry and Vladimir vodka; they're her praetorian guard. Laurence has lived with the geese since arriving as a duckling two years ago. He thinks he is a goose and attacks everyone, apart from Betty Topham whom he believes to be his mother.

Graham has had to develop a strategy to conceal his fear of these avian thugs from the eyes of the footballers.

Step one: glance over shoulder to check if being observed. (He is. The team monitors his progress with bemused expressions.)

Step two: accidentally on purpose drop a ball and sprint after it, quickly passing the door of the cage. The geese lower their heads and hiss, while Laurence spread his wings and lunges hungrily at Graham's ankles. There's nothing Laurence loves more than the chewy meat of a fat Achilles heel.

As Graham dances past the cage, Big Simon Coolidge shouts,

— Told yer. Sir's a wuss.

Once inside, Graham treads with caution along the corridor in his socks, muddy football boots in hand and a string bag of sodden balls over his shoulder. As he heads towards the staffroom, Taffy leans out of his study.

— Can I 'ave a word, Graham? Won't take a minute, boy.

Wearing an old rugby shirt and the pink, shrunken tracksuit bottoms, Graham doesn't feel dressed for an interview with the boss.

— Am I all right like this?

— Good question, lad. Good question.

Confused, Graham stands outside.

— Shall I leave my equipment here?

— Excellent question. And, yes, leave it there. In you come now. Close the door behind you, bach.

Joan, the school secretary, stationed behind Taffy's chair, stares hard at Graham's crotch. She screws up her eyes, shakes her head and slips a hand inside her blouse to adjust her bra strap before returning to her room. Taffy clears his throat.

— Graham, lad. Bit delicate, this one. Don't know where to start, boy.

— Delicate?

Taffy begins to swivel from side to side in his captain's chair as if he is warming up for a complete pirouette. He ruminates for a moment or two before reaching for the KitKat lying next to his mug of tea. Having stripped off the red wrapper, he peels back the silver foil and snaps off a chocolate finger which he proceeds to dunk repeatedly in his tea.

Eventually, he breaks the silence.

— It's about your dress, Graham.

— My dress? I don't wear a dress, Mr Jenkins.

Graham laughs. Taffy doesn't.

— Your tracksuit bottoms, lad. There's been... how can I put this? An observation.

— An observation?

He adopts the tone of a clerk reading out the charges in court.

— A female member of staff... no names, no pack drill, boy. A female member of staff has been to see me with a... complaint.

Graham's voice rises an octave.

— Why? What have I done?

Thoughtfully, Taffy sucks at the chocolate finger.

— No. Let's not say complaint, so much as… She has made a suggestion… She's suggested you invest in a…

He is searching for words and waves the soggy choccy digit in a minute upward spiral.

— Yes, a looser fit of tracksuit bottoms.

It still isn't clear to Graham what Taffy is on about.

— Looser fit?

— It's about the contents of your tracksuit bottoms, Graham, lad. Your tackle is too prominent, bach. She, who shall not be named, has had to stare into her lunchbox to avoid… puts her off her celery stick.

Graham feels himself blushing.

— So, says Taffy, a suggestion: how about a pair of new tracksuit bottoms? A more modest cut. School funds will pay for them. 'Ave a word with Joan, get a receipt. Nothing extravagant, no gold lame Liberaces, eh? And another thing, 'ow about getting changed in the sports storeroom next to your classroom, bach? Avoid the gents' cloakroom in the staffroom, then you don't 'ave to parade past the lunchbox brigade with their gobs full of sausage roll.

— I'm sorry… I put my red football socks in with them; they turned pink. They shrunk when I boiled them.

He recalls Abbi's look and the odd sound she made when she saw them. He feels sick; the blood drains from his face. Flustered, he exits and heads straight to the staffroom to say his piece. He opens the door; silence drops like a guillotine blade. They all know. He's unable to make eye contact with anyone.

Miss Broadstairs stands in front of the radiator next to the sink, her arms folded. She's giving his crotch THE STARE. Everyone is taking a shufti. Graham hastens to the toilets, emerging a few minutes later with his sports kit in a duffle bag,

Syd Formby barks,

— I'm still waiting for that cassette, Trotsky. The sounds effect tape from the play. Put it on my desk before you leave tonight. Or should I come and collect it?

Graham ignores him. It's evidence against Syd. Damning evidence. The only evidence he's got.

Thirteen

The Sorcerer

The rain races relentlessly down the high, metal-rimmed windows of the Teachers' Centre. The wind sprays in gusts, taking a breath then spitting out another spume. Squalls rattle the windows. Manchester meets its meteorological stereotype. Sitting on the back row of a raked platform, Graham is one of 30-odd teachers awaiting the arrival of the drama practitioner, Dorothy Heathcote. A hubbub of conversation fills the hall. Handshakes, waves, nods and thumbs up signs; everyone knows everyone else.

Graham looks around for Abbi and spots her on the other side of the room. He cranes his neck in the hope she might see him and acknowledge his presence, validate it, shrink his feeling of not belonging here. She's talking animatedly to a man in a pinstriped suit. Tall and suave, he stands with one hand in his pocket, seemingly agreeing with everything she says. He runs his fingers through his thick, silver swept back hair. He's cultured, sophisticated, supremely confident. He could easily pass as an Arena arts programme presenter, or a frequent, erudite guest on *Late Night Line-Up*. Graham sighs. He's out of his league fancying Abbi. Still, a day out of school, sharing time and space with her… Maybe… maybe, one day. She looks concerned and glances over the sophisticate's shoulder towards the hall doors. The drama specialist has not yet made her entrance.

The Teachers' Centre hall could do with a lick of paint and a spring clean. The walls are nicotine yellow, the brown parquet floor smudged with the skid marks of all the plimsolls in pursuit of shuttlecocks. There are no pictures on the walls and the long, faded, dark green curtains droop sadly.

The double doors swing open and, to Abbi's obvious relief, in strides Dorothy Heathcote. Abandoning her debonair companion, Abbi crosses the floor to greet the drama guru. As they exchange pleasantries, Dorothy slips off her dark blue woollen cape to reveal a white spotted, blue silky dress and navy cardigan. She is a sturdily built woman in her fifties, her grey hair pulled back into a bun. She turns to the rows of teachers and addresses them with easy authority in a Bradford accent.

— We haven't much time before the children arrive so I'll mention a couple of things.

Hands on her hips, she pauses, studies her audience.

— It will help the children if, while you're observing, you avoid communicating with them. Are you all right wi' that?

Mumbles of agreement are interspersed with coughs.

— That way, they'll be able to concentrate on the drama. So, no eye contact. If you have the urge to smile at them, resist it; this is not a performance. Am I making sense?

As she speaks, she folds her arms under her full bust. Graham is reminded of a big, friendly auntie who would clasp you to her bosom at Christmas, always surprised at how much you'd grown. Dorothy casts the room another warm smile.

— Good. Remember, it's a privilege to share children's work in drama. So show them the respect they deserve.

She acknowledges Abbi who's now standing by the main entrance next to a stack of coloured sugar paper, on top of which sits a margarine tub filled with fat felt-tip pens.

— I'm getting a signal the children have arrived. So, let's make a start, shall we?

Holding open the double doors, Abbi smiles at a tall, bespectacled female teacher who leads a class of seven and eight-year-olds. The sound of the wind and the beating rain sweeps into the hall with them. Abbi puts her shoulder to the door and shuts it after them.

The crocodile line meanders through the hall, heads twisting, turning, taking in the rows of faces, the walls, the ceiling, the sad curtains. They make their way nervously towards their new temporary teacher. Some observers smile, then stop self-consciously and return to scribbling.

One pupil moves with an embarrassed stuttering gait, another, pigeon-toed, is transfixed by the audience. A boy in a torn, faded blue anorak sways, like a sailor on the rolling deck of a ship. A tall girl puts her hand to her mouth to stifle a laugh while stooping, as if ducking under a branch of an invisible tree. They pile their coats on a wooden table at the end of the hall. A small hillock grows, patched green, red, grey, blue and black. Sleeves stick out; a glove hangs by a piece of string, attached inescapably to its twin. The teacher shepherds them until they coalesce into a clump of sitting, waiting, being-good children.

At the back, a boy in a tired blue woollen jumper with an iron burn prominent on the front, faces the wrong way, gazing at the watching teachers. His legs crossed, he rests his head in both hands, elbows balanced on his bare knees. With a tilt of her head, Dorothy alerts the teacher, who scurries over and gently grips the boy by his shoulders, swivelling him round to face in the right direction. Dorothy looks kindly at each child in front of her. When the final lamb is in the invisible pen, facing in the right direction, she begins.

— Good morning.

The class, in Pavlovian response, chorus their reply.

— Good morning, Miss...

They dissolve into embarrassed giggles. Dorothy smiles.

— Well, I know why you're laughing. Because I haven't told you my name, have I?

She pauses, then speaks slowly and deliberately.

— My name is Mrs Heathcote.

She pronounces it 'Ethcut'.

— Now, you're all wearing smart name tags. That's going to help me. Our names are important, aren't they?

A slim girl with a red Alice band and starch-white blouse puts up her hand. Dorothy's eyes dart from her label to her face.

— Yes, Angela.

— My mum's name is Angela. So my dad calls me Angie. Sometimes he calls me Angie Babe. Like in the song.

She laughs and bows her head. The class sniggers. Dorothy beams and lowers her chin, making her neck vanish. In the short time they've been together, reassurance has been spread like honey over hot toast. Dorothy sits up straight and clasps her hands in her lap.

— Right, we're going to do some drama today, and you're all going to be in the drama.

Her finger points down as she draws an imaginary circle over their heads.

— I'm going to be in the drama with you. Is that OK?

— Yes, Mrs 'Ethcut.

— But, before we start, I want you to have a look at all those grown-ups behind you. Go on! Turn around. Give them a right good stare.

Under the children's gaze, the teachers shuffle their papers, cross and uncross their legs. Again, they forget to not smile, then remember. Dorothy continues.

She leans forward in her chair to speak very quietly, intensifying the intimacy.

— Don't worry, because they're not looking at you, they're looking at me. They're interested in what I'm going to do with you. So you don't have to worry.

She gives them time to gaze at the rows of teachers.

— Right! Now turn around. We can forget them. They've got their writing to get on with and we've got our drama to make. Is that OK?

Her left hand seating her right elbow, her right hand seating her chin, she begins to wonder out loud.

— So, what shall we make a drama about? Any ideas?

Silence.

Dorothy stands, maintaining her chin-holding, wondering pose. Her broad smile indicates she is with them, on their side. They're in this together. Ideas begin to spill out and Dorothy echoes them.

— Cavemen.

— Cavemen?

— A princess.

— A princess? And what is this princess best at doing?

Dorothy writes up each idea on the blackboard. The wondering continues until a small boy with a close-shaved head attracts her attention.

— Castles! he shouts as if he's suddenly found the answer to a crossword puzzle clue.

Dorothy dips her head, her eyebrows draw together. She thinks there are possibilities here. Shifting forward, Graham's intrigued. Where is she going with this?

— Castles. That's an interesting idea.

She kneels on her haunches, close to the front row. Trust and proximity are sewn together.

— Shall we be in the olden days? Or now? Or in the future?

The shaved-head boy replies.

— Olden days, miss.

— So, our drama is a long time ago. Agreed?

Angela replies.

— Agreed, Miss 'Effcut.

— Good. In that case we're going to have to start by building our castle, aren't we?

The children clamour in agreement.

— Good. So what tools will we need to build our castle?

— 'Ammers, miss.

— Hammers. Mmmm. Well, pick up your hammers. Feel how heavy they are.

She mimes picking up a hammer, feels its weight. Some pupils mirror her actions; others are tentative, looking for permission to pretend.

— Place the stone you're going to work with in front of you.

Angela concentrates, a strained expression, her brow creased, lips pursed. She feels the weight of her great imaginary stone and then dumps it on the floor.

— Yes, they're heavy all right. Focus on your stone. It's there in front of you; use your drama eyes to see it. You need to shape it well. These stones need to fit together to make the castle wall. The boss won't be happy if it's the wrong size or shape.

Graham is on the edge of his seat. His head is crammed with questions. If this is drama, where is the script? Where are the props? The scenery? The costumes? When will she begin directing? Movement and music? Be a tree, big and tall. Be a mouse, as small as you can. All that drama stuff. Graham can see they are not doing 'little plays', but what *are* they doing? Something else is beginning to spill out. All in response to one question: 'What do you want to make a drama about?'

Dorothy moves through the class, now spread about, each working on their imaginary stone. She compliments, praises, questions, encourages. One boy, taller, with sharp, angular features, hasn't moved from the moment he sat down. His arms folded, shoulders hunched, he watches. He's not playing. Every now and again, he lowers his head and shakes it.

— Can you move your stones into a space? You're going to have to help each other.

The class moves. Pushing, lifting, working in pairs, carrying their imaginary worlds around with them. Dorothy notices the boy who hasn't budged.

— Can you all stop for a moment? One of our friends is finding it hard to believe. We need everyone to help, or we won't get this castle finished.

She approaches the boy and lowers herself, gets eye to eye.

— I'm going to bring out a big horse. Do you think you'll be able to believe it, John?

He shrugs his shoulders. Dorothy calls to Abbi,

— Miss Tomkins, could you bring me the grey mare?

Abbi strides to where the coats are piled high.

— Do you want it saddled up, Mrs Heathcote?

— Of course I do.

Abbi lifts the saddle, tightens the girth strap, clasps the imaginary reins and leads the horse to Dorothy who gently strokes its nose.

— The horse's name, blacksmith?

— Matilda, ma'am.

— Good. Come over here, Matilda, and meet John.

Her hands reach up, high enough for the children to believe it's a big horse. She continues to talk quietly to it.

— Now, John, if you can hold the reins and follow me, we can inspect the work the stonemasons are doing.

She raises her voice.

— Carry on, masons. John and I are coming round to talk to you. Show me your best work.

Casually she offers the reins to John.

— Take these, she says. I'm going to get the plans out of the saddle bag.

Sheepishly he takes the reins, all the while trying to gauge the reaction of the other children. They look serious; no one is laughing at him. His shoulders lift, his chest expands and he mimics Dorothy, stroking the horse's nose.

Dorothy mimes unravelling a scroll. She surveys the children, striking stones, wiping their brows. John follows her, his hands raised above his shoulders, gripping the reins of the invisible horse that everyone can see clearly. Graham sits back in his seat. No script. No lights. No rehearsals. A teacher at the fulcrum of pretending. In the drama with the class. As Andy would say, 'Yis and double yis.'

***

Graham walks the half mile back to school briskly, his pace quickened by a new found passion for drama and an eagerness to put today's learning into practice. He's a happy man, in a hurry. It's four-thirty and the children will have gone home but he still wants to touch base. The peace of the classroom will enable him to read his notes and plan a Dorothy-style drama. The only slight disappointment is that he didn't get the chance to talk to Abbi at the end of the day. She was too busy looking after Dorothy and bringing proceedings to a close. When he managed to catch her eye from a distance, she tilted her head, mimed holding a phone, and mouthed, 'Give you a ring'. At which his heart skipped a beat.

Reaching the school, he sees Dennis's car has gone. He must have zapped off early to pick up his kids from nursery.

It's a shame. Graham is desperate to share his excitement. But he'll have to wait until tomorrow. Once inside the prefab, as he heads towards the classroom door, he senses someone behind him. As he turns, a big hairy hand grabs his jacket collar.

— Want a word with you, you little shit!

Graham's being dragged, stumbling backwards into the boys' toilets. He struggles to stay on his feet. He's slammed up against a cubicle door which swings open. He tumbles in. Syd pushes him against the toilet wall. They fill the space and Graham can feel the sharp edge of the toilet roll holder digging into the flesh behind his knees. Syd hoists him higher as if they're performing a monstrous pas de deux, Graham's feet dangling in the air.

— For God's sake, Syd, let go of me.

He wriggles but can't extricate himself. Syd's too strong. And now he's spitting hatred in Graham's face.

— You fucking know what this is about, you slimy commie cunt. I want that tape. Where is it?

— I haven't got it, Graham lies.

Syd grabs Graham's testicles and squeezes.

— Do you want me to give another of your thickies a thwack? Because I will and, believe me, no one will see it.

Pain sears through Graham's groin; his bowels loosen. He holds his hands up in submission.

— OK! I'll get it. Let go. Put me down.

Syd drops him and shoves him out of the cubicle. Grabbing his tie, he yanks Graham out of the toilets and towards the classroom where he kicks open the door. Graham pleads, his voice high-pitched, strained.

— You can't do this kind of thing.

Syd pushes him up against the blackboard.

— Don't mess with me, you little twat. Take Taffy's advice and move on at the end of the year. Moss Side, Hulme – you could play the holy missionary boy somewhere like that, with all the little piccaninnies. You're poisoning the blood of this school. The kids in my class are meant for top-notch schools. Manchester Boys, Withington Girls. Where they were born to go. It's your job to keep the lid on the sump, but you're getting ideas above your fucking station. Now give me that tape.

Graham pushes past Syd and takes the tape from the back of his desk drawer. Syd snatches it and clamps Graham's jaw with his fingers and thumb.

— Don't even think about fuckin' blabbing. I know where you live, and there's no street lighting by that scruffy little bedsit. Top end of Demesne Road. So be warned. I've got lads watching you. You might wake up one night, screaming and cuddling your snapped legs. Think about it.

Syd lets go. Graham steps back and massages his neck.

Stuffing the cassette into his jacket pocket, Syd strides out of the classroom. Graham flops into his chair. Head in hands, snot bubbles from his nose; a whining grows from back of his throat. Terror embraces him.

— Christ! How can this happen? It's a school not a fucking borstal.

He considers his options. Take this to Taffy? He'd never believe him and, if he did tell Taffy, Syd would be certain to deliver on his promise of extreme violence. Should he talk to Don? No. What could Don do? Don had been in the war. Seen stuff. He'd wonder why Graham didn't fight back. No, he can't tell anyone about what happened. The only choice he has is to get this qualification and leave Union Street Juniors, move on. Until then he'll concentrate on the class. Immerse himself in the world of 4H, where he feels safe. He's no match for that bastard Formby, but he *can* protect the kids from him.

So that's decided. He'll lead his class through the wonderland of drama and keep them under his wing until they head off to Big School. Then, at the end of the year, he'll move on, qualified to teach drama. Is that cowardice? Maybe. But he is brave enough to do a Dorothy. Build a castle, feel safe. Steer clear of the fascist Formby.

Fourteen

The Apprentice

Adopting the drama teacher posture he's picked up from Dorothy – right hand seating chin, left hand seating elbow – Graham gazes out of the window in the school hall. The class, sitting in a huddle, look baffled. Graham strokes his chin.

— Now…

He pauses, giving a lighthouse lamp sweep of the head, catching the eye of every child, maintaining a fixed smile. He thinks Dorothy… therefore he is Dorothy.

— Now. We're going to do some drama.

Another pensive pause.

— You're all going to be in the drama, and I'm going to be in the drama with you. Is that OK?

— We know that, sir. You told us in the classroom, says Andrew.

Andrew doesn't realise Mr Harris is doing a Dorothy. Heads twizzle like wet mops. They misshape and twist their mouths, screw up their noses, shrug their shoulders. Graham moves to the blackboard, picks up a piece of white chalk, and readopts his Dorothy-is-wondering stance.

— What shall we make a drama about? Any ideas?

So far, so good. Graham truly is Dorothy. Yesterday has gone. This is what's important. This is where he belongs. Here he feels safe. He's asked the big question: 'What shall we make a drama about?' Now he'll get creativity by the bucketful.

Aaron's the first to pipe up.

— *Coronation Street*.

— Sorry?

Graham's refined wondering pose crinkles. Aaron repeats his idea with a hint of impatience.

— *Coronation Street*, sir. You know, Corrie!

This idea meets with a chorus of yeses and cries of 'Oh yeah, Corrie!'. That's not what he was hoping for. He wants mansions or ships, something they can build. Lorraine senses his hesitation.

— Sir, you said you'd write down all our ideas. You said, sir. So write down *Coronation Street*. Like you said you would, sir.

Graham resists tentatively.

— Any other ideas?

Silence.

— Surely that's not the only…

Sean interrupts.

— Yeah, but you haven't written down the first idea yet, sir.

Graham takes a deep breath and writes down *Coronation Street*.

— OK. I've written it down. Now, he says brightly, eagerly, any other ideas? Let's have some more great ideas.

— *Black Beauty*.

Karen's suggestion prompts a scattering of derisory moans and sighs. Andrew is contemptuous.

— Oh No! Not *Black Beauty*. She's always prancing around the playground is Karen, making neighing noises.

Karen sparks back.

— Well, it's better than you and your Stevie boring Coppell. Talking to yourself.

— I don't talk to meself!

— Yeah, yer does.

She mimics Andrew's fantasy football commentary.

— It's Wiseman to Coppell. Coppell passes back to Wiseman. Wiseman shoots! Goooooooal. It's another great goal for the Manchester lad.

She sneers.

— Manchester lad! Headcase, more like.

Pivoting, Karen folds her arms. Graham steps in.

— Now, now! Enough arguing. We agreed everyone can have their own ideas, OK? *Black Beauty* was Karen's idea, so it goes up on the board.

Graham writes *Black Beauty*. Marlon raises his hand.

— *Mr Magoo*.

— *Mr... Mr Magoo*, Marlon?

Janine cuts in.

— Well, you asked us, sir. Marlon's idea must go up.

Grimly, Graham inscribes *Mr Magoo* on the board.

Aaron is impatient.

— Can we choose now, sir? From the list.

— Haven't we any other ideas?

Silence.

— Like, er, I don't know, perhaps... er... castles, for example? Castles would be good.

The class throws back a collective grimace. They're all shaking their head.

— That's your idea, sir. Not ours.

Sally-Anne is business-like.

— I suggest we let sir write his little idea down, then we have a vote. Like you promised we would, sir.

Graham is hurt.

— My *little* 'castles' idea, Sally-Anne?

Marlon puts his hand up.

— Sir, you're both right. For sir, it's a big idea; for us… well, maybe not so big.

Graham draws four columns on the blackboard: Black Beauty, Mr Magoo, Castles and Coronation Street.

— OK. A vote. Who wants to do a drama about *Black Beauty*, then?

Two hands go up, Karen's and Susan's.

— Two votes.

Still reaching for the sky, Karen surveys the abstainers, her face distorted in disbelief. Graham writes the figure two under *Black Beauty*.

— Who wants to do a drama about *Mr Magoo*?

Marlon's hand shoots up, but when he sees he has no support, he retreats.

— OK, that's one.

Sally-Anne produces the rule book.

— No, sir. Marlon's put his hand down. He's changed his mind.

Marlon agrees that he has.

— She's right, sir. A mad idea, *Mr Magoo*. Who came up with that one?

The class laughs. Simon winks at Marlon appreciatively.

— That's zero, then. Right. Now, how about castles? Could be fun, this one, he says hopefully.

He surveys the sea of blank expressions. Not one vote. Pathetically, Graham puts his hand up and writes down the number one in the column. Then takes a deep breath.

— OK. How many people would like to do a drama about *Coronation Street*?

A forest of hands sprouts from the clump of bodies. Even Kathy and Susan join the Corrie crowd, and the vote is unanimous.

Kidnapped by his sham democracy, Graham introduces delaying tactics.

— I'm wondering. We need to make some big decisions before we can begin our drama. First of all, where are we in *Coronation Street?*

— Ken Barlow's kitchen, sir.

— Mmm. Well, that's an interesting idea, Katherine, but there are 30 of us.

— Yeah, you're right, she concedes, we wouldn't all fit in the kitchen. And Ken Barlow won't have enough mugs for tea, sir.

— So where could we all meet on *Coronation Street?*

And, before Graham can answer his own question, Andrew shouts out.

— The Rover's Return, sir!

Graham replies before fully comprehending what Andrew said.

— Yes, in the church hall… what? The Rover's Return?

— The Rover's Return, sir, says Aaron. The most famous pub in the world. Many a star has bought a pint in that bar.

— Yes, yes, Aaron. Quite.

Graham smells a burning fuse: it's winding its way to a barrel labelled drama disaster.

— Yeah, says Barry, a twinkle in his eye. And we could all have a p-p-pint, sir.

His suggestion meets with widespread approval.

— Yeah, Barry. Good one, kidda!

Graham continues to think Dorothy. What did she do once the children had decided on castles? She got the children to build it! Yes; they build. Graham has time to think. With any luck, these desperate delaying tactics will take so long that he'll be saved by the bell at the end of the lesson.

— OK. If our drama is in the Rover's Return, we're going to have to build it first. Tell me what it's like inside.

Aaron's hand shoots up.

— Sir, there's tables and chairs and a bar and a jukebox.

Lorraine has an idea.

— Yeah, one of them jukeboxes on the wall. I've seen 'em when I help me mam cleaning at the Dog and Duck.

Graham thinks *Mastermind*, Magnus Magnusson: 'I've started, so I'll finish.' His saving grace will be that they *won't* finish, he'll bring the drama to a halt, the bell will ring. Escape.

— Good. So, let's get to work. There's paper and pens for you to label things. Use the PE equipment and the chairs for the furniture. Let's do it! he cries. Let's build the Rover's Return!

They push PE platforms into spaces. Organise chairs into circles. Carefully lay scraps of paper on which they've scribbled 'pint' and 'pakit of crisps' on chairs. Graham turns the piano around.

— Is this the bar, sir?

Graham nods. Pauline writes the word BAR and pins it to the piano. Time for Graham to think. Ten minutes of the lesson to go. He decides to slow down the building process with a discussion about what they've done. Nine minutes to go.

— OK. Come over here, all of you.

Everyone gathers round, except Chinti who's still drawing enthusiastically. Mark taps him on the shoulder and makes a series of come and join us gestures. Chinti picks up his picture.

— What's Chinti been drawing, Mark?

— 'Ang on, sir. I'll check.

He signs for Chinti to hold up his drawing.

— What… this… picture of… Chint?

Chinti mutters something that Graham doesn't understand.

— He says it's a Kalashnikov, sir.

The Rover's Return meets the Tamil Tigers. Graham doesn't want to reject Chinti's idea but it's hard to see how it could be incorporated.

— What shall we do with Chinti's picture?

— Put it on the bar, sir, says Simon. Like they do with record-breaking fish in Scotland.

— Simon and Amy, can you pin Chinti's picture to the back of the piano? And let's give Chinti a clap for his... erm... idea.

They all applaud. A headline whooshes into Graham's thoughts. 'TEACHER PRAISES CHILD FOR ARMING THE ROVER'S RETURN.' Back to gritty reality.

Yesterday, Dorothy managed her drama by being 'in it'. Alongside the class. From the inside. Graham decides to do the same. Readopting his wondering stance, he fixes his gaze on the top of the hall windows.

— I'm going to be in the drama with you, OK? I'm going to be Fred, the landlord.

— Barman, sir. Fred's the barman.

— Thanks for that, Sally-Anne. So I'm going to be Fred, the barman. I want you to be customers in the Rover's Return.

Graham takes another deep breath. Checks his watch. Six minutes to the bell.

— I want you to make a still picture, a whole class photo of what it's like in the Rover's Return at half past nine on a Friday night. Decide who you are and what you're doing.

They chatter. Graham encourages ideas with questions.

— What sort of things do you think you might be doing? Anna?

— Having a drink, sir.

— Good. Who are you talking to, Anna?

— To me mates, Pam and Pauline.

— Right. Get into your places. I'm going to count down from 10 then clap my hands and you have to freeze.

The class starts moving around with purpose, clear about what they're doing. Unlike Graham. Labels are everywhere. Krisps, Pint, 'Arf Pint, Tekley's Bitter shandy, Babysham, Ciggies,

Peenuts, Blackcurant and Lager. Someone has pinned 'Gents and Ladies' on the doors of the PE store cupboard. On the floor is a large, circular piece of yellow paper with the words 'Careful – SICK' on it. Graham glances at his watch. Will they be able to hold a still image for five minutes? He begins a countdown.

— Ten... nine... eight...

Aaron takes up his position, leaning on the bar, a non-existent pint in his hand. Sean mirrors his stance.

— Seven... six... five...

Miriam, Lorraine and Alyson stand by the hall door next to a sign indicating that's where the 'jookebox' is. Underneath they've drawn a 45 rpm disc: 'Bye Bye Baby' by the Bay City Rollers. Ghazala and Anna join them and start to rehearse their backing group shuffle. Graham calls out,

— Four... three... two... and ONE. FREEZE!

Four minutes, 30 seconds to the bell. Moving slowly in and out of the frozen statues of his class, Graham narrates. *Very* slowly.

— It... has... been... another... busy... evening... at... the... Rover's... Return.

All is well. They are focused. Graham's feeling in control again. No way will they keep still for four minutes. Some are unsteady. Starting to wobble. The narration continues.

— It's been a hard week for Aaron. He's with his friend Sean, swapping stories about the biscuit factory. Janine has finished her shift and is meeting her mates. Fred, the barman, is pulling a pint of beer.

Graham moves to the piano with 'Kalashnikov' pinned to it.

— And now I want you to bring the picture to life.

With a clap he opens the improvisation floodgates. He's serving pints, crisps, pork scratchings, lager and black, responding to his customers' every whim.

— A pint of bitter, Fred, and one for yourself, mate.

There's delight on Aaron's face as he addresses his teacher as Fred.

— Certainly, sir.

Graham's starting to relax and enjoy the play. Another glance at his watch. Three minutes to go.

— Did you put anything on Noggin' the Nag in the two-thirty, Fred?

— I did, Andrew. Won a fiver.

Andrew catches David's eye and bends over, creased with laughter. Seated on a couple of blue plastic chairs, Karl and Mark mimic being drunk. Raucous hoots, squeals, the bang crash of toppling furniture fill the hall. The amusement bus is building up speed, trundling down the hill with a driver that's lost control. It's now the number 97 to Hysteria-ville. The jukebox trio have broken into 'Bye Bye Baby' and are dancing around three paper handbags. Sean has joined the drunks where he slouches, sliding ever so slowly off his chair to the floor. He sings 'Molly Malone', a song they learned in *Singing Together*, although that was without the hiccups and slurred words. The Rover's Return improvisation, without focus, learning or even a modicum of educational value, is bouncing around with all the energy of a space hopper on a trampoline. Graham is incapable of stopping it. This drama has developed a life of its own, a low life.

Graham glances through the glass panel in the hall door. His heart starts to thump madly. The headteacher! He strides purposefully along the corridor as the chaos of a lesson in freefall drifts outside. Laughter, joyful, drunken shouting, bassoon-ripe burping by Karl as he warms to his audience's joyous response. Something's not right in Mr Jenkins' well-ordered house of learning. Graham cries out in desperation.

— Order! Order, please!

— Two pints of Boddies, Fred. And a packet of cheese and onion crisps, mate.

At which instant the hall door swings open. Taffy stands there, frowning. Eyes as big as gobstoppers. The laughter, chatter and singing fade away and, in the silence that follows, only Karl's rasping burps echo around the hall. No one moves. No one speaks. Everyone is transfixed by the figure standing in the doorway. His aura demands attention, silence and fear.

Pause. Taffy surveys the class.

— Everything all right, Mr 'arris?

The sombre valley Welsh intonation gives a theatrical weight to the question. Graham's voice shifts to falsetto.

— Fine, thank you, Mr Jenkins.

— Fine, eh?

Slowly, he turns towards Graham, his brow creased in disapproval.

— Perhaps we might 'ave a word? At playtime tomorrow? Good lad.

Taffy straightens his tie, attaches his hands to his lapels and departs. The door slams heavily behind him.

Andrew knows something's up.

— Are you in trouble, sir?

— No!

The bell rings. The class pick up the debris of their truncated improvisation in silence and line up at the door.

— Sir?

— Yes, Aaron.

— Can we do drama again next week? It was top.

— We'll see, Aaron. We'll see.

The following day Graham dutifully appears before the beak at the appointed hour. Taffy leans, his fists pressed against the surface of his desk, like a gorilla on the starting blocks.

— We've 'ad this conversation before, boy. You seem to

take two steps forward and seven steps back. The jury is out on your future at this school, lad. This is Union Street Juniors, not the school for bloody scandal. As to your thespian ambitions, I'll back you all the way, lad, but you 'ave to keep your side of the bargain. Maintain some semblance of order. What with William Tyndale School closing down because the kids have taken over the wheelhouse.

Taffy takes off his glasses and pulls a white handkerchief from his breast pocket.

— As the Chinese would say, we live in interesting times.

He replaces his glasses and screws up his nose.

— As you know, I've agreed to Miss Tomkins coming to work with your class on their language development. It's important they talk proper, like. But we can't 'ave them turning into little rebels. Remember, drama and chaos give ammunition to you know who. Naming no names.

He doesn't need to. Word has got around regarding the *Coronation Street* fiasco. Miss Broadstairs asked Graham whether he had a licence to sell alcohol in his drama lessons. Syd caught him in the car park at the end of school and asked him if he'd been thrown off the Royal Society of Limp Wristed Farts course yet?

— All seems to be going to plan, Trotsky.

Fifteen

Stella

The children are writing letters to Taffy apologising for their behaviour in the drama lesson. Graham knows it wasn't their fault; it was his inexperience. Nevertheless, Andrew suggested it. He'd written to Mr Jenkins after he'd 'borrowed' the school trophies and his contrition had, he said, gone down a bomb. Mr Jenkins had patted him on the head and grinned at him every time they met.

— He likes kids saying sorry. Like what Sally-Anne's dad said – it takes a big man to say sorry.

Sally-Anne pipes up.

— And a big woman.

Like a mixed bed of annuals after a heavy shower, their bodies adopt different shapes, angles and positions. A variety of colours, textures, tones planted across the classroom. Lorraine is sprawled, wearily, head on the desk, watching her pen skate across the page in loops and lines. Sally-Anne sits stiff-backed in her Saturday morning ballet-class posture. Alongside her, Andrew is trying to mirror her position. As his form lapses, she nudges him, then frowns and lifts her chin, as if she is bidding at Sotheby's. He straightens his back; she bows her head, offering graceful approval. There is a sharp knock on the door. Joan Groom leans in.

— A quick word, Mr Harris?

She jerks her head, indicating the conversation should be in the corridor, away from prying ears.

— While I'm out of the room, says Graham, you can do a listening exercise. Write down every sound you can hear. And, Karl, no burping or trumping. Remember, you're sound recorders, not sound makers. Do you understand?

There is a less than enthusiastic chorus of 'Yes, Mr Harris'.

Outside, in the corridor, Graham finds Joan and two others: a young girl with flaxen hair, cut into a neat pageboy style, and an attractive, well-dressed woman. The girl's expression is sour; she's leaning back, elbows resting on the shoulder-high windowsill, legs crossed, in knee-high white socks. Tapping her blue Mary Jane shoes together impatiently, she stares down the corridor. She does not want to be here.

— Mr Harris, this is Mrs Tupper and her daughter Stella.

Stella bristles.

— I am not 'er daughter. She's not me mam, right? Me mam lives in Stockport.

Joan cockles her lips.

Mrs Tupper's blue, lace-trimmed, empire line dress gives her the look of a milkmaid. Wiping her jet black curls off her forehead, she reveals a furrowed brow. She bites her lip and massages the palm of her left hand with her right thumb. Undaunted, Joan continues.

— Stella has come from Stockport with her new mum. They've moved into Ventnor Street.

Stella tuts at the reference to her new mum, but Graham recognises the coded implication of a family break-up. He smiles at Stella, who doesn't smile back.

— That's handy, eh, Stella? Right by the school gates. Finish your Frosties, fall into our classroom. You're never going to be late, are you?

— Might be, and I don't like Frosties. I like variety packs, but she won't buy 'em.

She headbutts the space between herself and her mum.

— They're too expensive, Stella.

Her mum's tone is apologetic, patience under strain. Stella blinks slowly, heavily, fixing her gaze on something far away, out of the window.

Joan rolls her eyes. Mrs Tupper forces a smile, continuing to massage her palm. Graham turns to her.

— So, Mrs Tupper, when would you like Stella to start?'

— I was rather hoping she could join in straight away... if that's all right?

She bites her lip anxiously. This woman is clearly ready for a break.

— Er, well, I suppose so, if that's OK, Joan?

— Your decision, Mr Harris.

Graham turns to his new pupil.

— How about starting straight away, Stella?

— Suits me. Get away from *her*.

Stella jabs a finger at her not-mam.

— Don't you start, you little madam. I told you this morning, you cheeky beggar...

She breaks off, reluctant to lose her temper in front of Mr Harris. Graham's a bit taken aback by the outburst. Mrs Tupper's anxiety is obvious.

— If you've any concerns, Mrs Tupper, don't hesitate to pop in. I'm here 'til half five most days.

There's a minimal lift of her head in response. Graham gestures towards the class.

— We're a happy little band in there.

There is a crashing sound and a burst of laughter from inside.

Stella stares at the door and her eyes narrow. Mrs Tupper's brow smooths.

— Thank you for your help, sir.

Stella turns on her.

— You don't 'ave to call 'im sir, you know. 'E's not your teacher.

Then to herself.

— Me real mam wouldn't 'ave called 'im 'sir'.

Mrs Tupper reploughs the forehead, as Joan signals a quick exit.

— Right, we'll let you get on, Mr Harris.

She hands him a brown envelope.

— You might want to look at this. It's Stella's report card from her last school.

Mrs Tupper calls,

— Bye, Stell.

Stella swivels around.

— I told ya, don't call me Stell. Only me real mam calls me Stell, right?

Stella pushes the classroom door and goes inside. Graham reassures Mrs Tupper.

— Don't worry, Mrs Tupper. She'll be fine.

Mrs Tupper mouths, 'Sorry,' and retreats down the corridor.

It's already clear to Graham that his newest pupil is one very troubled bunny. She never asked for a new mum and the world is going to know how she feels about it. Stella announces her presence to the class by defiantly swinging her navy blue duffle bag over her shoulder. With one hand on her hip and her left foot tapping, she stands before them, glowering. Graham puts a hand on her shoulder, ready to introduce her. She shrugs it off. Lorraine bites her bottom lip, turns and shares a knowing look with Ghazala.

— Right, pens down, fold your arms, look this way. This is Stella, and she'll be joining us from today. Now, as you know, it's hard when you come to a new school. First of all, you don't know anyone, so you haven't any friends to play with. I want you to help Stella by keeping an eye open for her. Make sure she's not left out. If she's lost, help her out. And, Stella, if you're not sure about anything, don't be afraid to ask. We're a friendly bunch. Aren't we?

Andrew puts his hand up.

— Karl Connelly isn't friendly, sir.

Karl stands and points his finger.

— Watch it, Wiseman, or you're dead by dinnertime.

Andrew nods.

— Persecution rests, m'lud.

Sally-Anne laughs.

— Prosecution, Andrew.

Graham has unintentionally hit the banter button and quickly tries to switch it off again.

— Stella, excuse Andrew. He watches too much *Crown Court*.

— And Rumpole, sir. I love *Rumpole of the Bailey*. And Steve Coppell.

Karl interrupts.

— And Sally-Anne!

Sally-Anne squirms. Andrew bobs his tongue Karl's way. Stella prefers the view out of the window; foot tapping continues. Graham decides to allocate two 'sensibles' to watch over her.

— Miriam, Lorraine, I'd like you to be Stella's special friends while she settles in.

Stella grimaces at the words 'special friends' while Miriam and Lorraine frown uneasily at their new role.

— You can show her where everything is and make sure she's not left on her own at playtimes.

Stella's foot-beating irritation is now accompanied by arm

folding and impatient deep sighs. She mouths to Mr Harris, 'Get on with it'. Which he does.

— I'll sort out some exercise books, pens and pencils at playtime. If you could sit in that spare desk over there, Stella…

She walks haughtily to the back of the room; doesn't remove her duffle bag. Lounging with her legs splayed and elbow hooked around the back of the chair, she mimes a bored whistle. Graham decides it's time to shift attention away from the grumpy newcomer. He raises his hand to signal silence and one by one the class recognise the tradition and stop talking, raising their hands in a mirrored response.

— Good. Hands down, fold your arms, look at me and listen. Sally-Anne and Marlon, will you collect the letters of apology to Mr Jenkins and put them on my desk, please? While they're doing that, I want to tell you about our new drama.

There are hissed exclamations of 'Yis!' and 'Ace!'

— We'll start off in the classroom, then continue in the hall this afternoon with a drama teacher called Miss Tomkins. She's coming in to help me.

Lorraine turns to the class.

— She's well nice. I showed her where our class was, didn't I, sir?

— You did, Lorraine.

— If she's with you, Mr Jenkins probably won't tell you off, sir.

With desks pushed back and chairs forming a semi-circle, Miriam moves Stella's desk. Stella remains in her chair watching, then pulls her chair out of the semi-circle, creating a row for herself. Mark and Chinti make room and gesture for her to fill the space; she ignores them. Graham begins the drama.

— So our drama starts a long time ago. Before there were cars, electricity and gas, before televisions and cassette players. We're in a town called Hamelin.

Stella shouts out,

— Ham Lin? What kind of daft name is that?

Ignoring the muted giggles, Graham continues.

— Does anyone know how to make bread?

Stella tosses in an unhelpful question.

— What you wanna make bread for? Yer can get it from the Spar shop.

Stella snorts sarcastically. Sally-Anne looks at Graham for reassurance. Clenching his teeth, he looks away, drags in some air and instructs himself to stay calm. He takes Stella's question at face value.

— You're right, that's where you can buy bread, Stella, but how do we make it? I'm thinking about long ago, in olden days, before the Spar shop. So who can tell me how people got their bread then?

Stella shouts again.

— I dunno. I've never been to the olden days, 'ave I?

Unease ripples through the class. Graham sits on the edge of his desk, his patience with the new arrival wearing thin. It's time to draw some boundaries. Graham reminds himself to mask his true feelings. Rise above it.

— Stella, I know you're new, and you don't know our class rules, so I want you to listen carefully to what I say next. Firstly, we don't shout out; we put our hand up if we're going to say something.

She blows out her cheeks.

— Secondly, you don't have to have lived in the past to know about it. Can anyone tell Stella how we can know about the past?

Kathy raises her hand. Graham nods while keeping his eye on Stella.

— There's pictures and drawings of olden days in history books, sir.

— Good. Thank you, Kathy.

Stella mimics tauntingly.

— Oh, thank you, Kathy. Have a star, Kathy.

Kathy blushes while those around her titter. Graham makes a mental note: when the bell goes, get advice from Dennis the Wise.

***

Dennis is putting wooden mathematics counting rods into a tatty brown cardboard box. He's looking uneasy.

— Someone's taking a five-fingered discount on these, Graham. One of each colour goes missing every time I use them. Johnny 'The Grass' Caldwell says it's Janine Brook. Apparently, she drills holes in them to make bangles, then sells them for 20 pence a throw in the playground. Mrs Thatch would be proud of her. No evidence yet, but I've got me spies out.

Graham turns to the roller blackboard, spreads his hands and feet, like a suspect about to be body-searched. He headbutts the canvas, his voice getting louder with each jolt.

— New... Girl... Tupper... is... A... WINDER... UPPER!

With each thump of his head, chalk dust falls like snow and turns his hair grey. He's visibly aged in the half hour since he met Stella. A noise at the back of the class alerts Dennis to the fact that they're not alone.

— Gordon Farley, you can finish cleaning out the hamster cage at dinner time, OK?

Graham regains his composure. The boy eyes him uneasily and moves slowly, crab-like, out of the room.

— Sorry, Dennis, didn't realise...

— They're everywhere, mate. Kids, everywhere, there's no peace. Can't get anything done. Except in the holidays, that is.

My class runs like clockwork then. It's the kids that get in the way; I tell you, they're ruining my career in teaching.

Graham tells him about Stella.

— What should I do?

— Rule one, ignore her. She wants attention. When she does something good, praise her to the hilt. Simple psychology. Think rats. Or is it dogs? Think Pavlov – or is it Pavlova? It doesn't matter. Even if you end up saying – what did you say her name was?

— Stella Tupper.

— OK. 'Stella Tupper, you breathed well today.' If that doesn't work, tie her up, lock her in the PE storeroom and let her out on Friday. That never fails.

He smiles at his little joke before returning to his maths equipment audit.

— I'd better go. I've 30 acts of contrition to deliver to the boss. To be fair to my class, the *Coronation Street* calamity wasn't their fault but Andy assures me, pupil grovelling works wonders with Taffy. And he should know. Thanks for the advice about Stella, Dennis. I'll let you know how I get on.

Dennis holds up red and yellow wooden rods.

— Don't forget: check if any of your girls are wearing bangles made of these things. Vigilance, Graham. Vigilance. Don't let the buggers grind you down.

Sixteen

Mutiny on the Bounty

Andrew was right about the power of contrition: when Graham delivered the class's letters to Taffy, the boss was pleasantly surprised. Now Graham's pupils are settled and ready to start a new drama. Stella has returned to her seat *outside* the semi-circle of class chairs. Graham is going to take Dennis's advice and ignore her bad behaviour. He's going to go straight into role. Perhaps that will attract her attention and get her commitment.

He walks from his desk to the classroom door, turns dramatically and raises a chain of office above his head. A collection of old pin badges covered in tin foil and attached to an old toilet chain, it's a gift from Don, delivered by Aiden. Placing it ceremoniously around his neck, he strides purposefully towards his empty teacher's chair and climbs on it like a speaker mounting the hustings. Andrew cranks up the tension.

— Who *is* he?

Stella scowls. She looks askance, her cheeks pulsating as if she's building up a gob of spit. Which she might be. Graham raises his hands as if silencing a rowdy crowd.

— Thank you. Thank you. Can I begin by saying how grateful I am for your support throughout this campaign? You've placed your trust in me, and I won't let you down. As I've said before, I promise this town will, once again, be known as the cleanest, tidiest, smartest throughout the land. A place of which we can all be proud. Word will spread, good citizens, Hamelin town: healthy, clean and safe. Hamelin town: where everyone wants to live.

Stepping down from the chair, Graham takes off the chain.

— Who do you think that was? he asks.

Stella bellows.

— Some daft wally in a necklace!

Groans of disappointment ripple through the rest of the class. It's as if a spark has flown into the Bonfire Night family firework box for the third year running. Graham clenches his teeth.

— What did you say, Stella?

— This drama stuff is stupid.

Graham finally loses his cool.

— Stella, he yells, I will not have you shouting out and being rude. Do you understand?

Dennis's advice has left the building. Aiden covers his ears. Graham nods to Ghazala to go and sit by him which she does, putting her arm around his shoulders and pulling him into her. Stella folds her arms and smirks, avoiding eye contact and looking around the room as if admiring the décor. She's sensing victory over Graham's patience.

— Yeah, well, I don't wanna do this drama crap, right?

There's an audible sucking in of breath at her swearing.

— That's fine, Stella. You don't want to do drama, and I want you to go to the back of the class and watch, while those that do want to do it can get on with our story.

She slides down her chair and puts her hands behind her head, staring at Graham.

— Now, please.

Her challenging stare continues. The class is eyeing up the confrontation.

— I'm waiting. Go to the back of the room and you can watch from there. I'll speak to you at lunchtime.

She twists her body and stands up.

— Don't care. Not bothered. Didn't wanna come to this rotten school, anyway.

Stella tramps her way to the back of the class, clambers on to a stack of desks and wraps her arms around her legs, resting her head on her knees. She twists and with her back to the class, looks out into the girls' playground.

— Now, says Graham calmly, perhaps we can get on.

A mixture of agitated and apprehensive glances dart around the class like a pinball. Sucking in of cheeks, biting of lips, eyes widening, all indicate unease. Karl catches Miriam's attention and, tilting his head towards Stella, screws an index finger into his temple and makes a cross-eyed face. She smirks in agreement.

Graham continues.

— So who was he? The man wearing the chain?

Andrew, keen to return to the game of drama, explains.

— He was mayor of Hamelin. 'Cos he had a chain and gave a speech.

— Good. Mayor of Hamelin. What was his speech about?

Barry stutters his answer.

— He kept saying th-th-thank you and being de-de-dead nice to us. Like yer m-m-mam tells you when you go to a party.

Sean butts in with a decent impression of a nagging parent.

— Don't forget to say thank you. Say thank you when you get down from the table. Say thank you when you get a lucky bag at the end. Say thank you for 'avin me an' all that stuff.

Graham gets the discussion back on track.

— So he was very grateful. About what?

Sally-Anne sits bolt upright. Her finger points directly above her.

— There's been a vote, an election, sir. He's thanking the voters.

— Good, and what's he promised he'll do?

Graham's surprised to see Aiden has his hand up.

— Aiden?

— 'E's going to keep the town clean. 'Elfie and clean, fink dat's what 'e said. Like what Mr Miggleton does.

In the sin bin, Stella takes a peek over her shoulder and a red yo-yo out of her dress pocket. With a twist of her wrist, she spins it, and it sparkles as it falls. Graham continues to talk while walking over to her, holding out his hand.

— He did promise to keep the town clean, Aiden. Just like Mr Middleton keeps Union Street Juniors clean. Well done.

Stella tut-tuts her annoyance and hands over the yo-yo. Returning to his desk, Graham places it in the drawer.

— In the next part of our drama, we're going to make still images. In drama we call them tableaux. An art gallery of life in Hamelin town. Big paintings of something the whole family does together every week: making bread. Now, get into groups and find a space.

Animated negotiations for group membership begin. Popular class members, like Sally-Anne, Andrew, Miriam and Sean, point, beckon and nod to say, 'You're in.' An arm around the neck seals the deal. Everyone wants to be accepted, not to be left out but there are the leftovers, those never picked. Aiden waits patiently, hands in his pockets, silently pleading 'Pick me' by bobbing his eyebrows up and down. Karl isn't selected but doesn't appear to care: he rests against the wall and yawns, nonchalantly sliding his foot back and forward as if testing the doorstep for ice.

Aiden has too few ideas; he'll have to be carried along by others. Karl, too many ideas, too surreal, too dogmatic, not a team player. Graham intervenes and allocates the unpicked.

— Decide who you will be in your still picture: mum, dad, grandma or child.

Trying hard to disguise her interest, Stella subtly shifts her position so that she can watch her new classmates creating, imagining. They mime kneading, rolling, cutting and shaping. Sally-Anne, who has made bread with her dad, shows Andrew how to hold his hands. He then demonstrates to the rest of the class as if he's been doing it for years. They make an art gallery of their tableaux.

In the first picture, Ghazala's kneading the dough, wiping sweat from her brow with her forearm. Marlon is standing at the oven with a bread shovel, which bears a remarkable resemblance to one of the gardening spades that Don keeps in the storeroom. Elsewhere, Robert reads the paper, smoking a pipe. Karen and Susan are under the table, making boats with the unused dough. Stella slips down off her desk and opens the fire door at the back of the classroom. Sally-Anne sidles up to Mr Harris.

— The new girl has opened the fire door, sir.

— I know, Sally-Anne. Just ignore her.

The rest of the class are straining and pushing to get a view of what she's doing,

— Please, ignore Stella and come back and sit down.

They move back to the semi-circle of chairs. Graham opens a book and reads.

— 'Rats! They fought the dogs and killed the cats, and bit the babies in the cradles…'

Stella is bending over, unfolding her arms around a desk, lifting it and waddling to the fire exit. Graham continues his ignore her tactic.

— 'They ate the cheeses out of the vats and licked the soup from the cooks' own ladles...'

— Sir, the new girl's taking a desk outside.

— I know, Mark, and we're ignoring her. I want you all to ignore what she's doing.

At which every pair of eyes in the room immediately turns to gawp.

— I want you all to concentrate on me and ignore Stella, OK?

Reluctantly, 4H revolve to face their teacher as he reads the poem.

Rats!
Split open the kegs of salted sprats,
Made nests inside men's Sunday hats,
And even spoiled the women's chats,
By drowning their speaking
With shrieking and squeaking
In fifty different sharps and flats.

Stella hooks her arms around the next desk, lifts it and exits the classroom. One by one, she places each desk in a line along the path around the prefab. She's lost interest in the drama. Furniture removal is her sole focus now, as she rearranges her environment, changes the geography of her new and unwanted home. For the first time today, she's doing something *she* has decided to do. Something over which *she* has control. Miriam puts up her hand.

— I hate rats, sir. Me mam saw one in the back yard, and we had to get the rat man in. Mam blames the fried chicken carry-out on Maude Street 'cos the bins is overflowing. Me dad says yu' can't do nowt, 'cos there's rats everywhere.

— Very interesting, Miriam. Now...

— He says there's a rat for every square yard in Manchester. I don't know where he gets this stuff. Me mam reckons he's full of useless knowledge and if he spent as much time reading the jobs column as he does reading the *Sunday People*, we'd be a damn sight better off. That's what she's says, anyways.

— Yes, I'm sure that's right, Miriam. However…

— When she starts on 'im, 'e goes off to the bog to read the paper.

Graham holds up both his hands.

— Mmm, well, thanks for that, Miriam. Right. Back to Hamelin.

Miriam puts her hand up again.

— Sir, did I go on a bit then? Mam says I can talk for England.

Lorraine joins in.

— Yeah, our mam says that as well. She said that Miriam's a right chatterbox.

She turns to Miriam.

— But she likes you, 'cos you help with the dishes and once you changed our Craig's nappy while she was watching *Crossroads*.

Miriam's worried.

— But do I, sir? Do I go on a bit?

Andrew stands up.

— I think the evidence is before you, Your Honour. Guilty as charged!

— That will do, Andrew. No, no. Miriam, it was, how can I put this?

Graham pauses.

— Interesting, Miriam, with plenty of detail in there.

Stella continues to haul the desks through the fire door. They now encircle the classroom like a wagon train.

The bell goes.

— Right. As I said, Miss Tomkins will be with us this afternoon to help us with our Pied Piper drama.

There's a whisper of excitement across the room.

— Packed lunches go first.

The class scrambles noisily for the door; within seconds the room is quiet. Graham sits at his desk and opens the report card from Stella's last school. Dennis appears at the door and surveys the scene.

— What's going on?

Graham nods towards Stella who is wearily heaving the penultimate desk out of the room.

— You've taken my advice, then?

— Trying to. I'm not sure it's working.

— Stay resolute, mate. *No Pasarán*! Let me know if you need Pickfords. Better go, I'm on dinner duty.

Graham finishes reading the report card then turns to a pile of maths books and begins marking. Stella removes the final piece of furniture. She's exhausted.

— Sir, can I have a drink of water?

— Of course.

Graham hands her a small pink plastic cup which she fills at the sink before returning to stand next to her teacher. She gulps the water like a sheepdog at a stream.

— They're not hard, she says, looking over his shoulder at the maths books.

— Good.

— Baby stuff compared to what we done at my last school.

Her claim is backed up by what Graham has gleaned from her report card. She's bright. Particularly at maths. But there's a comment that's worrying; 'Stella's behaviour has deteriorated significantly since her mum and dad separated'.

— We'll have to sit you next to Chinti, then. He's best in the class at maths.

— Not bothered. Don't wanna be here anyway.

Graham has no emotional currency with which to negotiate. She couldn't care less what he thinks, who he sits her next to. The only person she cares about is her 'real' mum. She feels abandoned. She is angry and vengeful. Graham maintains his calmness.

— Do you want a hand putting the desks back?

She shrugs and looks out of the window.

Ignoring her rejection, Graham moves outside and picks up one end of a desk. She watches for a few seconds then joins him and picks up the other end. In silence, they return it to the classroom. Gradually they dismantle the rest of her protest barricade. When order is restored, Graham asks her,

— Are you on school dinners?

— No, packed lunches.

— Well, you can have your butties in the classroom. Then you can help me sharpen the crayons.

— That drama stuff is daft, sir.

— Well, the others like doing it.

— I don't wanna do it.

— That's OK. You can watch. Join in when you're ready.

Ghazala appears at the fire door and skips in.

— Do you want help… oh you've done it. After dinner, you can do skipping with us, Stella.

— I'm 'avin me butties with sir.

Ghazala's faintly surprised.

— Is Stella your new special assistant, sir?

— I suppose she is, Ghazala.

Ghazala's expression is a mix of confusion and hurt. Graham feels torn. A shrill voice from the playground cries,

— Ghazala, you're it!

— OK.

She brightens, turns and sprints towards the fun outside. Graham glances at Stella.

— Have you got any brothers or sisters?

— Yeah, there's our Stephen, me younger brother. But he's with me real mam. She said she couldn't take the two of us. There wasn't enough room. She told me I had to go with me dad and the witch.

— Why do you call her that?

— She's 'orrible to me. Not when me dad's there. She's dead sneaky. When it's me and her, she bosses me. I 'ate her and she's not me real mam.

She doesn't look at Graham as she speaks. The woman she's describing doesn't sound like the one Graham met. She seemed long suffering, meek. Although there was a moment when she became aggressive, but Graham had guessed she was just tired. He fishes out new exercise books, a dictionary, a pen, ruler and pencil.

— So how old's Stephen?

— Seven, and I 'ate 'im an' all. 'E's got me mum all to 'imself now. While I 'ave to go 'ome to... 'er.

Graham and Stella sit on the step outside the fire door. She scrabbles in her duffle bag, pulling out a brick of sandwiches wrapped in foil.

— What's in your butties, Stella?

— Fish paste.

— Who made them?

— Made 'em meself. She don't do nowt for me.

Stella describes her home life. She's picked on when Dad's not around. It's toxic but within the four walls of the classroom things can be different.

— Thing is, Stella, you can watch the drama as long as you don't spoil it for the others. When you want to join in, you can. Is that a deal?

She shrugs her shoulders. Graham will find out this afternoon. And so will Abbi. He'd better warn her.

Seventeen

The Pied Piper

Sitting astride a PE bench at the back of the school hall, Graham waits for Abbi to begin the next part of the drama. An exercise book for note taking rests between his sprawled legs.

The class sits on the hall floor in a bunch, around a bow-backed teacher's chair. Abbi hangs her brown leather bomber jacket on the back of it and rolls up her pillar box red sweater sleeves. She means business. Graham must concentrate hard on the lesson and not slip into Abbi daydreams. Imagining he's Michael Caine in the *The Ipcress File,* he presses a paper clip into the flesh of his palm. The pain will banish the fantasies.

Giggles and grins betray 4H's excitement. Excited whispers combine with nervous, stifled laughter. Lorraine and Miriam touch shoulders, rocking from side to side like two rowing boats in the wash of a passing launch. Others give Graham coy glances. He's a security blanket, left at the side of the room, available if required.

Abbi's ready. As she speaks, all heads turn towards her.

— We're going to continue with your drama about the Pied Piper today. Is that OK?

She inclines her head, awaiting a response.

Clenched fists accompany mutterings of 'Yis!

Abbi picks up a piece of chalk, blows the end of it as if it were a smouldering fuse on Bonfire Night. She writes in flowing, cursive script the words 'The Mayor's Parlour' on the board. Observing her profile, red jumper against the green board, waves of auburn tresses, her hourglass… Graham digs the paper clip deeper.

— Now, Mr Harris is sitting over there.

She points at him, as if there is any doubt about where he might be. With a coordinated swivel of heads, the class eyeballs him. Graham smiles, nodding bashfully in return. Andrew gives him a reassuring thumbs up and mouths 'Don't worry'.

Abbi continues.

— Now, he isn't watching you; he's watching me.

The paper clip is in danger of drawing blood.

— He's looking for new ideas for drama lessons. You'll see him writing them down. Later on, we'll use him in our drama, but for now you can forget about him. Is that agreed?

There's a timid chorus of 'Yes, Miss Tomkins.'

Sally-Anne's gaze flits between Graham and Abbi. Frowning in the way she does when working on a spot-the-difference puzzle, she whispers in Miriam's ear. Miriam glances over, bites her lip and then nods knowingly. Abbi straightens her back, pulls her sleeves further up her arms, now past her elbows. It's as if she's preparing to operate an old-fashioned wash tub.

— Mr Harris has told me how the story started, but I don't know how it ends. That's your job.

At the far end of the hall, Stella is lying on her stomach on a large blue PE mat. She rests her head in her hands and kicks her crossed legs back and forth. Since her playtime chat with Mr Harris, she's calmed down. She's happy to be Alice in Wonderland staring down the drama rabbit hole.

Abbi squats on her haunches; her voice becomes quieter, conspiratorial.

— In the next part of the drama, you're going to be the mums and dads of Hamelin town.

She stands and introduces a note of urgency.

— Rats are everywhere. The parents have decided to go and confront the mayor.

Miriam raises her hand.

— What's 'confront', Miss? Are we goin' to duff 'im up?

— No. It means we're going to ask him what he's doing about it, Miriam. When he sees the whole town outside his door, he'll be worried. But, before you can do that, we need to build the mayor's parlour. We'll use the tables, chairs and PE equipment.

Karl whispers something to Andrew, who raises his hand.

— Miss Tomkins, is there a bar? Are you going to be Bet Lynch the barmaid?

Graham winces. Abbi is firm.

— No, Andrew, there is no bar. This is the mayor's office. Are we agreed there is no bar in our Pied Piper drama?

There are a few 'tuts' and disappointed 'ahs' but they're drowned out by the chorus of 'Yes, Miss Tomkins.' Abbi picks up a roll of sticky labels.

— Before you talk to the mayor, I want you to 'use your drama eyes'. Tell me how luxurious the mayor's parlour is. How fabulous it appears because he spends the taxes you pay not on the town but on himself and his posh office.

Ideas spill out. There should be two big heavy doors with brass handles. A doorknocker in the shape of a lion's head. A big, dark, carved wooden desk, covered in red leather, with a gold ink pot and pen and pink blotting paper. A high-backed red leather chair to go with the desk. A coat of arms with two rats holding up a shield.

Karl waves his hand.

— A bottle of whisky hidden under the desk.

He's expecting the idea to be rejected, but Abbi likes it: just what you'd expect of a corrupt mayor. She writes the label and puts it under the PE table representing the desk. Karl nods his approval.

Aiden pipes up.

— He keeps his hat in the drawer. So it won't get nicked.

— What sort of hat is it?

Marlon's hand shoots up.

— It one of them three-cornered hats, like what Dick Turpin wears on the telly.

Marlon faces Mark and they high-five.

— Nice one, Marko.

— It's called a tricorn hat, says Sally-Anne.

Mark pulls a face at Marlon. The class stands in a group by the entrance to the mayor's parlour, represented by two chairs with their backs to each other. Abbi looks over to Graham and nods.

— Mr Harris is going to be the mayor in his office.

Graham gets up and ducks his head into the mayoral chain. Andrew waves him over.

Abbi continues.

— The people of Hamelin gather outside his door. How are they feeling? What's their mood?

Barry puts his hand up.

— They're right p-p-pigged off, miss. Wiv the r-r-rats and that.

Robert joins in.

— The mayor's a fibber. Said 'amelin would be clean, and it's crawling with rats. He tells porkies, miss. And he's our leader! You can't trust 'im.

— OK, so in the drama, the people of Hamelin have gone to the mayor's parlour to protest. The mayor can hear them coming down the street.

Abbi moves away from the class. She rests her chin on her hand. Thinking posture. She turns decisively to share her idea.

— We need a chant to show how angry they are. Let me hear your ideas and I'll choose one. Is that OK?

Abbi filters out the suggestions:

You said you'd make it clean.
Now there are loads of rats, and it isn't
Clean.

Abbi rejects this on the grounds that it doesn't scan.

Don't make promises
You can't keep,
Else we'll come round
And sort you out while you're asleep.

Rejected on the grounds of violent content.

Mayor, Mayor, you're a disgrace.
If you don't buck up
We'll smash up the place.

Also rejected on the grounds of violent content.

Finally, Sean's idea is met with unanimous approval.

One thousand rats and one fat mayor,
Answer the door if you dare.

Abbi continues.

— Now we need a spokesperson. If you pile in and all speak at once, the mayor won't hear you. We need someone who'll stand up to him and tell him why you're so angry. Any volunteers to do the talking?

Graham notices Stella has moved off the PE mat. She slips into the body of the class.

Andrew calls out.

— What about Sally-Anne, miss? She's good at telling people what to do.

Karl chimes in.

— Especially you, Wiseyman.

— Yeah, and sir, Karl.

Sally-Anne raises a thumb indicating her willingness to take on the role.

Abbi continues.

— We also need a signal to start the chant and another to get silence, so that we can hear Sally-Anne.

Stella shouts from the back.

— I'll stamp me feet to start it and wave me hands to stop it, like this.

She pushes her way through the crowd and counts herself in.

— And one, two, three, four. Then I'll do this.

She stamps three times then pulls her arms apart as if she were opening curtains.

— That'll tell everybody to shush.

Graham looks wide-eyed at Abbi, who voices her delight.

— Brilliant, Stella.

Stella beams a self-satisfied smile around the class. Abbi draws the planning stage to a close and introduces Graham's role.

— Now what we don't know is what happens next. So listen very carefully to Mr Harris as the mayor. You're going to have to deal with him.

Stella stands next to Sally-Anne, at the front of the class. Graham senses the importance of this moment. For the class and for Stella. There's a babble of excitement as Graham moves to the mayor's ceremonial chair. Abbi narrates.

— And so, all the mums and dads of Hamelin made their way to the town hall. They'd had enough. They've elected Sally-Anne to speak for them. They stand outside the town hall door and Stella starts a chant.

One thousand rats and one fat mayor,

The rest of the class joins in.

Answer the door if you dare.
One thousand rats and one fat mayor,
Answer the door if you dare.

It gets louder. The class relishing their role as outraged protesters.

One thousand rats and one fat mayor,
Answer the door if you dare!

Stella waves her arms vigorously. Finally, she pulls the curtains open to stop the chant.

Everyone stops, apart from Chinti, who hasn't understood, and his little voice pipes up.

— Thousand rat one fit mayor, answer the door I don't care...

Some of the class laugh, others give a sympathetic 'Ah!', but the tension is broken.

Mark raises his hands and puts his finger to his lips to explain to Chinti what he was supposed to do.

Chinti moves his head from side to side. Mark reassures him.

— Don' worry, Chint. Remember, you're the only one who is on purple book three in maths.

Abbi intervenes.

— Right. Let's do it again. That's what's great about drama: we can make a mistake and then put it right. This time, raise the hall roof. Let's get Mr Jenkins out of his room.

Graham's not too keen on that suggestion and swallows hard.

The chant erupts, much louder than before. Graham moves over to a bench labelled the balcony window and voices his concern.

— Oh dear me! The whole town's out there. They don't sound very happy.

With a mischievous grin, Stella signals to stop, this time accompanied by stamping her foot three times, sending reverberations across the hall. Three loud stamps for Stella. One huge stamp of approval for Graham. He sits on the front edge of the desk, smiling amiably.

— Come in, good people of Hamelin.

Sally-Anne marches in with a thunderous expression. The rest tumble into the space behind her. She points her finger at Graham.

— You! You're a disgrace!

Stella, encouraged by Sally-Anne's righteous fury, joins in.

— Yeah, you are.

Graham raises his hands in contrition.

— I know. I know. I've let you down. I made promises I should've kept. You're right; I'm a disgrace. I am so sorry.

The class, not expecting such deference, are confused. Graham continues his sycophantic bleating.

— It's the rats, isn't it?

Sally-Anne rejects his pathetic penitence.

— Yes, Mayor, they're everywhere. One bit Lorraine's baby yesterday. What you going to do about it?

Stella echoes.

— Yeah, what you going to do, eh?

— I've called a rat catcher. He's called the Pied Piper, and he's on his way now.

Stella steps between Sally-Anne and Graham, folding her arms.

— Well, he'd better be. How do we know your Pied thingy person is any good?

Sean addresses the class.

— Well, if he can't do the job, then he doesn't get paid. If he doesn't get paid, then you get the sack. Isn't that right, Mayor?

There is laughter followed by mumbled agreement.

Stella breaks into a new chant.

— We'll be back to give you the sack.

She turns to the class and conducts.

— We'll be back to give you the sack, we'll be back to give you the sack.

They all join in enthusiastically.

Stella is pleased with herself. Abbi holds up her hands.

— We've got to stop there. That was really great.

Alyson's disappointed.

— Ah, sir! We were just getting into it.

Taffy is standing by the hall door and he's smiling. Graham removes his chain as Abbi announces,

— Alyson, the next time we do this drama will be for some important people. We're going on a big day out. Mr Harris will tell you all about it when we get back to the classroom.

Graham sees Andrew rubbing his hands together.

— Is this our special treat, sir? Can I be the Pied Piper, sir?

— No, Andrew.

— Sir, you get all the best parts.

— Yeah, but you get to shout at me, don't you?

— Good point, well made, as me dad would say.

The strapping girls clear the table and equipment. Stella, without being asked, joins them.

As Graham passes Taffy, he catches his eye.

— New girl settling in, Mr Harris?

— Early days, Mr Jenkins. Early days.

He holds up his crossed fingers. Abbi is collecting her coat and bag. She looks over to Graham and smiles broadly. Graham feels flutters in his stomach. Sally-Anne looks up at him.

— Are you all right, sir. You've gone red.

Eighteen
The Big Day Out

Eight-thirty in the morning. As the spring dawn crawls reluctantly over the red brick terrace houses, 4H gather outside Union Street Juniors, under Graham's watchful eye. Some stand in groups of three or four, stamping their feet, hugging themselves or, in the case of Ghazala and Miriam, each other. Graham cups his hands to makes a loudhailer.

— The coach will be here soon, he reassures them.

David Bignall rummages in his haversack and pulls out a packet of crisps.

— David, no! shouts Graham. Save them 'til break time. Now put them back in your bag.

— Ah, sir. I'm hungry.

— Bag, David.

Sally-Anne and Pauline scrape a large heart with their boot heels in the frost. Mark, Andrew, Sean and Marlon are having a kick-about.

— Boys. Header tennis only. I don't want a gang of mudlarks on the coach.

Andrew picks up the ball.

— What's a mudlark, sir?

— You, if you fall over. Header tennis, please.

Aiden skips around like a faithful pet dog, retrieving the ball.

A large white coach swings into view down the street.

— OK, gather round, everyone.

Grabbing their bags, they skip, run and saunter towards Graham. It's their big day out. A trip to York to finish the Pied Piper drama in front of Her Majesty's School Inspectors. Abbi has kept her promise to Lorraine for a special treat.

Mark runs in the opposite direction to everyone else. He's retrieving Chinti who's counting the railings in the field. It's for his Prime Numbers Are Everywhere project.

— While we wait for Mark to get Chinti, says Graham, can I remind you that on the coach you will sit girl–boy, boy–girl.

— Do we have to, sir?

— Yes, we do, Janine. You can be next to your friends on the way back.

— But *why* do we have to sit boy-girl, sir?

— Because, Lorraine, you'll be better behaved. You'll arrive ready to do some work. Not wound up like clockwork mice. Remember, today you're an advert for Union Street Junior School. You're on your best behaviour.

Simon gives a thumbs up.

— Don't worry, sir. We'll be good.

He pauses.

— You won't have us much longer, will you, sir? It's Abbey Wood for us after the summer term.

Graham tries not to think about their move to secondary school. Sally-Anne puts her hand up.

— Actually, Simon, Ghazala's going to Saltacre High School for Girls, and Chinti's off to Manchester Grammar.

Simon closes his eyes, spreads his arms and speaks into the cold, clear blue sky.

— Blimey, Sally-Anne. If I put my socks on the wrong way round, you'd be round to tell me mam!

Sally-Anne blushes and Andrew jumps in.

— Leave her alone, Simon. She was only saying.

Mention of secondary school always prompts a mood of anxiety. But Sally-Anne won't let Simon off the hook.

— It's impossible to put socks on the wrong way round, Simon. Inside out, yes. The wrong way round, no. Shoes, yes. Socks, no.

Simon starts pulling at his hair.

— Aaarrrghh!

Andrew's pleased.

— Yeah, nice one. You tell 'im, Sal.

— Sally-Anne, please, Andrew.

Andrew purses his lips and frowns. Mark and Chinti join the back of the group. Chinti is stuffing a reel of white sticky tape in his pocket. He's marked three more of the railings.

Found some primes, Chinti?

— 71, 73 and 79, Mr Hurries.

The coach revs its engine. The doors open and Abbi comes down the steps. She's wearing brown boots, culottes and a red bolero jacket over a white blouse. Graham feels ill-dressed in his black Team Suzuki anorak and corduroys.

— Good morning, Mr Harris's class.

The class chorus 'Good morning, Miss Tomkins' and file onto the bus.

The boy-girl seating arrangement is still causing resentment. Grumpy faces, hands in pockets, they avoid contact like trams on different lines.

Apart from Andrew and Sally-Anne. He chats away eagerly.

— We're off to Magaluf, Sal. It's me first time on a plane. Mam says I'm in charge of our Wayne. She says she's 'aving a couple of lagers. She said, 'I want to start off as I mean to go on.' Where are you going for your hols?

— The Cinque Terre.

— Where's that? Is it near Hong Kong?

Sally-Anne shakes her head.

— I'll draw you a picture when we're on the bus.

— Cheers, Sal.

— Sally-Anne, Andrew. Not Sal.

Behind his hand, Graham discreetly asks the driver where he keeps the sick bags. He doesn't want the children to hear the 'S' word. There'd been an incident in the canteen when a first-year shouted, 'Alyson Healey's puked over her Manchester tart, sir' and the domino effect took hold. Table by table, retching, heaving and regurgitating. Soon the smell of vomit and boiled cabbage had filled the canteen, followed quickly by the whiff of Dettol-laced mops as the dinner ladies fell into action.

As the coach moves off, Abbi turns towards Graham who's sitting beside her. Her breast presses against his upper arm. He swallows hard and makes a small but audible sigh.

— Are you alright? Not another pilchard, I hope.

— No, erm, I was thinking about… erm, my roles in the drama… as the boy who gets left behind and then the Pied Piper.

As she talks, her scent, softly spiked with wood and musk, invades Graham's senses. He realises he's making short snuffling noises and takes out his hanky to blow his nose as a cover up. As she leans forward to pull a clipboard out of her turquoise rope bag, her blouse falls forward offering a glimpse of cleavage. Graham averts his gaze instantly. Sally-Anne, in the seat across the aisle, is staring hard at him. Miriam speaks to her from behind her hand. They giggle. Abbi scans her checklist.

— You've got the pipe, Mr Harris?

— Yes, Ms. Tomkins, and the shoe for the boy.

— And you're clear about the attitude you'll adopt when the class meets you?

— Yes, I'm disappointed not to get into the mountain when I'm the little boy and when I'm the Pied Piper, I'm ill-tempered and blaming the parents for the children's disappearance.

— Sounds good but listen carefully to what they say. We'll talk after the session.

Graham feels he's putting the pain and disorder of recent events behind him. Here's someone who knows what she's doing, who has the same desire to make learning a creative exploration. Who treats the children as co-adventurers. His portfolio of drama write-ups is full of questions. When he looks back at his earlier entries, he sees descriptions without analysis. Things are looking up. Coming into school, he's no longer saturated with fear. The stomach-churning anxiety as Syd Formby approaches in the corridor is diminishing.

Graham's confidence is growing and so is the self-assurance of his class. He can see it in the way they move about in the school, the way they walk into the hall. He's filled with pride when they raise their hands to answer Taffy's questions in assembly. Drama is undermining the elitist structure, and the woman sitting beside him is making it happen. Oh to spend time more time with her. Just listening to her ideas, her commentary on classrooms, learning. Schools as they are and how they could be.

***

Travelling through the affluent suburbs of Manchester during rush hour, the warm coach and crisp, cloudless sky are a welcome change from the classroom.

A commotion at the back of the coach has caught the driver's eye.

— Sir, will you tell them kids to sit down, please?

Marlon, Lorraine and Simon are kneeling on their seats,

Janine and Robert are in the aisle looking out of the window. Janine points.

— That house has got a swimming pool in the garden.

Simon shouts from the other side.

— That one there, as well.

There are whoas and wows.

— That car! It's a Merc.

— A what?

— A Mercedes, dummy.

Karl shouts.

— Sally-Anne, you live round here, don't you?

He laughs. With a huff, Sally-Anne folds her arms and reddens. Andrew leaps to her defence.

— Hey, Karl, put a sock in it.

— Ooh. Wiseyman's got a cob on. Sally-Anne your girlfriend?

There are more sniggers, then Robbo shouts out.

— Hey, over there. Look at her, gettin' in the milk. Oooh! She's in her dressing-gown. She doesn't work, does she? Just got out of bed, by the look of it. Andy, can you see? Them's big... you-know-whats!

Marlon completes his sentence.

— Bazzoomas.

Everyone's laughing, except Sally-Anne.

— Andrew, ignore them. They're childish.

Instead, Andrew ignores her and, rising in his seat, his eyes like the fat end of binoculars, he frantically scans the passing houses.

Lorraine spots something on the other side of the road.

— There's a bloke in a cap cleaning that posh car.

Graham marches down the aisle.

— You're not allowed to stand when the coach is on the move. Everyone, sit in your seats, please.

They all slump back into their seats. A reflective silence falls.

— It's not fair, is it, sir? says Marlon.

Graham smiles resignedly, sits back in his seat and pictures the council estate most of these kids go back to every night. That's too simple. If houses were the size of the joy and happiness inside, wouldn't some of these be two-up, two-downs? Aiden's house would be even smaller than it is now, but Miriam's? Ghazala's? Andrew's? They'd be mansions.

Abbi interrupts his stream of thought.

— So, Graham, as I was saying, in drama you throw in the tension, the rest will follow. Believe me.

She gives him a comfortable smile.

***

Abbi stands on a raised platform in the main lecture theatre of the College of Ripon and St John. The class huddle around her. The entrance to the Pied Piper's cave is made with paper labels, chairs and two parallel benches. Leaning against a wall to one side of the room, Graham studies the rows of inspectors who make up the audience. All men, save one. All dressed in pinstriped or dark suits with white or blue shirts. All wearing ties. The lone woman is in a navy twinset, reading glasses teetering on the precipice of her nose. She's wearing a cameo brooch, the edges of which glint when she moves.

The class is pensive. Abbi reminds them of where they're up to in the story.

— The greedy mayor has cheated the Pied Piper out of 200 guilders. The Piper is furious; he plays his flute. This time it's not the rats but the children who follow him. The parents, frozen by his magic spell, watch helplessly as the children skip along behind the Piper. Finally, when they can move, they dash to catch up with children. But it's too late: they've gone.

Graham moves to the front of the hall.

— Mr Harris is going to take the role of a child. You'll be the parents. You meet him as he comes down from the mountain. You'll have a chance to ask him what's happened to the others.

Andrew raises his hand.

— How do we know he's not lying?

— We'll have to agree he tells the truth. OK?

Abbi narrates and pulls the class into the drama.

— The mums and dads are trudging up the mountain path. In the distance, they see a boy carrying one of his shoes heading towards them.

Graham takes off his shoe and limps toward the chair.

— It's not fair. I said, 'Barry, wait for me! I've got a stone in me shoe'. By the time I'd got it out, they'd all gone.

Sean's puzzled.

— Gone where?

— Into the mountain.

— Into the mountain? What d'yer mean?

— That piper bloke. He said a spell. A large stone rolled back, and that's when you could hear it.

— Hear what? asks Miriam.

— The music. The fairground. You could smell the doughnuts. Hot and sweet.

Miriam's doubtful.

— What? Doughnuts inside the mountain?

— Yeah. There were lights and a funfair. There were trees with toffee apples dangling from them. Ice-cream vans were playing 'Greensleeves'. My mates were running inside cheering. Barry shouted, 'It's free. It's flipping all free, kids'.

Andrew leans forward, his eyes piercing, alert, intrigued. Katherine clasps her hand and starts sucking her thumb. Graham continues.

— The last one in was the piper man. I shouted, 'Wait up'. He didn't hear me. He lifted his arms. The great stone rolled back, and that was it. Closed. No funfair. Not a sound.

Pauline wonders.

— Did you hear any magic words?

Kathy takes her thumb out of her mouth and speaks in a lowered voice.

— Yeah. Were there spells? There's always spells in these stories. What spell did he use? Was it abracadabra?

— I shouted, 'Piper, what about me? Open up the door, please'. I tried all the spells I knew; abracadabra, shazam, izzy wizzy. Even 'Invent a door where there wasn't one before'. Nothing worked. They're in there, having fun and I'm out here, having none.

Graham puts the shoe down and freezes. Abbi steps in.

— So all the children are in the mountain.

Khalid puts his hand up.

— Sounds good. Fairground. Free nosh.

His best friend, David, breathes in deeply, inflating his bulk.

— Yeah, and doughnuts.

The topic of food has roused him.

— The thing is, how long would this fun last before the children got fed up and wanted to go back home? Graham asks.

Sally-Anne puts up her hand.

— It'd be great for a while, but I'd want to see my mum and dad after a bit.

Stella laughs.

— I wouldn't.

— I wonder if the little boy would get fed up. Miriam, will you ask him?

She nods enthusiastically.

Stella jumps up and, standing on one leg, begins pulling the buckle on her shoe.

— I'll be the boy.

Her volunteering for this role is a risk. Graham stands and moves to one side. She sits. Will she try to destroy the drama? She pulls at the heel of her shoe. Abbi says,

— Stella's going to be the little boy.

There seems to be some doubt about whether this will work, but Miriam is keen and leans into Stella, adopting a compassionate tone.

— Little boy, are you sad?

— No, I'm pigged off.

She throws a hitchhiker's thumb over her shoulder.

— I wanna be in there, with me mates.

Miriam raises her hands, palms open.

— But you'd miss your mum and dad if you were stuck in that mountain for ever.

Stella starts laughing.

— Ha! Well, first off, my new mam is useless, right, and like, in that mountain, I'd be well out of her way. And, like, I'm gonna miss all the jobs she gives me? Get the coal in, wash the pans, make yer bed, do the hoovering.

All this pours out with such conviction it appears her mum is not the meek woman Graham met on Stella's first day. There is apparently a darker side to the new Mrs Tupper.

— Miss her? On at me all the time, them two, sending me to bed at eight o'clock. Listening to them laughing, getting drunk. Miss them? I don't think so.

There are sympathetic nods and murmurs among the class. Abbi says,

— In the next part of the drama, you're going to have a chance to speak to the Pied Piper.

She stands in the centre of the parallel benches and points to the space in between.

— This is the size of the boulder that covers the entrance to the mountain. The mums and dads are in a crowd outside. But how do we get him to come out and talk to us?

Miriam puts her hand up.

— That piper bloke plays a pipe, right? He likes music. What about me and the girls sing him a Rollers song?

Andrew leans back, throwing his hands up in the air.

— Well, that will defo bring him out, sir. Where's me earplugs?

Miriam isn't laughing.

— Ha ha. Got a better idea, Wiseyman?

Abbi jumps to her defence.

— I think it's good, Miriam. Let's try it.

Lorraine, Ghazala, Anna, Alyson and Miriam take up positions in front of the door to the mountain. The four stand side by side, at an angle, their hands on their hips. Miriam places herself in the front. A sixties girl group. Miriam is the leader of the pack.

— What are you going to sing?

— We'll sing 'I Only Wanna Be with You', sir.

Miriam begins to click her fingers and count them in.

— One and two and three and four.

The backing singers start to 'Bop shawaddy' rhythmically before Miriam breaks into song, pitch perfect.

When they're finished, the class applaud. Abbi looks pleased.

— Blimey, Miriam, girls, that was splendid. Perhaps Mr Harris will get you signed up for the next dance and drama evening.

— Miss Broadstairs won't let us.

— Why not?

— She said I wiggled like a hussy. I told me mam, and she said if she saw her she'd smack her one. Anyway, we're gonna do 'Chants on the Moor' instead, 'cos it's French and we do the Harlem Shuffle with no wiggling.

— Do you mean 'Chanson d'Amour'?

— Summat like that.

— Well, let's see if the Rollers' song brings the Pied Piper out of the mountain. Listen to the story, and you'll know when to begin.

Graham picks up his wooden pipe and moves behind the cave entrance, ready to march out angrily. Abbi narrates:

— The singers stepped forward. They were going to test the Piper's curiosity and entice him out of the mountain.

Miriam clicks her fingers, counting in her backing singers.

— One and two and three and four.

They sing the first verse and chorus again. Graham strides in, shouting,

— WHAT? What do you want? What's all this noise?

Stella pushes her way through the band, pointing an accusing finger at Graham.

— Right, Mr Piper, or whatever they call you. Listen, 'cos I've had enough. We want our kids back, right?

Sean shouts from the back of the crowd.

— You tell 'im, Stell!

Encouraged, she ups the ante.

— We done nowt wrong, pal. We weren't the ones promising 200 guilders or whatever you call 'em. If you've got a problem with the fat mayor… sort it with him, right? But don't take it out on us. We've done nothin' wrong. Give us our kids back.

The class breaks out into a spattering of applause and shouts of 'Go, Stella'. She speaks from a point of hurt, with passion, authenticity. The Piper challenges her.

— You sort the mayor out. He's your mayor, not mine.

— What d'ya mean, he's our mayor?

— You elected him.

She puts her hands on her hips and pulls a face of disbelief.

— You're a joke, Piper.

Abbi steps in, addressing the whole class.

— What the Piper says is true. You did elect him. So, isn't it your problem?

Stella's miffed. Abbi asks,

— So... what are you going to do?

Karl comes to the front and addresses the class.

— I say we rush 'im. Andy does like he's had a heart attack. That distracts the Piper man. Then we rush 'im and Marlon does his martial arts stuff.

Karl raises his flat hand and cuts the air with a karate chop.

— Ah... so! Like that.

Marlon is shaking his head, profusely.

— Not allowed. You lose your licence if you do karate at school. And martial arts people don't say 'Ah... so!' Karl. That's just cartoon stuff.

Karl's disappointed. Abbi confronts them with the logic of their reasoning.

— Even if Marlon did that, your children would still be in the mountain. And, worse, you'd have no Pied Piper to open it up. So, you're going to have to be smarter than that.

Miriam spreads her hands in a gesture of clarification.

— The Piper hates the mayor, we hate the mayor. So we're on the same side.

— Go on, says Abbi. That sounds interesting.

— Let's tell the Piper we'll sack the mayor. 'Cos he a crook. We raid his safe, it's our money, pay off the piper man for getting rid of the rats.

Stella spins around and stamps her foot.

— No! He's taking it out on us. We're getting the blame for what the mayor did.

She turns on the Piper.

— Right, Piper, listen up. Who promised you 200 guilders?

— The mayor.

— Not us, right?

— It's not the money. It's 'cos he's a cheat.

Sally-Anne moves in.

— What if we elect a new mayor? Someone who's fair? Someone who doesn't cheat?

— Show me.

Sally-Anne looks over at Abbi for help.

— Any suggestions?

Ghazala has a suggestion.

— What about Aiden? He's fair. Never fights. Likes doing the drains with Mr Middleton. Will keep rats away. Doesn't support City or United, so won't quarrel.

Aiden looks aghast.

— Who, me?

Marlon agrees with Ghazala.

— Why not?

There's a muttering of agreement.

— Will the Piper help me do the drains like Mr Middleton?

— Of course, I will. In fact, I wouldn't mind retiring to your town if you'll have me. I'll set up my fairground for your kids.

Abbi holds her hands up.

— Let's stop there.

There are groans of disappointment at having to finish. Murmurs of approval issue from the audience of HMIs.

— I'd like you to finish with a still image of Aiden as mayor. Where's the chain of office and his tricorn hat?

Mayor Aiden, enthroned on a chair, on a table, in the centre of the room, looks pleased with himself. His hat at a curious angle, the chain down past his waist, he basks in the attention he's getting. The class position themselves around him. Abbi kneels and takes a Polaroid photo. The class have forgotten the room full of inspectors. All that matters is the story they've helped to write, the problem they've solved and the child who is empowered by their collective imagination.

Nineteen
The Dog and Duck

For the return trip to Manchester, the class can choose where they sit on the coach, and the great gender divide yawns open again. Miriam, Lorraine, Ghazala and Anna slip Bay City Rollers scarves on to their wrists and march to the back seats where Aaron and Sean are swapping footie cards. Miriam flicks her wrist, like an impatient hitchhiker.

— Play elsewhere, little boys. The girls are back in town.

Mercilessly evicted, they sidle off to find other seats.

Graham intervenes.

— Excuse me, Miriam. That was quite rude.

She hoists an eyebrow at her friends.

— Don't worry, sir, says Sean. We don't want to sit next to them. They'll only start squawking Rollers songs.

Aiden sits alone, wearing the mayor's tricorn hat. Sally-Anne has slipped a label, Mayor Aiden, into the band.

To finish the drama Abbi had asked,

— What happened to Hamelin after Aiden became mayor?

Ghazala replied.

— He's a good mayor, miss.

— Why do you say that, Ghazala?

— 'Cos Aidey doesn't fight, he's kind and wouldn't be mean to anybody. Would you, Aidey?

— I'm rubbish at scrappin', miss.

The children made a tableau entitled 'Hamelin five years later'. Aiden sat on a chair, wearing his tricorn hat and chain, surrounded by the rest of the class, kneeling and bowing their heads. Graham took Polaroids and the class bunched around him to watch the images emerge. He could feel their warmth, excitement, togetherness.

Aiden stares out of the coach window with a smile hooked onto a memory. His lopsided hat remains on his head for now, but he'll have to hide it from his dad. Mr Harris will keep it safe in his desk.

The only children who haven't swapped seats are Sally-Anne and Andrew. They chat away, sharing snacks. It's unlikely Andrew has ever eaten raw carrot before. He stares at it like an antique dealer examining a netsuke.

— Hefner would like these.

— Who's Hefner?

— Oh, he's our rabbit.

Sally-Anne twists her mouth.

— Why is he called Hefner?

— I don't know. It's my dad's joke.

As the coach pulls away, Abbi and Graham settle down in the front seat. Their legs touch, but neither of them pulls away.

— How do you think it went today, Graham?

— Good.

Was that the right answer? She takes her glasses off and wipes the lenses with a frilly white hanky with a pink flower in one corner. Graham notices her emerald eyes and green eye shadow. Her pupils enlarge. His stomach sinks pleasantly. She nods thoughtfully.

— What makes you think it went well? I agree, but it's

essential to articulate what worked and why. Your RSA portfolio must reflect your ability to analyse a lesson.

Graham takes a deep breath. He hasn't thought it through.

— Well, the children never lost their concentration.

She agrees. Encouraged, he continues.

— Because they're in a collective role, they're not as exposed. There's 28 of them trying to work things out and not set against each other or on their own.

— I like that. Put the children in a community.

Her approval is fuelling his confidence.

— Ghazala's idea about making Aidey mayor was great. They loved carrying him on the chair and making the tableau.

— So, Ghazala's idea is presented back to her by the rest of the class. Very satisfying for her and for her classmates.

Conversation with Abbi is stimulating. She knows so much. She turns her intense gaze on him and he feels his stomach sink again. Her tone becomes softer.

— Where do you live, Graham?

He becomes flustered. She wants to know where he lives! He hesitates.

— Erm…

She smiles.

— You're not sure where you live?

— No. I mean, yes. Demesne Road, next to Alexandra Park, Whalley Range.

He feels another wave of warm anticipation.

— Why don't we meet up later for a celebratory drink? Talk through how it went today.

Graham's enthusiasm is betrayed by the lightning speed of his reply.

— Wow, yes. Dog and Duck, Withington? Eight o'clock?

Her eyes possess him. Her voice is sultry.

— I think we deserve it, Graham.

Graham never imagined he could move on from the Ice Queen Cheryl, but the big day out has delivered thrilling new possibilities. Abbi shifts in her seat to survey the antics at the back of the bus.

— I think the girls have started their celebrations already.

The re-formed *Coronation Street* jukebox quintet is delivering a tuneful rendition of Bye Bye, Baby. As they sing, they sway from side to side, their Rollers scarves raised above their heads.

Abbi sinks back into her seat with the trace of a smile. Graham can smell her perfume. Ma Griffe? Cheryl's Christmas present 1975. Graham still carries the wish list she wrote for him in his wallet. He'll bin it tonight.

— It's Miriam. Any opportunity to do a Rollers song.

She gives Graham another green-eyed stare.

The Bay City Rollers song peters out and is replaced with a snickering commotion. Graham swivels in his seat. Heads pop up all the way down the coach as the children take a peek then sit down, covering their mouths to stifle their laughter. Lorraine catches Graham's eye and, with a tell-tale smirk, nods towards Andrew and Sally-Anne.

She has fallen asleep on his shoulder, her arms wrapped around his. Andrew, wearing a sizeable grin, puts his finger to his lips. Miriam breaks into 'Puppy Love'. More Brenda Lee than Donny Osmond, her voice breaks in mock desolation. Lorraine and Ghazala join in. Miriam moves up the aisle to serenade the couple, kneeling beside their seat like a tenor in a Sorrento restaurant.

Andrew ignores the snorts and giggles of his classmates; he's deeply contented. A ghost of a smile flits across Sally-Anne's face and she snuggles closer. Graham taps a heartbeat rhythm with his hand on his chest.

— Ah, sir, whispers Ghazala, biting her lip. That is so sweet.

The driver barks his frustration at the coach's big rear view mirror and punctures the mood.

— Could Marie Osmond take her Puppy Love back to her seat, please.

Miriam obeys.

Graham can't help comparing Sally-Anne and Andrew's touching pre-pubescent romance with what might be developing tentatively between him and Abbi.

Parents gather by the school gates. Aiden's mum, in slippers, stands apart from the others. Dad's at work, patrolling the biscuit factory perimeter fence, searching for someone to, as he would put it, beat the shit out of. Graham lifts Aiden's hat from his head as he gets off the coach.

— Shall I take care of this, Aidey? I can show it to your mum on parents' evening, eh?

— Fanks, sir.

Aiden taps it, as if to check that what happened actually did happen.

— Sir? Can I see it at playtimes?

— Of course, Aiden. I'll be the security guard.

He frowns.

— The caretaker, I mean. I'll be the caretaker. It'll be safe in my drawer.

— Sir, that was the best day of my life.

— Good, Aiden. You were a real star today. Well done.

He jumps down from the steps, and Mrs Wright waddles forward.

— C'mon, buggalugs. Let's gerr'ome.

He follows like a last surviving duckling.

Sally-Anne and Andrew hold hands as they walk away down the street. As her dad swings around the corner in his Rover 3.5, she lets go of Andrew's hand and breaks into a run towards the car. She doesn't look back. Her dad pulls up and leans across the front seat to open the passenger door. As she scrambles in, smiling, he tousles her hair.

Andrew watches, his mouth slightly open. He half lifts his hand to wave, but she doesn't see him and the white Rover rolls away into the distance.

Sean walks up behind him, puts an arm round his shoulders and pulls him into step; the car carrying his new love disappears. Andrew's obsession with Stevie Coppell is over. It'll now be Sally-Anne who fills his thoughts.

***

You couldn't swing a vole in the snug of the Dog and Duck. There's room for one table and two chairs. A hundred years ago, it was a shop window display space. Boots, clogs and shoes. Now the words 'Hydes Brewery' are etched into the glass.

Graham sits like a shop window mannequin on his night off. This is the perfect spot for his first date with Abbi. He's planted a pint of Anvil bitter as a claim to the table. Through the half open door facing the bar, a skinhead stares at him. He has a swastika tattooed between his eyebrows and the letters NF needled into his neck. Coiled around him, like a denim-clad python, is the girlfriend, her hair shaved close to the sides of her head and topped with a Mr Whippy purple and pink, inverted cone hairstyle.

To avoid the Nazi's intimidating glare, Graham heads to the jukebox at the far end of the bar. Flicking through the plastic pages of songs, he constructs a soundtrack to the Abbi fantasy he's editing in his head. A couple of drinks here, then a candlelit dinner at his bedsit. In his imagination, the scent of foo yung and special fried rice mingle, a perfumed garden of carry-outs.

Passion lubricated with a bottle of Mateus Rosé. Cut to leaning across the table in mirrored poses, slipping After Eight mints from their glossy sheaths and placing them on each other's tongues like black communion hosts. This is my body. It's all yours.

He taps the numbers into the jukebox. Number 152, the sultry trumpeting of Herb Alpert 'This Guy's in Love with You'. Number 94, no-nonsense, straight-to-the-point 'Shaft' by Isaac Hayes and, in one last flick of his fantasy showcase, 'Express Yourself' by Charles Wright and the Watts 103rd Street Rhythm Band.

When he returns to the snug, the Hitler Youth has annexed the territory by removing Graham's pint to the bar. He's sitting on Graham's stool, grinning defiantly, his legs wide apart, the Pink Python stroking his shiny scalp.

Graham raises his finger as if politely making a point of order at a debating society.

— Excuse me, I was sitting there. I only left my seat to put some music on, so if you don't mind...

The youth's smirk slides into a scowl.

— Fuck off, pal. You're takin' up two places, right?

— My friend will be here any minute.

The skinhead's eyes lock on to the Rock Against Racism badge Graham is wearing. Graham looks down at it and back at the skinhead, whose jaw pulsates with irritation.

— So where is this girlfriend, pal?

Before Graham can stop himself, he's sounding teacher-ish.

— I didn't say it was a girlfriend, and anyway it could be a boyfriend.

The skinhead rises, slipping his thumbs inside his studded belt.

— You a fuckin' 'omo?

— Do you mean, am I a packet of washing powder? Or am I homosexual?

He sings the slogan from the TV commercial.

— 'Omo adds brightness to cleanness and whiteness.' You should try it.

The Nazi pulls back his arm, fist clenched. Graham, anticipating a punch, lifts his forearm across his face, then switches to running his fingers through his hair, in a weak attempt to conceal his fear.

The Nazi's purple-haired partner steps between the two of them.

— Leave it, Brian. 'E's a knobhead.

— Fuckin' won't leave it.

The pub door swings open. In struts Tug. Oily overalls, work boots, blue bobble hat and impeccable timing. Closing in behind Graham, he grabs his mate by the shoulders, spins him around and announces, in a thick scouse big voice,

— Bomber Harris, reprobate, ne'er-do-well and hinter-lectual, *This Is Your Life*.

— Oh my God, what are you doing here?

— Said I'd come up to see you, didn't I? Your Brummie landlady said this was your local. Correction: she said this 'am yowm' local.

Graham looks back at the boot boy and Tug follows Graham's line of sight. Tug's brow wrinkles; his eyes switch back and forth. Nazi to Graham, Graham to Nazi. All is not well. Finally, as slowly as a drowsy jaguar, he looks the youth up and down and, maintaining his gaze, he says,

— Everything all right, Bomber lad? This specimen bothering you?

Emboldened by Tug's presence, Graham says,

— This young man was about to return the table he was… so very kindly, saving for us.

Graham throws the words towards the Nazi-like a frisbee edged with razor blades.

Now allied to Tug, the sapling of Graham's cowardice has grown into a giant sequoia of bravery.

Tug catches sight of Graham's Anti-Nazi League badge. His tone changes.

— Cool, man. What's the badge?

Graham doesn't take his eyes off the youth as he answers.

— Rock Against Racism. There's going to be a concert in Alex Park. Buzzcocks, Steel Pulse, Exodus. They're all going there.

Tug slips his fingers behind Graham's jacket lapel to lift the badge. The skinhead, watches, listens and scowls. His cheek muscles continue to twitch. Tug enthuses,

— Oh yeah! Fancy going to that, mate.

Tug jabs a thumb over his shoulder.

— We could take him.

He turns to the youth.

— Fancy coming with us, cosh boy?

The Nazi pushes past Graham towards the door.

— Fuck you.

Tug calls after him.

— Take it that's a no, then?

The skinhead disappears, his purple python slithering after him. A murmur grows into a hubbub throughout the bar. Graham grabs Tug's arm and moves him towards the snug.

— Thanks, Tug.

— I can't leave you for a second. Where would you be without your old mate?

— If you hadn't walked in, probably warming my cheek on the floorboards.

Tug laughs. Graham opens the snug door and guides his friend away from the attention of the crowd in the bar.

— Look, I need a word. Let me get you a beer; you sit down in here.

— Don't drink, lad. Get me a pint of orange.

Graham's eyebrows rise.

— I told yer, Bomber. Fit as a butcher's dog, me.

Tug moves to the window and presses his nose to it.

When Graham returns from the bar, he places Tug's glass with precision on a small cardboard mat advertising Anvil Bitter: 'Brewed in the Traditional Manner'. Tug is still squinting into the street. He snorts,

— He's still out there, the tosser. Looks like he's waiting for someone. Us maybe?

— Never mind him. I need to talk to you.

Tug sits and lifts his orange cordial; he takes a sip and nods for Graham to continue. Graham takes a slug of his beer.

— Thing is, Tug, I've got a date tonight.

Tug drops his jaw in mock shock, then smiles and says,

— Not a problem mate. I'll be your chaperone. Make sure she doesn't try anything on.

Graham laughs. Tug raises his glass.

— Who is she, anyway?

— A colleague.

— Ah. A colleague. Not a workmate, not a girlfriend, eh? Drinky-poos with a colleague, is it? Just remember, Mr Teacher, I knew you when you had fuck-all. A colleague!

Tug is about to take another sip, then stops. His lips remain close to the glass, he narrows his eyes.

— Not ashamed of me, are you? Want me to vamoose?

— NO!

— You do! She's posh, isn't she? Me in me oily overalls. Well, you don't have to worry. I'll talk proper and then fuck off back to me slum in Tranmere.

— Tug, c'mon! I'm here because *she* suggested we went out for a chat. We've been working together; I asked her for some feedback.

— Feedback? What the fuck's feedback? Is that a posh word for preliminaries to getting your end away? Feedback!

The snug door swings open. Graham stands abruptly. Abbi, out of breath, presses the snug door closed.

— Hi. Sorry, I'm late. I had to take evasive action. There's a skinhead kicking seven bells out of a dustbin out there.

Abbi looks at Tug. Graham looks at each of them in turn.

— Ah, yes. Abbi, meet Tug.

He turns to Tug.

— Abbi's the colleague I was talking about.

Tug leans back in his chair, spreads his long legs, raises his glass and winks.

— All right, Abbi girl.

— Pleased to meet you.

She proffers her hand. Tug waves. Graham explains,

—Tug and I met at school. We started work together. Inseparable.

Tug leans back in his chair, crosses his legs and puts his hands behind his head.

— Certainly were. Before he ran away to the circus.

Graham looks flustered. He points to his chair, inviting Abbi to sit down.

— What can I get you, Abbi?

— Half a lager and lime. Thanks.

Graham regards the two of them once more. He's nervous about leaving them alone together.

— I'll get another chair.

He moves to the door then stops.

— I won't be long, he says urgently.

As he opens the door, the brass and bass of 'Express Yourself' boom out of the jukebox. Tug watches Graham exit, then looks directly at Abbi.

— Don't mind me, love. I won't get in your way. I'll finish me drink then get on back to Birkenhead. I only came up on the off chance he was free. Should've rung him, but you know, shared payphones, you can never get through.

She raises her hands.

— No, don't rush away. I'd like to hear. You were at school and then you worked together.

She shakes off her duffle coat. Tug pulls his chair in and places his hands palms down on the table as if he's about to give a team talk before a big match.

— OK. I'll stay on a bit.

Abbi pulls her chair nearer the table and steeples her hands.

— So, tell me, how did you meet?

Tug rubs his hands together and screws up his face, relishing the chance to tell the tale.

— Well, it was our first day at grammar school. A playground full of 12-year-olds, new caps, blazers, school ties, white shirts. Snobbed up. Not me, like. Me mum and dad couldn't afford all this new gear.

— OK.

— Anyway, I was the only one from my primary school so I didn't know anyone. I was feeling on me own. It was the same for Bomber. He didn't know anyone either. Anyway, most of the kids were little toffs. Kids whose dads wore shirts and ties to work and whose mums stayed at home. I remember thinking, they might be posh but these don't frighten me. I was big for me age. A porker. Anyway, we all moved into the cloakroom waiting to be told which classes we were in. I saw this lad playing hoopla with his cap on the coat hooks. And there was this little crowd 'oohing' and 'aahing' at the near misses, clapping when he landed it on a hook. You could see he was enjoying the audience. He was performing. Then this teacher called Williams appears. Grey, greasy hair plastered across his fat head. He clocks what's going on and says – Tug affects a posh accent – 'What in God's name are you playing at, boy? That's your new school cap!' Everything stops. Silence. Bomber's oblivious, lost in his performance. He just carries on. He's doing fancy moves, reverse throws from behind his back. This lad taps him on the shoulder and says, 'Look out! Stench is here', Bomber sees the teacher, freezes, notices everyone's staring at him. So, he pipes up, like a choir boy. 'Sorry, Mr Stench,' he says, not realising that Stench is the kids' nickname for Mr Williams. And the kids are wetting themselves. Williams goes ape. He pushes through the other lads to get to Bomber. 'What did you call me, you idiot?' 'Mr Stench, sir.' 'You call me that once more and I'll swing for you, you little piece of excrement. What are you?' 'I'm a little piece of excrement, Mr Stench.' It was mad. I thought, this lad's fucking crazy. But, you know, in a brilliant way. Anyhow, the next time I see him is at the rugby trials for the school team. He's playing full back. Last line of defence and all that, and this fat kid runs over him, flattens him. So Bomber grabs his ankle and hangs on. The fat guy is dragging him along. Bomber won't let go. Eventually, the lad falls over, but Bomber's still got his boot in his hand, so the fat lad says, dead posh, like, 'Give me my boot, you fucking Pikey' so Bomber gets up and chucks it over the fence into someone's garden.

Bomber jogs off and this lad hares after him. So, I grab the fat one and tell him, if he lays a finger on Bomber, I'd personally stuff his other boot up his bum. And he says, 'What's it got to do with you?' so I tell him me grandad was a gypsy. Which was a lie, like. And that was it. Me and Bomber got into the team. We were inseparable. I looked after him, and he made me laugh. I knew he'd always make a stand. You know, if things weren't fair. Have a go. Speak up. He knew I'd back him up.

Abbi throws her head back, laughing. Graham returns carrying a chair and a mud coloured lager.

— Oh no, he says. What's he been telling you?

Graham slides a mat across the table and places the drink in front of Abbi.

— He's telling me about Mr Stench, the rugby team. How the two of you met. I love it.

Graham closes his eyes slowly.

— Oh, Christ. It'll be the day the rain came down, next.

Abbi looks excited at the prospect of another story.

— The day what?

— Forget it. Don't encourage him.

She pleads with him,

— Do, Tug. I can't wait.

Graham retreats.

— I'm going to the gents. I can't listen to this. Too embarrassing.

Graham exits hurriedly as Tug pulls himself closer to the table.

— Right, we're in the school navy cadets. Bomber likes the uniform: bell bottoms, white shirt. Random girls come up and touch your collar for luck. And I join, 'cos he has. What we don't realise is we'll be stuck indoors, every Thursday night for the next five years. Tethered to a Rowenta iron. Surrounded by damp cloths and steam clouds. Pressing our Class II naval uniform. Designed by someone with a degree in pointless tasks. Five horizontal creases down each trouser leg, an inboard, an outboard on the white dress shirt, three more on the collar. Bloody mental. Death by a thousand creases.

OK, in the first year we were dead keen; by the time we'd got to the fifth form, we're a couple of able-bodied scallies. We've done our O-levels and the last day at secondary school arrives. An inter-house, cadet marching competition in front of Rear Admiral Sir Snotty-Nosed Tosser, OBE. The great and the good are sat on the balcony of the cricket pavilion. Ready to pass judgement on our ability to march meaninglessly up and down. Me and the lad himself are in Drake House. You know, Drake, Churchill, Wolfe, Clive. Usual crap. Bomber's been up 'til midnight getting his uniform ready. To save time, instead of scrubbing his white hat, he slaps on a bottle of Blanco. You know, that cream stuff you put on your plimsolls to make 'em whiter than white. After all, it's summer term, blue skies, sun baking down. He'll have the whitest hat on parade.

What could go wrong? Well, it only pisses down. Bomber looks like a gallon of Dulux emulsion has been poured over his head. White raindrops bouncing off his cap. Blanco dripping off his hat like a white chocolate fountain, dribbling down his Buddy Holly specs so he can't see where he's going. He's marching in the wrong direction, down the wrong gap in the lines. A complete shambles. We finish with three cheers for Rear Admiral Sir Double-Barrelled Who Gives A Fuck. Bomber chucks his cap on to the roof of the pavilion: a spinning, white Catherine wheel of shoe cream spattering the top brass, who are livid. Of course, when we get back to the changing rooms, the loyal Drake chaps are all shouting, 'Bloody disgrace, Harris. You let the house down.' All that crap. Anyway, I told them, it was our last day, and if anyone wanted to take it up with Bomber, they'd have to get past me first. That shut 'em up. It was the pinnacle of our grammar school career. I knew I wasn't going back. Me dad had died and no matter what the results were, we couldn't afford for me to go back into the sixth form. So that was it. Our last hoorah! Great moment. Bomber did us proud. Unforgettable finale.

Abbi is shaking her head.

— So, you stayed close after school?

— Yeah. I was into politics. Bomber's dad got us to join the Young Socialists. Leafleting, ward meetings, that kind of thing. And we worked together, too. Lots of jobs. Wirral Concrete, making paving stones, Kirkham's, making wooden pallets. Did our civic duty grafting for the council on the bins, down the sewers, then off to Vauxhall's at Ellesmere Port. Then he met this girl, Cheryl. Filled him with ideas, going to college and all that.

He pauses. Looks away.

— But seriously, he's done well. I'm made up for him.

Graham returns. His face is white.

— What's up, lad? says Tug.

— It's that fascist teacher I told you about. Syd Formby. He's here. With the boot boy. I spotted them as I was coming through the bar. I did a U-turn but they followed me into the gents.

Abbi is confused.

— Who's Syd Formby?

Graham closes the door and swallows hard.

— Tug knows. He's a teacher from school. He threatened me. It's rumoured he has National Front links. Well, it's no longer a rumour. They've got a meeting upstairs. I overheard them.

Tug moves to the door.

— Did they see you?

— No. I climbed out through the window in the gents and came back through the front. Talk about the odd couple. Him in his suit and the lad in his Doc Martens.

— That's how they work, says Tug. The suit does the strategy and the boot boys do the kickings.

He opens the snug door a crack and peers into the bar.

— Let the dog see the rabbit. Just in case we meet again. I want to clock 'im. Get a picture in me 'ead.

Abbi looks confused.

— Who? What's going on?

— It's that teacher I told you about at school. The one who hits the kids.

— Not just kids, says Tug. Didn't he have you up against the wall?

Abbi looks alarmed.

— What!

Graham shakes his head. Tug spots them in the bar.

— That's them! The skinhead and a big bloke in a tie and blazer. Smooth-looking prat, isn't he? It's all part of the cover-up. A Nazi dressed like a double-glazing salesman.

Graham's tone is urgent.

— Tug, don't do anything rash.

— Don't worry. I won't. Need to think this one through. Come up with a plan.

He returns to the table and picks up his glass.

— I better get off anyway. Leave you two to... feedback, bounce off each other or whatever it is 'colleagues' do.

Graham gives Tug a fierce look to shut him up. Then turns to Abbi.

— I'm not too keen on hanging around here. Have you eaten?

— No. I thought we were getting fish and chips?

— That was the plan. We can get some on the way to the flat. Tug, do you want to get some chips with us?

— No, count me out. Like I said, I've got to get back to Birkenhead. It'll be quiet on the East Lancs this time of night. Look, I need a favour. I'm trying to get this damp coursing thing going. You know, start me own business, like. I could use some help over Easter. If you're up for a bit of real graft, eh?

Cash in hand. How about it? We can maybe have a chat about our Nazi friend, eh?

— I'm up for it. Forget the cash in hand. I owe you one after tonight, anyway.

Tug leans forward to shake Abbi's hand.

— Nice to meet you, Abbi. Look after the boy. If he gives you any grief, let me know. Corlett Damp Coursing.

He opens his wallet, slides out a white card and offers it to Abbi.

— Bloody hell, Tug, a business card! says Graham intercepting it.

— Corlett. Damp Coursing. Very nice.

Graham hands the card to Abbi, who gives it a cursory glance, smiles and hands it back to Graham. Tug buttons up his overalls and lifts his collar.

— Give me a ring on Friday. We can talk through the damp course thing. After eight, when I get back from karate club. Have a good evening.

He winks.

— Be good!

Tug pulls on his bobble hat and steps out of the snug.

— What a character, Graham. Looks after you, doesn't he?

Graham nods.

— It's true.

Abbi downs the dregs of her lager, stands and drapes her coat across her shoulders.

— Now, let's get some chips, a bottle of something pleasant and away from here before the third Panzer division move in. On the way you can fill me in on the racist in your ranks.

Twenty

The Bedsit

A newspaper-wrapped fish supper warms Graham's lap and steams up the passenger window next to him. At the wheel, Abbi cranes her neck in search of Demesne Road.

— Which way now?

— Straight on, down to the end of the park, then left.

Her left hand massages the gear stick. For a moment, Graham imagines a romantic scene unfolding in his bedsit which, right now in his imagination, is a seductive, candlelit love nest. Then reality rudely intrudes as he remembers the scene he left hurriedly at seven-thirty that morning. The sort of pigsty a Gloucester Old Spot would be ashamed to call home.

What will Abbi think when she walks in to be confronted by a Baby Belling adorned with a trickle of burned milk down the oven door; an unmade bed draped with off-white sheets in urgent need of a hot wash; a bottle of milk, now turned to cheese, on the table; 32 exercise books scattered across a grubby carpet that longs to be caressed by a hoover; a lumpen eiderdown he'd dragged over himself as sleep overtook him in the middle of marking; a waste bin filled with fat-smeared polystyrene containers that once held egg foo yung and chips?

His fanciful notion, the romance of a fish and chip supper for two, accompanied by a bottle of Mateus Rosé and with Jacques Loussier tinkling away in the background, dissolves rapidly. Then, most dismaying of all, Graham remembers the Pirelli calendar hanging on the wall. June's naked body on a Barbados beach, her tanned breasts sprinkled with white sand. The azure, cloudless sky, the aquamarine sea lapping her bikini bottoms. Why, oh why, did he take down the poster of Che Guevara which is now squeezed into a gap in the sash window as a draught excluder?

— Is it next left?

— Erm… yes.

Abbi's Austin Allegro swings into Demesne Road.

— Which one?

— On the right. Number 48.

Pulling over, she mounts the pavement in front of a cream and grey brick Victorian semi. As she turns off the ignition, Graham slaps his forehead in theatrical gesture of remembering.

— You know what we've forgotten? The wine.

She shuts her eyes.

— Sorry, Graham, my fault, I was so busy nattering.

— No worries, he says as he grabs the fish and chip supper and pushes the car door open. The off-licence is next to the chippy. You go and get the hooch, I'll put the food in the oven and light the gas fire. Get the place warmed up – it'll be bloody freezing in there.

— OK. What number flat are you?

— Five. My name's on the bell. The upside-down one.

Graham strides across the road, sprints up the steps and opens the front door. In the murky darkness of the hallway, he pats the wall on his left until he finds the timed light switch which will grant him 30 seconds of yellow dinginess before it clicks off. Through the gloom, at the end of the corridor, he spies the dimly illuminated figure of Jenny, the landlady. He can just see that tonight her dyed black hair is tied up with a red scarf, a black bra visible through her white blouse. Her Brummie voice sings down the hallway.

— Oo-ah, it's little Graybobs. How am yowm, petal?

As thin as a sweetpea stick, she leans against the wall for support, one hand cupping her right elbow, in the V of her index and middle fingers an ash-drooping cigarette. She sways drunkenly, squinting through the half-light. Graham calls out.

— Can't stop, Jen.

— Ah, no time for your Auntie Jenny, then?

Graham flicks her an embarrassed smile. Her face is pasted thick with pastel orange make-up and pale pink lipstick. Behind her, deeper in the gloom, is her latest man, Tone-oy. He folds his hazel-brown arms, which are covered in dark-blue tattoos. He looks Graham up and down but remains silent as he drags in some sweet-smelling smoke, holds his breath, then blows it out slowly.

The problem is, Jenny likes to chat. Rent collection days are the worst. Her conversational subjects, explored between lung rattling coughs, include knocking the smokes on the 'ead, happy days as an evacuee to Rhyl, the delights of Tipton and the proposition that all men are bastards ('Present companoi excepted, Graybobs'). He tries to make his exits polite, but he's running low on get-outs. He's used:

— Sorry, Jenny, left the milk on the stove.

— Got to go, Jen, soup's on the boil.

— Bloody hell, Jenny, I can smell me toast's burning.

Aware that they are about to be plunged back into darkness, he dashes up the stairs, chased by the sound of her crackling smoker's voice and slurred words.

— Is that big handsome Scouser coming back for supper? I told 'im yowm were at the pub.

— No, he's gone home. There'll be... er... someone else, though.

— Oh, arr. It's a laydoi friend, ain't it? Is her going to share your chippois? Them smell bostin, Graybobs.

She falls backwards.

— Oops!

Followed by a loose phlegmy cackle.

— Hold me up, Tone, yu' bugger. I'm shlidin' down the fuckin' wall.

Tony grabs her arm and pulls her roughly towards the ground floor flat. Graham shouts,

— If you hear the bell, Jenny, I'll get it.

— Don't worry, my love, I might have a little gander. Just make sure she's...

Tony slams her door shut. When Graham is halfway up the stairs to the first floor, the lights go out. He feels for the lock and inserts a key. The door opens to reveal the scene of mayhem frozen in time. Nothing has moved for 12 hours. He stuffs the chip supper into the oven and leaves the door open to warm the room. He tosses the eiderdown on to the bed then neatly piles the exercise books on the table, pours the cheesy milk down the sink, then runs hot water to dissolve the curds blocking the plughole. He squirts washing-up liquid liberally, sprinkles bleach over the basin then, in desperation, sprays the great smell of Brut everywhere, finishing under his arms and down the front of his trousers. In spite of all his efforts, the smell of curdled milk hangs around wilfully.

He lifts the sash window to rescue Che, the draught excluder, and Blu Tacks him over June's bare-breasted beach beauty. The tarnished 1930s mirror above the fireplace is realigned to the horizontal. After cleaning the cutlery with a quick wipe in his armpit, he lays the old oak table for two.

Finally, he strikes a match to light the gas fire and sighs

with relief at the thrump of its ignition and the hiss of burning North Sea gas. Clear-up mission completed in four minutes.

A buzz from above Graham's door signals Abbi's arrival. Jenny shouts up the stairs.

— Graybobs. Shomeone at the bloody door, mate. Can yer gerrit? I'm busy wi' Tone-oy.

Graham skips down the stairs two at a time, like a 10-year-old heading for a newly delivered pile of birthday cards. He grabs the newel post and spins around into the hall. It's a race to get there before Jenny's business with Tone-oy is trumped by her curiosity. Easing back the heavy door, he ushers Abbi in. She slides a bottle of Mateus Rosé from her hessian shoulder bag, saying,

— What kept you?

— Sorry, I was hiding…

— Hiding?

Graham shuts his eyes and headbutts the palm of his hand.

— Tidying! I was *tidying*.

Jenny is peeking around her door.

Tone-oy shouts from inside, 'Come back in here, will yu?'

— Just 'avin a little gander, Tone.

The lights go out just as Graham and Abbi reach the first floor.

— Bloody hell, Graham. Where are you?

— Give me your hand.

Graham reaches out and clasps Abbi's hand. An intense rush surges from the pit of his stomach. He guides her towards the horizontal line of light under his door. Pushing the door open, and keeping hold of her hand, he turns to her. They're very close. Their glasses clash in an awkward moment. Abbi's skew and lift to an angle on the bridge of her nose. She readjusts them, coughs, heads to the sink and pulls back the grubby floral curtain to reveal the cluttered draining board.

— Shall I use these plates?

Taking a dinner plate from the rack, she begins to wipe it with the limp, damp towel. After examining the cloth, she grimaces and abandons her efforts.

— Let's eat them in the paper, eh?

Graham nods. He squats in front of the oven door, trapping Abbi in the corner, the moist rag still in her hand. As a wave of warm air from the oven wafts into Graham's face, he jerks his head back and brushes her hip. The urge to wrap his arms around her waist and nuzzle her tummy triggers him to shout,

— No, Graham!

She looks down, bewildered.

— No, Graham what?

— Erm... No ketchup. I was talking to myself. Sorry. I'm out of ketchup.

There's a long pause.

— Are you going to stay there? she asks.

He grabs the warm bundle from the oven.

— No, right. Sorry.

He hands her the food and retreats to the sideboard to take two place mats from the drawer. They're decorated with orange dandelions and white ox-eye daisies. He tries to remove a scab of brown sauce with his thumb, but it refuses to budge. Abbi pulls open the newspaper wrappings to reveal a steaming golden clump of chips crowned with a battered cod. The smell of vinegar is strong enough to challenge the odour of North Sea gas coming from the fireplace. Abbi forks a lump of fish and examines it hungrily.

— Oh my! Am I ready for this!

She pops it into her mouth, closes her eyes and hums her satisfaction.

Graham reaches over to the draining board and grabs two squat glasses that look remarkably like the ones they use in school canteens.

— A glass of wine? he asks.

— Just a small one. I'm driving.

Before he can stop himself, he blurts out

— You can stay over if you want to.

Abbi frowns.

— Not tonight, Graham.

He starts digging a hole.

— Of course. I wasn't trying to… you know… erm. I can sleep on the floor… erm.

As Graham fumbles for words, Abbi places her hand on his knee.

— Don't worry. I didn't take it the wrong way.

Graham drowns the faux pas with a large gulp of wine. Abbi swirls a chip in a puddle of vinegar. She frowns.

— What was all that business in the pub? A teacher from your school at a National Front meeting?

— Oh, God, don't go there.

— Go on. I'm intrigued.

— He's called Syd Formby, a nasty piece of work. Do you remember the guy playing the piano at the Ants performance?

— Vaguely.

— He smacks kids. I tried to expose him, but it went… very wrong.

He retells the whole sorry tale of a play within a play, a tragedy within a tragedy, then pauses and looks hard at Abbi.

— Not only is he free with his hands but he's also a racist. You know, Ghazala? He called her a…

He can't say the word and spells it instead. It feels less offensive than saying it.

— "W-O-G"

— Bloody hell, Graham.

— It's all hidden from view, covered up, the usual.

His jaw tightens.

— Does Mr Jenkins know? asks Abbi.

— I don't think so. All he's worried about is the school's image. Don't look for trouble, don't rock the boat and all that.

She pokes her fork into her chips.

— You have to do something!

— Honest to God, I've tried. But Syd's threatened to have me done over. You saw his boot-boy friend?

Her eyes widen in shock. Graham nods his head slowly.

— I mean it. All the heroes are dead, Abbi. I'm not brave enough.

In the silence that follows, they eat like strangers at the same table in a café. Eventually, Graham speaks, his tone defeatist.

— I'll look after my class 'til the end of term, get through the RSA, then I'm off.

Abbi glares at him.

— Great. So, he carries on smacking kids. That's OK then. And the streaming system you hate so much? Well, that will carry on but no matter: you're out of it. Why should you care?

She skewers another chip. Graham sounds wounded.

— So, what am I supposed to do? I've tried. Honestly, I have. I confronted him, tried to expose him. Everything I do makes it worse. Worse for me, worse for the kids.

Graham lays down his fork and refills his glass. He holds the bottle over Abbi's drink; she shakes her head, then asks,

— What about the other members of staff?

— Like me, they're intimidated by him. And Formby has a big ally, Miss Broadstairs. She's another monster. Even Taffy is scared of her. Insists his door's open when she's with him. It's her and Formby that run the school. They boss it. They set up the streaming system; they write the tests and mark them. Select the kids. It buys off any opposition from parents because they're desperate for their kids to get into the top set. So, they don't complain. Well, that's not quite true. Sally-Anne's mum and dad did, but...

His words trail off. Abbi puts down her fork and pushes the mound of chips and half-eaten fish across the table. Reaching into her bag, she pulls out a small packet of paper tissues. As she dabs her lips, she stares through the grime-streaked sash window. After a few moments' thought, she turns back to Graham and fixes her gaze.

— OK. There is a way out. This is how it works. You can't confront this fascist directly?

— No way.

— Mr Jenkins doesn't want to know. So, you've got to be smart. If he's all about the school's image, that's what you work on. That's his Achilles heel. You work at your dramas. Keep the children at a safe distance from Formby and Miss Whatever she's called. At the end of the summer term, you take your RSA drama exam, don't you?

— So you say. Do you think I'm ready for it?

— I'll make sure you are. The guy who'll do the final adjudication is an inspector called HMI Waverley. Not a local authority inspector but an HMI. A big wig. Do you know how powerful these people are?

— No. Not really.

— Well, they're gods. Think Poseidon. Think Athena. Think Zeus for goodness sake! They can close a school with a flick of the wrist.

—All well and good but why would they be interested in a mere mortal like me?

— Because, mere mortal, HMI Waverley carries a trident with the words 'mixed ability classes' etched into each prong. It's his mission. His raison d'etre. He will step down from Mount Olympus to watch your drama lesson... your final exam.

— Yeah. That's the bit that worries me.

— Which will be brilliant. Because your class is brilliant.

We've seen that today. And you'll be good. Good enough. Well, at least you will be by the time I've finished with you.

— How's any of this going to change things at Union Street?

— Because, by the time I've primed HMI Waverley, he'll know how things work in your school. When Mr Jenkins invites him into his lair for a sherry and a chat, the inspector will start asking some penetrating questions.

Out of the corner of his eye Graham notices the Che poster is starting to peel away from the wall, revealing the nakedness of Miss June. Abbi follows his gaze, then gets up to take control.

— It's a sign, Graham. You think Che has bitten the dust?

She tears down the beach babe, rolls her up and drops her into the cane woven basket on the hearth then reattaches Che to the wall.

— Voila! And how is this done? HMI Waverley will launch into his well-rehearsed, brilliantly argued diatribe against streaming in primary schools. Mr Jenkins, desperate to enhance the image of his school and ingratiate himself with the powers that be, dumps apartheid for justice and fairness.

She turns, both hands held open like a conjurer who's just made her assistant vanish into thin air.

— Mixed ability classes! The fascist is outmanoeuvred. He'll have to teach mixed ability classes… real teaching and, as we know, he'll be lost. Up the no streaming creek minus a paddle. Of course, HMI Waverley will be back in a matter of months, to check all has been implemented. He's like that.

— Wow. OK, I'm up for it. A plan, at last.

There's a commotion outside the door. Voices, deep laughter, a clumping up the stairs, followed by a loud knocking. Abbi looks at Graham. He shrugs his shoulders and opens the door. Jenny, her blouse buttons in the wrong holes, announces,

— The big bugger's back!

Tug moves around her and into the room, a broad smile on his face.

— Sorry to disturb the lovebirds. Upstairs and downstairs.

He arches one eyebrow in disbelief.

— Me van's knackered. A port in a storm and all that. Hope you don't mind if I kip down for the night Bomber, me old mate?

Graham closes his eyes. His voice is flat, dull.

— Great.

He looks at Abbi and shakes his head. She smiles.

SUMMER TERM

———∞∞∞———

1978

Twenty One
Rising Damp

The common house brick is eight inches long and four and a half inches wide. Four and a half inches is the right size to be picked up with one hand by a bricklayer.

Graham is keen to share this newly discovered fact. He looks up from his reading.

— Tug, do you know why a brick is four and a half inches wide?

Tug ignores him. Sitting cross-legged, elf-like on dirty grey flagstones scattered with dog faeces, he sucks a plastic tube, eyes bulging, cheeks concave, an inverse Miles Davis; he turns a kind of blue. Damp course liquid rushes to his taste buds. Thumb in mouth, he's ready to block the end when the foul-tasting chemical arrives. When it does, he jerks out the tube, stemming the flow as he spits out a mouthful. He grabs a bottle of dandelion and burdock, takes a swig, swills it around his mouth and sprays it over the flagstones. A yellow dog turd edges away. The principle of the pipette is usually associated with pristine, white-walled laboratories, not crumbling Victorian terraced houses in Tranmere, one of Birkenhead's poorest districts, where Tug and his assistant Graham are outside 28

Gladstone Street. Around here, there's plenty of work for the jobbing builders of Merseyside: housing improvement grants abound. Tug pushes the tube into a plastic bottle and fills it with the damp proof liquid. Graham frowns.

— What yer doing?

He gives Graham a wink.

— Remember Pettigrew at school? Brainbox. Well, he's a chemist. Works in St Helens. I'm sending this stuff to him.

He holds up the bottle.

— He's going to analyse it. See if we can't make our own. Increase me margins.

— Increase yer what? Bloody hell, Tug. You're turning into a right little entrepreneur. You'll be voting for that Thatcher woman next.

— Steady on, lad. Anyways, how's me new apprentice? Ready to do a real day's work?

It hadn't taken Graham long to accept Tug's invitation to 'give him a lift' over the Easter holidays. He's now 60 miles away from ball squeezing fascists and the loneliness of his shabby bedsit. He's joined Tug in his new career as a damp courser, helping his old friend achieve his ambition of running his own show. The move follows Tug's dramatic exit from employment as a bus conductor. He rang the bell on that career when a particularly officious inspector was about to step onto the platform. Tug signalled the bus to move off and left the inspector chewing the tarmac. The inspector exited stage left to Birkenhead General Hospital, Tug stage right to self-employment and a bank loan.

Graham returns to the instruction booklet for his Hilti TE 17 power drill.

— 'Bricks are usually placed end to end and in alternating courses. Placed like this, they are called stretchers. Sometimes you will notice one brick is placed longways; these are known as headers'.

Graham looks towards Tug. In his plummy, Home Service radio voice, he says,

— Welcome to *Animal, Vegetable, Mineral?* Today's object is mineral. Mineral. And, for our listeners at home, here is our mystery voice.

He shifts to a Brummie accent.

— Today's object is a brick. A brick.

Tug spits out another mouthful of damp course liquid.

— For Christ's sake, Bomber. You're a good act, but you're on a bit long.

Graham tosses the instruction booklet into a box of masonry bits. He checks the weight of the drill by raising it up and down with his middle finger. He squeezes the trigger producing a muffled machine gun rattle, the percussion hammer action bouncing the drill bit in and out.

He swings it, like a Sten gun, towards the backyard wall and fires a burst. His voice now has the timbre of a High Court judge,

— Sydney Aloysius Formby, you will be taken from Revolutionary Courthouse No. 6 to 28 Gladstone Road, Tranmere. There to be mown down with a Hilti TE 17 hammer drill 'til your bloodied shirt is in shreds and your potato face is splashed with ketchup. Take him down.

Tug's impatience spills out.

— What yu' doin, bollocks? You're like a big kid, yoos. Make yourself useful, grab a brush, and turn this yard from Dog Poo Rovers to Tranmere Palace. No wonder you work with 10-year-olds: you fuckin' are one.

Tug digs in his duffle bag and pulls out a damp meter.

— I'm going to have a word with her inside. So, while I'm giving her walls a prick, will you stop being one and do a bit of graft? I want this yard looking like the floor of the Sistine Chapel when I come back.

By the time Tug emerges from the kitchen, jotting down measurements in a small green notebook, Graham has swept all the shit away and is once more perusing the drill manual. He waves it at Tug.

— No mention of health and safety in here. Says nothing about your wrists turning into arthritic twigs and your eyes jiggling in their sockets.

Graham slots a drill bit into the chuck. An indistinct voice calls from the kitchen. Tug responds.

— Don't worry, luv, we'll clear up.

Then to Graham, his voice lower,

— Since when's she been bothered about mess?

Tug rolls up the feed pipe from the plastic drum and wipes it with a rag. He flicks his head back.

— So, you were saying? This Formby character, what did he do? Held you against the toilet wall and squeezed your goolies? Why didn't you stick one on him?

— Because both my feet were off the ground. Plus, I was scared shitless. He's five inches taller than me.

The drill bit squeals as it penetrates a house brick. Tug waits for a pause and points the metal injection tube he's holding at Graham.

— You want me to come up and sort him out, don't you?

— Jesus, no! I'm in enough trouble. I need to be subtle, cleverer than that. Abbi has a plan.

— Never mind Abbi. You handed over the cassette tape! The fucking evidence. You daft twat!

— I told you, I had no choice. He threatened to have my legs broken.

Graham drills some more, drowning out Tug's remonstrations. When the drilling stops, Tug's still talking.

— What about the kids what got smacked? They're witnesses, aren't they? Get their dads to sort 'im out.

— You've got to be joking. Aiden's dad is a fellow member of the beat 'em and thrash 'em brigade and Chint's dad is just pleased his kid isn't being shot at.

— If you're too scared to confront him, freeze the bastard out. Ignore him.

— Well, I'm doing that. That's part of Abbi's plan. All enemies have a weak spot. Don't show him you're scared and *then* blow his cover.

— Is that what Abbi said?

Graham starts drilling again but this time Tug shouts over the noise.

— Number one: you *are* scared. Number two: you couldn't blow the hat off a chocolate mouse, mate.

Tug gives up. He takes a lump of white chalk from his bag and draws a line on the layer of bricks above the old damp course.

— Don't go above this line. I'll make a start in the back room.

He picks up a second drill and leans against the wall, pointing the drill at Graham.

— I tell you what I'd do with him, brother: put his knob in a vice and whack it with a lump hammer.

— Ah, the subtle approach. I think I'll stick with Abbi and clever.

Tug shakes his head then pauses at the kitchen door to make his final offer of help.

— I could be up to Manchester and on me way back in two hours.

— Yeah, and I could lose me job. Though I suppose that'd give me plenty of time to visit you in Strangeways.

Tug looks at his watch.

— We'll have a brew at 11.

He taps his temple with his index finger.

— OK, this is how it works. You've got Abbi's plan, plan A. But you haven't got a plan B, a backup. Me 'ead's werkin on it, brother.

Twenty Two
Insurrection

The staffroom, Union Street Juniors, five to eight in the morning. The hot water boiler on the wall gurgles into life. Hissing and billowing steam squirts into a mug and an instant coffee aroma fills the air. The staffroom door creaks open and Syd strides in. He takes a sly look around before focusing on Graham. He contorts his face, screwing up his eyes then lifts one leg and emits a long, rasping fart.

— Speak up, Brown. You're through.

He snorts at his little joke. Graham's plan to avoid him, freeze him out, has been scuppered.

— In early, Trotsky.

As Graham grabs his coffee and makes to leave, Syd puts one arm on the door frame to block his exit. Avoiding eye contact, Graham reaches for the door handle.

— Excuse me, Mr Formby, I'd like to get back to my classroom.

Syd growls.

— Not so fast, drama queen. Firstly, there's a couple of jobs in Moss Side in this week's bulletin. Suit you. I can see you carrying your missionary flag into the jungle.

Graham stares at the door hinge behind Syd's left ear. Freeze him out. Syd continues.

— You're on your way at the end of the year. I'm going to see to it. OK?

The door handle rattles. Syd braces his foot against the door to stop it opening. He makes a 'V' sign in front of his eyes then swivels his wrist and points the two fingers at Graham.

— We're watching you, Trotsky.

Dennis appears on the other side of the door and pushes in. He sounds impatient.

— Syd, you're blocking the door.

— Just giving the apprentice some advice.

Dennis turns to Graham.

— Can you let me have your damp coursing chum's phone number? Sheila and I want to get an estimate.

Dennis looks at Syd, who's still staring at Graham.

— What's going on?

Syd smirks.

— Now there's a career that would suit you, Trotsky. Damp coursing. Inject thick bricks with something useless. Continuation of your current occupation, don't you think?

Syd chortles and leaves. Dennis takes his red Maxwell House mug from the draining board and refills the boiler.

— Ignore him, Graham, he says.

— That seems to be what everyone's telling me to do.

— He's an ignorant prat.

***

Back in the cloakroom, outside his classroom, in two jagged lines, the children of 4H await Graham's signal to enter. The sun floods the corridor, and their clothes are splashed with summer. Flowery dresses, brightly coloured skirts and tops shift and slide. Miriam's flared skirt of turquoise hoops brushes past Pauline's dress with its sky blue squares, while Ghazala's salmon pink trousers seem to glow. At the back of the boys' line, Chinti's animated chatter contrasts with the impenetrable silence that characterised his early days at the school. His conversation and confidence have grown. For the boys, long trousers have been banished, as they return to their younger selves in shorts.

— Marlon, when you get inside, can you wedge open the fire door with a chair? Otherwise, we'll cook in there today.

As the class streams into the hothouse, Janine hangs back. Graham waves his arm and bows in a theatrical gesture of courtesy, to usher her in. She shakes her head and doesn't move. She lowers her eyes to the floor.

— Janine? Are you OK?

She shakes her head once more.

— Stay here while I sort the class out, he says.

Standing inside the open door, he addresses the class.

— Take out your diaries and write down the three best moments of our day out to York. Ghazala, will you work with Aiden? And, Mark, will you work with Chinti?

Graham closes the door. Janine is studying the cracks in the concrete floor. She looks up at him and her face crumples, tears streaming down her cheeks.

— Oh, Janine. What's up, kidda?

— Hilda's dead, sir. And me mam said I've got to tell you 'cos she's not touching it... and... Oh sir...

She begins to wail then turns, flops onto the windowsill and buries her head in her arms.

Graham puts a hand on her shoulder.

— Hey, Janine, it's a guinea pig. They die. It's not a problem.

— But I was...

She draws in a slurping, shoulder juddering breath.

—... supposed to be...

Another slurp of air, ending in a falsetto wail.

—... taking care of her, sir.

She rocks in waves of grief.

— Hime, hime, hime... sorry, sir.

Without taking his eyes from her, Graham pushes the classroom door open with his foot and shouts into the classroom.

— Sally-Anne, will you get the Kleenex off my desk, please? I need your help here.

Box of tissues in hand, Sally-Anne comes to the door and sees Janine. She eyes Graham accusingly, hands him the tissues and wraps her arm around her classmate, pulling her away from Graham.

— What's up, Neen? she says softly.

Janine can't speak and Sally-Anne fixes Graham with a what's going on? stare.

— Hilda died while Janine was looking after her.

Janine lifts her head, Sally-Anne whips a tissue from the box and dabs her cheeks. Graham stands helplessly, holding the box, upright as a butler, awaiting instructions from Lady Sally-Anne. She takes charge and grabs Janine by the shoulders.

— Don't worry, Neen. All guinea pigs die one day. Andy's Horace Rumpole died last term. They'll be together now. Horace and Hilda.

Janine is still sobbing.

— Yeah, but it was our Brian what done it. I told him not to let Bullseye into the telly room.

She throws her hands in the air melodramatically. Sally-Anne hugs her.

— Neen, it's not your fault.

— It is! I shouldn't have let her out of the cage. I was only givin' her a run round on the carpet. Then Bullseye comes in, barks at her, she does a poo and dies.

Sally-Anne bites her bottom lip. Janine turns back to Graham.

— Me mum said I had to tell you, sir. Our Brian said you'd yell at me and give us the strap.

— The strap! I don't do that, Janine.

She returns to freefall sobbing. Sally-Anne reassures her.

— But sir isn't shouting at you, is he?

— No, but Mum said she's not touching it, and sir has to come and collect it or there'll be trouble in the camp. We can't even watch telly 'cos Hilda's still lying there next to the poo. And if we open the door Bullseye'll get in there and…

The words 'eat her' slide into a wail.

Graham's not sure what his role is beyond dispenser of tissues. Sally-Anne, however, is clear. In a calm and reassuring tone, she explains,

— Sir will go around to your house at lunchtime and collect Hilda. We'll bury her at school this afternoon, won't we, sir?

— If you say so, Sally-Anne. I'll go around and collect it – I mean her – Janine. No need to get upset.

Janine blinks her big, blotched panda eyes.

— Thanks, sir. You're my favourite teacher this week.

Arm in arm, the girls return to the class as Sally-Anne continues to comfort her friend.

— He wasn't cross, was he? Sir will sort it out.

Janine snivels and nods. Ghazala and Lorraine, followed by others, gather around in a scrum of sympathy. In the wafting of a Kleenex, Graham's role has changed from butler to undertaker.

***

It's lunchtime and Graham is standing in front of the matt green front door of the Copley family's council house on the Hepsworth Estate, in his hands a garden shovel and an empty Tesco carrier bag. He rattles the aluminium letterbox cover. Inside, a yard dog snarls ominously. The door opens. Before him stands a woman, probably in her thirties with permed curly black hair, wearing a white T-shirt emblazoned with a picture of Johnny Cash. Graham shifts his gaze to her ankles and delivers the speech he's rehearsed repeatedly during the 10-minute walk from school.

— Mrs Copley? It's Graham Harris, from school. I've come to collect Hilda.

Graham looks up. Mrs Copley's puzzled.

— Who?

— Graham Harris, Janine's…

— I know who you are, but who's Hilda?

— Your Janine, she was looking after…

Mrs Copley throws her head back as she connects the corpse in her front room with the man on the doorstep carrying a shovel and Tesco bag.

— Oh, thank God you're 'ere. We can't watch telly with 'avin to keep the dog out of the room. It's just a snack to him, right? Kill it, eat it, that's our Bullseye.

A bull terrier, with a mean eye, stands at the far end of the hall. Bill Sikes's orphaned pet. It bounds down the hallway, paws scraping, falters and slides to a halt. Its head is half white, half dark brown, with splashes of pink around the mouth. Blood? Saliva froth dribbles from its jaws.

Mrs Copley screams and traps its head in the door.

— Bullseye!

Growls turn to a yelp. Graham shuffles backward uneasily. Mrs Copley tries to reassure him.

— He's all right. Big softy, really.

Yeah, thinks Graham, they all say that before they call for an ambulance. Mrs Copley turns and shouts down the hallway.

— Brian! Put this fuckin' dog in the back yard, will ya?

She puts her mouth to the crack in the door.

— 'Scuse my French. He's a lazy twat, our Brian.

Despite the dog's head still being trapped in the door, its legs skate on the lino as it continues its attempt to sink its teeth into the visitor. Out of the corner of his eye, Graham sees the front room curtain opens. A face appears and, to his horror, he realises it's the Nazi from the Dog and Duck. Janine's brother! The boot-boy throws the curtain closed. The dog's still struggling to get its head free, its blood red eyes keep flicking up at Graham, malevolently. Then, in an instant, an unseen hand drags it backwards and Bullseye, still yelping, is removed.

Mrs Copley lets Graham into the hall. At the far end, the Nazi throws the hound into the kitchen and slams the door shut. Leaning on the door frame, he takes a deep drag from the butt end of a tab and blows the smoke with a twitching movement so that it streams out in several directions.

— I know you, don't I?

— I don't think so.

Brian narrows his eyes.

— I'm sure it was you.

His mother turns on him.

— Never mind that, Brian. I want this dead animal out of the house.

She turns to another door in the corridor. Brian mouths 'Fuck off' behind her back while she directs Graham.

— Right, the pig-guinea thing's in here.

She holds the door handle ready to let Graham in and shut it as quickly as possible. Graham asks,

— Can I have a cloth, a bucket of hot water and some Flash?

Travelling carpet cleaner can now be added to Graham's CV. He adds,

— Oh, have you any rubber gloves?

— What d'yer want them for?

— I'll be having my sandwiches after this.

Graham's words trail away. Mrs Copley gives him a long hard stare, turns on her heels and heads to the kitchen. Brian pushes the telly room door open with the toe of his Doc Martens. A pungent smell rushes out.

Under the television lies a brown lump of fur. The TV is still on, entertaining the empty room with an episode of the animated children's television programme, *Mary, Mungo and Midge*. Graham takes a deep breath of air from the hall and turns to the scene of Hilda's demise. Holding his breath, he approaches the corpse, sliding the shovel under it. As it rolls over, small white mites leap from the fur. Graham deftly slips Hilda's inert form into the Tesco bag.

Mrs Copley stands at the door with a bucket.

— There's a cloth in the bucket. Haven't got no rubber gloves.

She places the bucket outside the door.

— Do yer wanna a cuppa soup, Mr Harris?

Graham glances down at the last will and excrement of Hilda.

— No thanks, Mrs Copley.

***

The afternoon's lesson is the start of a new drama. Graham writes on the blackboard, in his very best Marion Richardson print: 'The Village of Eyam and the Plague'. He can see lots of drama potential in this story of moral cowardice confronted by moral courage and bravery. The class sit in silence reading the blackboard, save for Ghazala who reads words out loud for Aiden. Graham picks up a Bible and is about to go into the role of the vicar of Eyam when the classroom door swings open with such force it bangs loudly against the radiator. Miss Broadstairs marches in, dragging along the notorious Chris

Darby, who wears a thin lipped smirk, his red, yard brush stiff hair standing to attention. In the staffroom, he's regarded as the naughtiest boy in the third year juniors. Infamy at nine. He wears a T-shirt with a picture of Clint Eastwood holding two six-guns and screaming with rage the words, 'Outlaw Josey Wales'.

Miss Broadstairs booms with the force of a court usher.

— Mr Harris!

Graham thunders back.

— Miss Broadstairs?

— This boy, Mr Harris.

— This boy, Miss Broadstairs?

Still holding Miss Broadstairs' hand, Chris points at himself, grinning inanely.

— This very rude boy, Mr Harris.

— Very rude boy, Miss Broadstairs?

— I've told him, Mr Harris.

— You've told him what, Miss Broadstairs?

This exchange would not go amiss in a panto at the Children's Theatre, Oldham. Every phrase his jailer utters, Chris mimes in response, signing as if he was at an event for the hard of hearing.

— I've told him what happens to VERY RUDE boys, Mr Harris.

Chris makes a throat cutting gesture. His warder holds up a large pair of stainless steel scissors and snaps them open and closed, like a barber who fancies himself as a flamenco dancer. Graham is bemused. Chris Darby hasn't blinked yet. At the sound of the snipping, the smirk grows into a grin. He raises two fingers, scissor-like and waggles them.

— And, Mr Harris [snip snip snip]. Do you know what this RUDE BOY was doing in the line at the end of playtime?

Graham takes a deep breath. It started off well but now it's getting Pythonesque, and he wants to get back to the drama. His tone becomes wearisome.

— No, Miss Broadstairs, I cannot guess what this rude boy was doing in the line at the end of playtime. Pray relieve me of the burden of my ignorance.

Miss Broadstairs lowers her voice and does a convincing impression of Dame Edith Evans.

— He was showing his WINKY to some of your girls, Mr Harris.

It dawns on Graham. Winky?! Scissors?! She *is* mad. Graham's unease grows by the second.

— His winky? To some of my girls, Miss Broadstairs?

— His [snip snip snip] WINKY, Mr Harris.

Graham hears a stifled laugh from Karl sitting next to him. He throws him a don't you dare look, then turns to the girls.

— Is this true, some of my girls?

Miriam, Sally-Anne and Ghazala nod grimly. Miss Broadstairs raises her scissors again and snip, snip, snips once more. There's a high-pitched whimper from little Aiden.

Stella begins to squirm; her face moves to pre-detonation red. Miss Broadstairs looks down at the accused. Her BROAD STARE is switched on and her head moves slower than a Kabuki actor on Valium to confront her prisoner.

— I've told him what happens to little boys who wave their winky, Mr Harris. SNIP SNIP, Mr Harris. Snip, snippety, snip!

Chris Darby contorts his face. Robert, Andrew and Karl cross their legs in unison.

— So what do you have to say for yourself, Chris Darby? [Snip snip.]

Pulling at his trousers and rocking back and forward, he grins.

— Sorry, Sally-Anne. Sorry, Miriam. Sorry, Ghazala.

— You don't sound sorry, Chris Darby.

— Y'am sorry, Miss Broadstairs.

— You don't look sorry, Chris Darby.

His eyes cross and uncross.

— I always look like this, Miss Broadstairs.

She leans into him like a warthog examining a grub.

— Just thank your lucky stars, Chris Darby, Mrs Topham couldn't find her PINKING SHEARS!

Stella leaps to her feet. Red faced and wide-eyed she screams,

— 'Ang on, you can't do that. Yer daft bat!

Graham's stunned. Stella's lost it and nailed it all in one utterance.

— What did you call me, young lady?

— You can't cut his… thing off.

— Stella, says Graham, I'm sure Miss Broadstairs has no intention of… doing what you said.

— She's a psycho!

The class and Chris Darby are aghast. Miss Broadstairs is aghast and in opened mouthed shock. No one in the history of Union Street has confronted Miss Broadstairs like this. She's dumbfounded. The king of bad behaviour, Chris Darby, is dead; long live Queen Stella.

Miss Broadstairs lunges at her with her clicking scissors.

— I'll give you psycho, madam. You'll go home bald if I get near you.

Stella's voice changes. Low, gravelly, from deep in her throat, a gurgling utterance. Slow. Menacing.

— Do it! Go on, do it.

This has gone far enough. Graham has to get Stella out of the classroom.

— Stella, go to the sports stockroom and count the shinty sticks. Now!

— Right. I'll be back with enough sticks to arm the class.

Stella moves slowly, eyes fixed on Miss Broadstairs; she

walks sideways then backwards out of the classroom, a grin stapled to her face. Who will blink first? Stella widens her eyes and with a cackle, retreats to the sports storeroom.

Miss Broadstairs is disturbed. She swallows hard. Graham pulls Chris Darby towards him by his shoulders. He gazes into his contorted little face.

— Chris, listen to me.

— Yes, miss. I mean, sir.

— You've done very well to say sorry to the girls. That's really good.

He's confused. His eyes dart to one side. Miss Broadstairs is looking at the classroom door in anticipation of Stella's return.

— It was a little joke, wasn't it, Chris?

— Fink so, Miss…sir.

— It was, Chris. But you have to remember, with little jokes…

Graham looks up at Miss Broadstairs.

— They might be funny to you, but they're not always funny to other people.

Miss Broadstairs whelps with disgust at Graham's peace negotiations. She pulls the boy's arm and wheels right. With the same theatrical flourish with which she made her entrance, she exits. Chris trots behind her, beams, gives the class a little wave and stumbles out.

The door slams. The class does a collective broad stare. A wide-eyed, unblinking, mad glare. They become rigid from the neck up and rock to and fro, like skittles about to topple over.

Miss Broadstairs' unexpected appearance and the kangaroo court trial of Chris Darby have the same effect as a tablespoon full of Space Dust washed down with a can of Coke. Stella returns with an armful of shinty sticks.

— Where is she? Has she gone? Bugger.

Graham postpones the drama and opts instead for a game of tag on the back field to defuse the trauma.

Twenty Three
Resurrection

In the school potting shed, Graham wraps Hilda in a Wonderloaf greaseproof shroud and places her in a white shoebox. In his best gothic script, he writes on the lid in a black, fat marker pen: 'Hilda, guinea pig 1975–1978, wife of dearly beloved Horace Rumpole, guinea pig 1972–1977.' Graham's dug a hole about a foot deep outside the classroom, alongside Dennis's gardening club potato patch. Sally-Anne and Andrew volunteered to make a cross out of two wooden rulers and twine. Sally-Anne had decided to paint them white. When Andrew suggested adding splashes of red to show she'd been murdered, Sally-Anne said that would be sacrilegious and Andrew asked if that was a type of holy body bag. She didn't reply.

The class, solemn and respectful, mill around the empty grave. Mark and Rob stand like sentries, each shouldering a gardening spade. Janine holds the shoebox. When Stella drapes a dishcloth over her head as a veil, nobody laughs.

Graham asks the children how they wish to proceed.

— Well, we need a song, sir.

— Good idea, Miriam. A hymn?

— What about 'Chants on the Moor', sir?

'Chanson D'Amour' is her party piece.

— That's fine.

In his left hand Graham holds a copy of the BBC *Come and Praise* hymn book. His right rests on his heart. He extemporises on the theme of 'Chants on the Moor'.

— We'll start the service with Miriam's group singing 'Chants on the Moor'. We know how Hilda and Horace loved this song when they stayed at their little cottage near Hollingworth Lake, above Rochdale.

Sally-Anne frowns.

— Sir, Mr Middleton looked after them last summer holidays.

Graham waves away her protestations.

— I'm waxing lyrical here, Sally-Anne.

She shoots him a look of wide-eyed disbelief.

— As I was saying, a small cottage on the moors. How fitting this song is to remind us of their devotion.

Andy leans into Sally-Anne and whispers,

— What's he on about, Sal? I mean, Sally-Anne.

Sally-Anne shakes her head and shrugs her shoulders. Graham dips his chin slowly, a signal to Miriam, who takes one deliberate pace forward. Lorraine, Ghazala, Alyson and Anna form a semi-circle behind her. Miriam raises her conductor's hand, her thumb and index finger in a pincer movement, precisely mimicking Miss Broadstairs' pose at choir practice. A hum grows into a steady G note. Ghazala counts the group in. As they sing, they Harlem Shuffle their shoulders, twice to the right, twice to the left.

Chants on the Moor,
Rat a tat a tat
Rap the door.
I bend me ear.

Rat a tat a tat
Rap the door.

After two choruses, Miriam lifts her hands, bringing the performance to an abrupt close. The silence is broken only by snivels from Janine. Chinti blinks hard behind his gold-rimmed specs.

Graham hands the hymn book to Andrew and, lacing his fingers together, adopts his plaintive vicar intonation.

— I'm sure we've all got memories of Hilda and perhaps now is the time to share them. If you can think of one, start it with the words 'I remember when...' Who'd like to share a guinea pig memory?

— I will, sir, says Andrew. I remember when I had to look after Hilda over the Christmas hols. She ate through the TV aerial cable and we missed the Queen's speech. Me gran were so pigged off, she went home with a cob on her. Me dad gave Hilda a piece of melon as a treat, then he whispered 'Thanks' so me mam couldn't hear and winked at me.

— Well done, Andy. Anyone else?

Karen steps forward and sweeps her long black hair off her shoulder.

— I remember during Anna's 'How to look after a guinea pig' project, we all had a turn to stroke Hilda. When Melanie done it, Hilda pooed on her hand, and she screamed and dropped her into sir's waste bin.

Melanie pulls a face of disgust, wiping her hand on her thigh.

— Thanks, Karen.

Ghazala squeezes sideways through the group to the front.

— I remember when Hilda went missing, and sir said we've got to do a search and find mission. Me, Marlon and Aidey was looking in the gardens on Semple Street.

Aiden laughs. Marlon is unable to hold back and butts in.

— We was singing the *Mission Impossible* tune. Doo-Doo, Doo Doo, Doo-Doo.

Ghazala continues.

— Yeah, then Sue came out. She'd found her behind the sink cupboard eating the poster paints.

Everyone laughs, before falling into a respectful silence. Eventually, Sean offers mournful homage.

— She made me laugh, sir.

Then Ghazala.

— She was soft to cuddle.

Silence again. Graham nods to Janine, who kneels and places the shoebox in the hole. Rob and Mark shovel soil on top of the box, creating a small mound, and Graham brings the ceremony to an end.

— Come on, team, let's go back to the classroom.

With a flurry of waves and cries of 'Bye, Hilda' they trail back inside.

***

Half of the class are standing at a display table, finishing off their model cottages. It's all part of their Great Plague project. The other half sit at their desks drawing maps of the village of Eyam. The sudden death of Hilda and her burial have given the project poignancy. Graham chivvies up the children to finish before home time.

His tour of the room is suddenly halted by a sound coming through the open window, a scraping and scratching sound from the vegetable garden. He looks out on a scene that turns his stomach. Bullseye, the Copley hound, is desecrating Hilda's newly created resting place. The cross has been uprooted, the shoebox excavated and Bullseye has Hilda, still wrapped in her

Wonderloaf shroud, in his jaws. With a whip of his fat head he tosses her into the air, then leaps on the body, tearing, ripping, gnashing and growling in an outburst of frenzied fury. Bullseye is oblivious to Graham's stare. Andrew is not.

— What you looking at, sir?

Graham must grab the class's attention before they realise what's happening. Striding purposefully to the opposite side of the classroom, he stands on a chair and returns to his role as an overemotional cleric, specifically, the Vicar of Eyam. He throws his hands in the air and howls a pitiful lament.

— *O me miserum*!

Sean, distracted from his modelmaking, asks,

— Who's May? Who's Miss Orum, sir? Is she the vicar's wife? The one what tried to sneak off in the cart, so she didn't catch the plague?

Graham, arms raised to the heavens, presses on, imploring the class,

— Villagers of Eyam, gather around. Please. Now.

Sean relays the message to the rest of the class.

— Over here, everyone! Sir's doing a mad vicar thing.

He turns to his teacher.

— He's cracked up, an't he, sir?

Stella, Robbo and Sean stand beside Graham's improvised pulpit. Others follow until all, save for Chinti, are gathered together. Graham's voice is tinged with melodrama.

— This is our punishment! I've not led you well enough. I've let you down.

He climbs down and sits on the chair, head in hands.

Miriam offers consolation.

— Vicar, it's not your fault, mate. Plague's a disease.

On the other side of the room, Chinti stands transfixed, staring out of the window. Having spotted the mayhem in the graveyard, he raises his hand and, with increasing volume, he calls out.

— Sir. Sir. SIR!

He spins around.

— Mr Hurries, Hilda, she…

He can't find the words.

Graham jumps back on to the chair.

— Yes, villager, we have lost our dear friend Hilda. To the plague. She is…

Graham addresses the heavens.

—… with her maker. And we must pray for her.

— Mr Hurries, she on her way now, I've seen her.

Graham, sensing a downside to Chinti's improving spoken English, kneels and puts his hands together. The class follow suit. Chinti advances and then retreats, to and from the window, confused. Graham cries,

— A vision! Villager Chinti has had a vision.

— But Mr Hurries, Hilda… she's up in air.

— Yes, citizen. Up in that great cage in the sky. The plague has taken her.

— Yeah, but Mr Hurries, she keep comings back.

Graham chucks Christian beliefs overboard and opts for something more Eastern.

— We will all come back, we know not what as…

— She's come back as dog's dinner, Mr Hurries.

In desperation, Graham swaps the role of vociferous vicar for that of calm narrator.

— So, the good citizens of Eyam closed their eyes. Closed their eyes tight, very tight and prayed.

The class take their cue as Graham spots through the window the figure of Don Middleton lumbering across the playground. It's the cavalry on the horizon. Brush and shovel in hand, Don's armed and ready for his evening classroom rounds. How can he be discreetly diverted to the terrible scene in the vegetable garden? A plan forms in Graham's head. Conscious of Miriam's irrepressible desire to sing, he'll use this to further draw attention away from Bullseye's grave robbing antics. He continues his narration.

— And so, villager Miriam broke into the hymn, 'Chants on the Moor'. Two, three, four...

Miriam, leaping at the opportunity to perform once more, slots straight in, singing sweetly.

While the class sway to the song, Graham moves behind them, opens the fire door and intercepts Don.

— Don! Bloody mayhem around the corner. Dog guzzling class guinea pig. Can you sort it out?

— What the bloody hell are you on about, Bomber?

— Have a gander.

As they talk, Bullseye sprints between Don's legs, his takeaway lunch sticking out of his mouth.

— Bugger me, Bomber. What the hell was that?

— Class guinea pig, just buried it.

Graham points to the scene of devastation.

— If you could do a cover up before the kids get out for home time. It's got to be worth a couple of pints at the Dog and Duck.

— Will do, old man.

Behind Don, Graham spots a figure in braces and Doc Martens clambering over the wall. It's Brian, Janine's Nazi brother! Back in the classroom, the children are clapping a gospel rendition of 'Chants on the Moor'. Wrapped in the happy clappiness of it all, they ignore Chinti who is pirouetting in confusion, index finger pumping heavenwards. Graham pulls the fire door shut, turns to the class.

— And so it was that villager Miriam, with one sweep of her conductor's arm, brought the singing to a close.

The singing stops followed by a ripple of self-congratulatory applause. Mark rescues Chinti, resisting his efforts to drag him to the window by insisting he listen to Mr Harris's instructions.

— To end the lesson, let's make a whole class still image of the tragedy of Eyam.

Chinti places a desk at the centre of the picture and climbs on it, holding a wooden board duster labelled 'Hilda'. Don, returning from his emergency clear up operation, taps on the window and gives Graham a thumbs up. Sally-Anne pins an orange piece of sugar paper to the wooden desk. She's written in large capital letters,

'HILDA HEADS TO HEAVEN'

The class gather, extending their arms towards Chinti. Graham kneels to take Polaroid photos. However, he's prevented from doing so by Chinti who keeps moving. He's throwing Hilda the board duster into the air and chanting

NAMO TASSA

BHAGAVATO

Andrew asks,

— What's 'e saying, sir?

— I don't know. Maybe it's because of all the singing we've been doing.

Stella joins in. Her face is serious, concentrated. Miriam's next, then the others. One by one, the whole class unite in Chinti's mantra. The rhythm is infectious. Graham lets it grow as he continues to take photos from different angles. As each one slides out of the camera, he pins it to the blackboard. The outsiders are kings. First Aiden as the mayor; now Chinti as a Buddhist monk. The chant peters out before Mark speaks up cheerily.

— Top for that, Chint!

The class crowd around the Polaroid images to watch them magically appear.

The home time bell rings. As the children file out, Graham stands at the door to say goodbye, dispensing reminders and compliments to be repeated at home.

— Chinti, don't forget to tell your mum you've moved on to purple book five in maths.

He gives a mini head bobble then puts his arm around Mark.

— Thanks for remembering your library book, Pam. Karl, well done – not one rude sound today.

He burps.

— Sorry, sir.

They continue to stream out.

— Well done, Ghazala. Great ideas in the drama today.

When all the others are gone, Aiden and Stella remain standing by Graham's desk.

— Sir, can I put me mayor's hat on?

— Of course, Aiden.

Graham takes the hat from the drawer and hands it to Aiden who places it on his head, smiling broadly. Stella's confused.

— Why doesn't he take it home?

— It's safer here, Stella.

Aiden returns it to Graham.

— Thanks, sir. See yer.

As Aiden leaves, Stella peeks into Graham's desk drawer.

— Mr Harris, can I have me yo-yo back?

— Of course.

Graham scrabbles about for it. Dennis is at the door.

— Have you got the gardening spade? It's gone missing.

— Ah, yes. I borrowed it to dig a grave.

— Oh God, I've accused Aaron Randell of nickin' it to bury the wooden maths rods. Could you drop it back in the gardening shed *now*? Don's on his way to get it. He'll blow if it's gone missing.

Dennis turns and goes outside to catch up with a boy whose hunched shoulders and sad demeanour indicate one falsely accused.

Graham, conscious of the huge favour Don has just done for him, makes the return of the spade a priority.

— Wait here, Stella, he says, heading for the door. Just got to...

She tuts and folds her arms. Graham dashes across to the garden tool shed on the back field. Don's already there.

— You looking for this?

— Ah, good man.

Graham hands him the spade.

— Thanks for covering up the grave robbing, by the way.

Graham turns and walks quickly back to the classroom.

Stella's gone. In his desk drawer lies Mayor Aiden's hat. It's been cut into shreds with pinking shears.

Twenty Four
J'accuse

It's Monday morning. Graham is standing with Sally-Anne and Karl in the corridor outside the school hall where morning assembly is in full swing. Their task: to remake Mayor Aiden's hat before he discovers what happened to it.

— I've spoken to Mr Oldham. He said you could work at the back of his classroom. If you work quickly, we'll have it done by break time and he'll never know.

Sally-Anne is upset. Vandalism disturbs her concept of order.

— But who did it, sir?

— It's that headbanger Tupper, isn't it, sir?

As he says this, Karl nods his head, slowly, knowingly.

News of this crime must not leak out. Graham doesn't want Aiden to be upset; neither does he want Stella to be Bay City Rollered in the playground by Miriam and co. He wants a tidy cover up, and he'll sort the culprit out himself.

— Say nothing about this to the others. I'll deal with... whoever.

Graham's class, sitting in assembly, crane their necks as they try to work out what's going on. They can smell trouble.

Karl and Sally-Anne, the newly formed Guild of Cardboard Handicrafts, stride purposefully towards Dennis Oldham's class.

Back in the packed hall, Graham gives Dennis a wink and Taffy a nod.

Miss Broadstairs lifts her conductor's hands and the choir takes a deep breath before plunging lustily into 'Crown Him with Many Crowns'.

One reconstructed mayoral hat will do.

***

The class is back in the prefab. Silent reading is accompanied by a soundtrack of yawns and coughs and, from Andrew, barely suppressed snorts and giggles as he flicks through the 1976 Beano Annual.

Stella holds a copy of Roald Dahl's *Danny Champion of the World*. She's slumped in her chair, legs splayed out, waggling her feet back and forward in opposition, like balance wheels in a clock.

— Stella, can I have a word?

She frowns, smacks closed her book and stomps over to the teacher's desk.

— Yeah?

— 'Yes, Mr Harris.'

She rolls her eyes.

— Yes, Mr Harris.

Graham speaks quietly so that the others won't hear.

— Stella, when I left you last night, you were standing by my desk. I went outside to the gardening shed and when I got back, you'd gone. What happened?

— Nowt. I took me yo-yo and went home.

— So, you went into the open drawer and took the yo-yo?

— Yeah. Well, I wasn't gonna hang around, or she'd tell me dad I was late home, and then he'd start on me. 'Why were you late?' and all that stuff he does.

— Your mum would tell your dad you got home late?

She snaps back.

— I told yer, she is not me mam!

Her raised voice alerts the class and they look up in unison. Graham realises this conversation needs to be continued away from prying eyes.

— 4H, can I have your attention? I'm going to talk to Stella outside. Carry on with your reading. And not a peep do I wish to hear.

Andrew stretches across his desk with his hand up.

— Where's Sally-Anne and Karl, sir?

Miriam calls from her desk.

— Oooh. Jealous, are we, Andy? Think Karl's run off with yu' girlfriend?

— Shuruup, Miriam.

Graham intervenes before it gets ugly.

— Enough, Andrew. They're doing a job for Mr Oldham.

— A special job, sir?

— A job. Now get on with your reading.

Graham opens the door and waits for Stella. Hands stuffed into her pockets, she marches out, peeved. Once in the corridor she leans her back on the windowsill, arms folded, avoiding eye contact.

— Now tell me about the mayor's hat. The one I look after for Aiden.

She pulls a 'what are you talking about?' face.

— Don't know anything about stupid Aiden's stupid hat.

— Stella. I know you cut it up. It was in a thousand pieces by the time I got back to the class. You were the only one in here when I left. Why did you do it?

— I never did! Did he say that? 'Cos I never!

— Stella! You were the only one in there.

— The little... Well, I never touched it. I'll 'ave him, the little prat.

She turns, bursts back into the classroom and, in so doing, knocks Andrew over. He's been earwigging behind the door. He buckles, crumples, holding his head. The class laugh but the laughter is short-lived as Stella strides towards little Aiden. Graham advances after her.

— Stella! Come back here.

It's to no avail. As Stella reaches Aiden, he pushes his chair back and covers his face with his arm, cowering as if he is about to be hit. She grabs his arm.

— I never touched your daft hat. Right?

— Don't hit me, Stella.

Her voice is shrill.

— I didn't cut it up, you weed.

Graham moves to get in between them, but Stella releases her grip and heads towards the fire door. Ninja-style, she lifts a leg to waist height and kicks the metal bar. The door flies wide open, smashing against the back wall. Flouncing out, she heads for the girls' playground.

Aiden's pathetic voice pipes up.

— Is me mayor's hat cut up, sir?

His words descend into a wail. He falls forward on to the desk, resting his head on his arms, shuddering with sobs and howls.

Miriam stands and looks out of the window in the direction Stella has taken.

— We'll 'ave her at playtime, girls...

Graham cuts her short.

— None of that, Miriam. I'll sort this out. It's bad enough having one bully. I don't want a classful.

Stella comes into view, striding angrily across the playground. She hesitates, folds her arms and stares at the school gates. The whole class are now watching.

Lorraine summarises.

— She's gonna do a runner, sir.

Barry says,

— I think she's ch-changed her m-m-mind, sir. L-l-look at the way she's st-standing. She's fl-fl-flummoxed, sir.

— What's flummoxed, sir? Has Barry made that one up?

— It means she can't make her mind up, Lorraine. OK, back to your seats. I think we'll get on with our reading and Mark, could you do a Stella watch? If she heads towards the school gates, tell me.

Ghazala has her arm around sobbing Aiden.

— Don't worry, Aidey. Sally-Anne and Karl are making a new one.

Mark stands like a cabin boy in the crow's nest, eyeing Stella's movements.

— She's frightened to go home 'cos her new mam will tell her dad, and he'll give her a leathering.

There's a general murmur of agreement. Marlon's not impressed.

— I hope she stays there 'til home time.

Graham decides to deploy Dennis's ignore Stella tactic.

— Let's put on our forget Stella cloaks. Back to silent reading everyone.

Half an hour later, the bell goes for playtime. Stella has moved to a corner of the playground where she can't be seen by passing teachers or children. Mark still has her in his sights.

— She's sitting with her arms around her legs, he reports. Looks well pigged off, sir.

— Now, nobody is to say anything to Stella at playtime until I've sorted this out. Not a word. Did you hear, Miriam?

She purses her lips and reluctantly agrees.

— Yes, sir.

As the class leave, Andrew hangs back. He's still rubbing the back of his bruised head.

— I earwigged what you said to Stella. You've got to be careful, sir. You don't *know* she done it. It just looks like she did.

— What makes you say that, Andrew?

— Me dad reads loads of whodunnits. He's told me all about circumcised evidence, sir.

Graham frowns.

— It's no skin off my nose, sir, but you have to be careful when you's accusing someone.

Andrew walks away. Graham says nothing but realises he may have a point.

***

Graham is walking with Stella towards Taffy's office. She made no fuss when he collected her, and he was surprised how willingly she'd accompanied him. It could be she wants to be as far away as possible from Miriam who'd given her the evil eye in the playground. Graham presses his nose against the headteacher's window. Taffy's busy with a parent and a child: Mrs Darby and her boy Chris. Voices are raised. Mrs Darby smacks the back of Chris's head. He cowers, waiting for more. Taffy booms out.

— Diawl and Cariad, Mrs Darby. No need for that!

Graham ushers Stella down the corridor, out of earshot.

— Stay there. Mr Jenkins is busy. I'm getting my cup of tea. I'll be right back. Don't move an inch.

She crosses her arms, sucks in her cheeks, skews her mouth to one side and looks away. Standing on one leg, a foot pushing the wall, she's unrepentant, defiant. In the staffroom, there's a hubbub of consternation. Miss Broadstairs is holding court. Samantha Greenwood is shocked at what she has heard.

— He didn't! The little bugger.

Miss Broadstairs waves a booklet cut into shreds like jagged paper fingers.

— It was the most valuable programme of my collection. Signed by Sir Malcolm Sargent. I only brought it in to show the choir. I'll swing for him, I bloody will. And he's cut up Betty Topham's Victoria Wine vouchers. She's seething. So angry, in fact, she's going to the Dog and Duck for a Ploughman's.

Syd's at his Churchillian worst. Pouting bottom lip, hunched shoulders and narrow-eyed rage.

— Little bastard needs a damn good thrashing.

He looks over towards Graham.

— 'Course, that's not allowed under this bloody softy Labour council, is it, Trotsky? How can you keep order without discipline?

Graham raises his hand tentatively like a new pupil asking their first question.

— Miss Broadstairs. You said 'he'. Who's 'he'?

— The Darby boy, of course. Chris Winky-Waving Darby. Haven't you heard? He's been wreaking vengeance with a pair of pinking shears. So much for your protecting him.

Graham feels the blood draining from his face. Andrew was right; he'd been relying on circumstantial evidence. He backs away muttering,

— Oh dear, excuse me.

As Graham makes his way back to Stella, Mrs Darby, with Chris in tow, troops past.

— Wait 'til I get you home, you little sod.

— It were a joke, Mam.

— I'll give you joke. Suspended for a week. I'll bloody suspend you.

Ignoring the threat, Chris cheerily greets Graham.

— Hiya, sir.

Stella is biting her lip, shaking her head. She's livid.

— See, it wasn't me, she says, putting a hand over her face. There's a snuffle. She's holding back the tears. Graham moves as if to comfort her, but she swings around and flicks her hand at him.

— Don't you touch me!

He steps away, pressing his hands together as if in prayerful supplication.

— I made a mistake, Stella. I just thought… what with you in the classroom…

She spins around. Her voice is raspy, harsh.

— Yeah, right. Can I go?

— Of course. You've still 10 minutes of playtime.

She strides away, wiping her nose with the back of her hand.

***

Graham stumbles into his bedsit, door key in his mouth, Tesco bag of shopping in one hand and 26 exercise books under his arm.

— Thank God it's Friday.

There's a faint smell of gas mixed with the more pungent whiff of unwashed socks and underwear. They're maturing nicely in the old sewing machine case that doubles up as a laundry basket.

As he dumps the books on the unmade bed, they splay like oversized playing cards. An unwanted hand. He won't bother with them tonight. He wants to forget school. Stella Tupper, falsely accused, queen of the malevolent confetti makers. Not guilty. God Save the Queen and the guillotine machine.

Graham spreads the meagre ingredients of tonight's feast on the dining table: a small tin of Heinz sausages in beans, bread, milk, half a dozen eggs and a packet of butterscotch powdered dessert.

He flips over the calendar revealing Ophelia's seagrass tendrils shimmering on a cornflower blue liquid mattress. Che Guevara has returned to his draught exclusion duties under the sash window. Rain lashes the loose glass panes.

Graham regards his dejected expression in the bevelled mirror hanging above the gas fire. With its pockmarked silvered surface, it distorts enough for him to let his imagination take him far away from today's events. He will Whicker around the World. His party piece. He grabs a black and gold clothes brush, carved in the shape of a Guinness bottle, and holds it like a microphone. With a Whicker-ishly nasal rise and fall in his voice, he introduces the report.

— Welcome to the dismal gloom of Whalley Range's bedsit land. Where food is tinned and a gas meter is a slot machine with only one winner. The landlord. Tonight, a small tin of sausages and beans is lovingly immersed in boiling water, bursting the bubbles of high expectations. For pudding, Butterscotch Whip-Me-Quick Delight, aka Seagull Shite. A chemistry set, shaving cream and vanishing kit in one packet. Leave it for 10 minutes and watch it disappear. All to be washed down with a can of Boddies best bitter. The two course meal for the impoverished bedsit dweller.

There's a light tapping on the door.

— Yowm all right, Graham, me owld duck? Yowm gorra little friend in there?

— No. No, Jenny. I was just...

Graham squeezes his eyes shut as if he's about to have an injection in the bottom.

—... just talking to myself.

— Oh ah. Well, mind yowm don't have an argument and beat yowmself up, me lovely.

She moves away from the door, her laughter dissolving into a wheezing, phlegm shifting rattle.

The dishes on the draining board lean on each other for support. Previous aromas have finished their shift but insist on hanging around. Burned toast and the North Sea gas have clocked on. Graham sighs. Nothing's going right. His fixation with Cheryl has faded, to be replaced by an unrequited passion for Abbi. Only for the realisation of this dream to be checked by Tug's unannounced arrival at a crucial moment in its incubation. And now today's events. The trust carefully nurtured through drama with Stella destroyed by a false accusation. It's time to bury guilt, plaster over events and vanish into a sweet sickly mist of escapism.

Like a dutiful altar boy preparing for mass, he positions the paraphernalia: candle, box of matches, half-inch woodscrew, round glass jar. He rolls up the grey and blue Welsh blanket that covers the bed and presses it up against the gap at the bottom of the door. He moves the Garrard record deck to the centre of the table, lays the headphones in front of it, switches on the lava lamp. He takes the album – Jethro Tull's *Stand Up* – slides it out of its sleeve and makes his track selection. 'Nothing Is Easy'.

Slipping his hand under the mattress, he feels around for a small wooden snuff box, opens it and takes out a nugget of hashish, wrapped in silver paper.

It stands like the statue of liberty, skewered on a brass screw. A spiked crown of dope. He sets it alight and traps the fumes in the glass jar. He slides the headphones on to his head and places the needle in the groove. The flute wails, the bass pumps, the drums gallop. He sucks in the holy smoke. Mass begins.

Father Ian Anderson puts aside the flute and leans over the pulpit to remind him again that Nothing Is Easy. The liturgy.

Holy smoke rises. Graham sucks in the incense. A rush fills his head, the music swells. He watches meandering fumes refill the glass. Taking another hit, he holds his breath, leans back and balances on the back legs of the chair. Eyes still closed, he crashes to the floor.

Whatever was not easy is easier now. The flute warbles. Graham is a giggling bearded tit in a Welsh blanket nest. There's clumping up the stairs. Sing-song Jenny Brummie Wren.

— My God, Graybobs, that was an 'ell of a bang. Yowm sure you aren't got a little friend in there, moi lad?

Graham spits and splutters uncontrollable giggles into the fetid, crumb-covered carpet.

Nothing is easy.

Twenty Five
The Goose Girl

Stella is now a heroine. The class has witnessed her journey to Calvary, carrying the cross of blame. They empathise with her experience. What pupil has not seen or felt the injustice of a teacher's false accusation or mistaken identity? All the class want to be her friend, want to be in her gang. Miriam recognises this. She has Stella as her second lieutenant in the Bay City Rollers Collective. She told her,

— You can have me old Rollers scarf. Les chucked me his, outside the Piccadilly hotel. I had to scrap a girl for it, though.

Like a chihuahua passing an Alsatian, Aiden continues to give Stella a wide berth. Graham sits on the edge of his desk and raises both his hands, the signal for all to listen.

— Before you go to the hall for hymn practice with Miss Broadstairs…

As soon as her name is mentioned, the class pulls a collective Broad Stare.

— Thank you, that will do. Miss Broadstairs can't help… being Miss Broadstairs.

Marlon is indignant.

— Yes, but she doesn't have to drag kids around, waving scissors and threatening to give them the snip, sir.

More Broad Stares, accompanied by scissor-cutting fingers waved above the head.

— Sir, says Andrew, my dad's had the snip. I asked my mum what it means, and she said he doesn't have to spend as much money at the barbers. I don't understand it, but Sally-Anne says she does and she'll tell me on the last day of term.

Aaron rises like the leader of the opposition to make a point.

— Yeah, but at least Miss Broadstairs isn't as bad as Beat 'Em and Thrash 'Em Formby.

Graham corrects him.

— Beat 'Em and Thrash 'Em *Mr* Formby, Aaron. And you understand the word slander, don't you, Andrew?

For a legal judgment, Graham turns, as ever, to Lord Chief Justice Wiseman. His pupillage was at the TV series *Rumpole of the Bailey* and he's delighted to share his expertise. He stands to attention, thumbs and forefingers pinching an imaginary gown.

— It's a tricky area, slander, sir. Take the number of times Miriam has slagged me off. I have to prove me reputation has been damaged and... well, as I haven't got one, Miriam can continue calling me Wiseyman the Weirdo and get away with it. There again, Stella *does* have a reputation and blaming her for summat she had nowt to do with...

Graham cuts him off.

— Thanks, Andrew. I think we'll move on now.

He sits down, beaming contentment like a victorious silk.

— Now, back to this afternoon. Miss Tomkins is coming in to watch me do some drama.

Graham gives an involuntary nervous cough.

— It's part of a course I'm doing.

Aaron's hand shoots up.

— Is it an exam, sir?

Graham's voice wavers.

— Sort of, Aaron. I will be doing an exam later this term. And I'll be needing you to help me.

— We'll help you, sir, says Ghazala. You won't have a problem there. You're ace at drama.

Stella adds,

— You better not blame me if you fail, sir.

Which Andrew appreciates.

— Good point well made, Stella.

Again, Graham moves on quickly.

— We don't usually have the hall at one-thirty this afternoon, but I'm sure Miss Broadstairs won't mind swapping. Sally-Anne, will you remind me to send a note at playtime?

She takes a small red notebook out of her blouse pocket and writes.

Ghazala raises an index finger.

— So Miss Tomkins is going to watch you doing drama with us, is she, sir?

Lorraine turns to her.

— Remember that *Coronation Street* drama, Ghazala? A top lesson that one, sir. Karl burping like a good 'un. Chinti making weapons. Sean falling off the chair drunk…

Graham tries to restore order.

— OK. OK!

Sean's eyes grow big.

— Ooh, Miss Tomkins. She sat next to you on the coach, didn't she? When Wiseyman copped off with Sally-Anne. Is she your girlfriend, sir?

A chorus of *Oooh*s fills the classroom. Graham replies briskly.

— Miss Tomkins is a teacher and a very good one, so show some respect, please.

Graham feels himself blush. Andrew turns to Sean.

— Hey, Sean! Don't be cheeky. Sorry 'bout that, sir.

Rob adds his reassurance.

— You'll pass your exam with us, sir. Especially now Stella gives some gob to the baddies.

Stella swivels around and jabs a finger at Robert.

— Less of the gob, Rob.

He shrinks in his seat.

— Stay cool, Tiger. I was just saying...

Graham averts a kerfuffle by calling time on the proceedings.

— Right. Off to hymn practice, and don't forget to sing up for Miss Broadstairs.

They all rise, a sea of wobbling skittle people. Bumping and rocking, they line up at the door, chanting 'Up, up, up. Up, up, up.'

***

The class are at lunch and Graham, at his desk, bent over his notes, is mugging up on his plan for this afternoon's drama. He's stolen it from a BBC School Radio programme, *Beowulf.* There's a knock on the door and Joan Groom steps in.

— Miss Tomkins to see you, Mr Harris.

Abbi marches in, confident and stylish. Graham realises he is gawping like a first-year spotting the head girl in her glad rags. Joan lingers a little longer than necessary, scrutinising them with an expression she reserves for new parents.

Abbi gives Graham a finger-unfurling wave.

— Hi, Graham. All ready for this afternoon?

Joan leaves with more coals to throw on the staffroom rumour furnace.

Bemused, Abbi watches Joan leave as Graham waves his lesson plan in the air to attract her attention.

— I've pinched an idea from a drama radio programme. Hope it works.

— Go on.

— Beowulf and the monster Grendel.

She lifts her eyebrows and tilts her head.

— What role have you given the children?

— Beowulf's warriors.

— All of them? You haven't split them into opposing factions?

— No. I remembered what you said after the Pied Piper drama.

— Good. And your role?

— Well, first of all, Hrothgar, King of the Geats, then a servant of Beowulf.

— What are you hoping the children will learn?

Graham's floored.

— I'm not sure… but I know they'll be enthusiastic.

— You need to think about it. HMI Waverley will want clear learning objectives. He'll ask you in the viva after the exam.

She collects her bag and heads towards the door.

— I'll wait for you in the hall. Have you a copy of your lesson plan?

— Erm… no, sorry.

— Again, the inspector will expect you to give him a copy before the lesson. Try to remember next time.

She leaves. Any hopes Graham has of rekindling something beyond a mentor/teacher relationship are binned. His thoughts turn to the class and their current mood. Since he falsely accused Stella, levels of cooperation are likely to be in short supply. Success will depend on her attitude and behaviour this afternoon. He's in her hands.

***

Abbi sits with a large notebook at the back of the hall. Graham's done the introductions. He's already dropped his clipboard twice. Stella weighs him up.

— You're nervous, aren't you?

He gives a small nod of the head.

— Is it 'cos she's watching?

Graham remembers what Dorothy Heathcote said in the demo lesson.

— Miss Tomkins is watching me, not you. So you've no need to worry.

— *I* ain't worried. *You* want it to be good, eh? So *you* get top marks.

— It'll be as good as you want to it to be, Stella. I can't make it work on my own. You'll decide whether it works.

She shrugs her shoulders.

— We'll see, sir.

Graham walks to the side of the hall, pauses, then returns in role with regal aloofness. He puts on a purple cardboard crown, lifts his chin then bows his head. His expression is solemn, his voice grave.

— Greetings, brave warriors of Beowulf. My name is King Hrothgar. Welcome to the Castle Herot.

Marlon's not convinced. He looks around the hall, his nose screwed up. Graham continues.

— Your reputation as fearsome warriors precedes you. Word has travelled about your great deeds, your terrifying reputation in battle and your courage. We're in great danger, and it grieves me to tell you that a horrifying creature – a fiend, an ogress – is in our midst. The great warrior Beowulf has promised to help. He is, at this very moment, searching the swamps for…

Graham adopts a half-whispered tone.

—… for the monster, the appalling beast they call…

He stands and pauses briefly before bellowing,

— Grendel's mother!

The door swings open and in strides Miss Broadstairs. She puts her hands on her hips. Her flared white dress is spattered with large pillar-box-red cherries. Or are they splashes of blood? Behind her, the long winding trail of her class. The child at the front, the tallest, struggles under the weight of a teacher's chair. The smallest, at the back, can be seen through the glass wall, clasping the class register. Chinti is wide-eyed and stiff necked. He starts rocking from side to side, doing the Broad Stare routine.

Mark grabs him with both hands.

— Don't! She'll clock you!

Too late. She swoops in like a kestrel that's spotted a field mouse.

— What's your game, little boy?

Chinti, completely ignorant of the rule, 'Never perform the Broad Stare while in her sight-line', has done exactly that. It's the equivalent of selling Caligula's favourite horse to the knacker's yard, then handing him the receipt.

— I'll deal with you after I've had a word with Mr Harris.

Chinti looks at Mark who shrugs his shoulders. Miss Broadstairs screws up her face and speaks to the hall clock.

— *My* PE lesson, I believe, Mr Harris.

Graham glances at Abbi.

— Didn't you get my note?

— What note?

Sally-Anne shoots up her hand.

— Mr Formby took it off me on my way to deliver it. He said he'd make sure Miss Broadstairs got it.

Graham sighs.

— Did he indeed.

He takes a deep breath.

— There seems to be an error, Miss Broadstairs. I wonder if you wouldn't mind swapping…

She interrupts, her tone haughty.

— The school timetable does not alter at the whim and caprice of you and your muddled arrangements.

She then adopts an accusatory spikiness.

— I hope you've not inconvenienced Miss Tomkins by dragging her out here on a fool's errand.

She gives Abbi the stare, then turns back to Graham to deliver the final volley.

— If you make arrangements to use the hall, do so through the *proper* channels, not by a last minute scribbled and misdirected missive. Now, if you and your happy band can vacate the hall, I can bring my class in, and we can get on with some rigorous PE exercises.

There's a small whimper and mewl from members of her platoon. Miss Broadstairs isn't finished.

— Mr Harris, I would like the dark-skinned boy, the one with the National Health specs

to be at my desk tomorrow at morning playtime.

— It'll have to be the two of us, Miss Broadstairs. Unless you can speak Sinhalese?

She narrows her eyes suspiciously.

— Oh, don't bother.

Bending her wrist and pointing to a space alongside a stack of PE mats, she indicates where her throne must be placed. An elevated position from which she can observe her tedious, soul destroying drills.

Graham leads the drama caravan as it winds its way out of the hall like an unwelcome circus evicted from an ill-tempered farmer's field. Abbi doesn't know what to make of it.

— Who was *that?*

— *That* was Miss Broadstairs.

— I see what you're up against. Why don't we start again in your classroom?

— Unfortunately, Agatha Day is using it for the slow readers' group. We could go on the back field.

Abbi's unsure.

— There's no other space?

Graham shakes his head.

— Oh, very well, then. It's not ideal, but it saves cancelling the lesson.

With the lost tribe in tow, they trail around to the back of the school. As they pass Graham's classroom, he can hear Mrs Day shouting,

— Don't yer get it, lad? 'E' and 'e' together make 'ee'… like in 'feet.' Look 'ow big your feet are. Or 'reet', like in, 'You'll 'ave a reet good time at t'party'. The 'ee' sound. Now choose a card. What do you need?

A little voice speaks out.

— Can I have a pee, miss?

— No, you don't need a 'pee', you need a 'ee'.

Sean, a former member of the slow readers' group, explains.

— They're playing Mrs Day's version of Scrabble, sir. She invented it. I always wanted a pee when she brought out that Scrabble game.

The next station on their exodus involves passing the cage that holds Betty Topham's birds of prey, Liz, Richard and the demonic duck, Laurence. Stella leads the class line. Graham's noticed the birds withdraw to their hutch when she approaches. They reach the enclosure.

— Remember, shouts Graham, don't look them in the eye.

The class edge guardedly around the pen except for Stella, who stops at the cage door and rattles the latch. Andrew jumps back.

— Don't, Stell. You'll wind 'em up.

Grinning, she rattles the latch again. The geese hiss and withdraw to their covered shelter, followed by Laurence. Once the class is past the guardians of the playing field, they head towards the far corner, where the school's green railings butt against a sandstone wall. The wall is a metre and a half high and encloses the back gardens of a row of three storey Victorian semis that have been divided into flats. Abbi plonks her chair down near the railings. When she sits on it, it sinks into the damp turf. Graham places his chair opposite her, leaving the class sandwiched between the two of them. He addresses the children while Abbi tries to get her body and chair perpendicular. Graham restarts Beowulf.

— I'll begin just as I did before, as King Hrothgar. Listen carefully as His Majesty talks to you, all those years ago.

A British Airways 747 rumbles overhead on its final approach to Manchester Airport. Graham waits for the noise to fade before rerunning his imperial approach to the throne which, like Abbi's, sits lopsided.

— Welcome, brave warriors of Beowulf. My name is King Hrothgar. I welcome you all to the castle known as Herot.

Marlon looks up at the jumbo and frowns.

— I know of your reputation as brave warriors and servants of the mighty Beowulf. I've heard of your great deeds in battle. I've asked your leader Beowulf to help me. The castle and yourselves are in danger. A frightening creature lurks in our midst. The great Beowulf is, as I speak, searching the swamps for the monster, the terrible beast they call...

Graham leans forward and roars the dramatic crescendo.

— GRENDEL'S MOTHER!

— Who the fuck's Grendel's mother?

A husky voice from behind the sandstone wall shifts attention from the drama, like the arrival of a naked guest at a Mary Whitehouse birthday bash. The remark is followed by a crackle of raucous laughter. A Greek chorus of five lads are looped over the wall that forms the boundary between the back field and house gardens. They're grinning and tap-tapping ciggy ash from their twig-like liquorice paper roll-ups. Graham immediately recognises one of them as Janine's brother, Brian.

Consumed with embarrassment, Janine closes her eyes and places a splayed fingered hand over her face.

Graham stands. His crown is lopsided, covering one eyebrow. The leader of the gang calls once again.

— Hey, Elvis? Still the fuckin' king, eh?

More loose phlegm laughter from the Greek chorus which encourages him.

— Give us a song. You ain't nothing but a dick'ead…

More coughing and wheezing then a looping gob of saliva. Graham's face muscles twitch as he struggles to turn the other cheek. Janine laments, under her breath,

— Oh no. My stupid brother. Me mam will kill him when I tell her.

Abbi sighs. Her eye rolling impatience triggers an outburst from Graham who takes two strides towards the hecklers.

— You boys, instead of spoiling this lesson, why don't you crawl back into the dark cave from whence you came and give the kids who want to learn a chance to do so?

— Who the fuck do you think you're talking to, Elvis?

The leader of the pack climbs over the wall and snorts derisively as he strides towards Graham. This isn't looking good for the teacher. Tug is 60 miles away.

Unannounced, Stella stands up, turns towards the school building and marches away. Graham is caught between chasing after her and dealing with the approaching menace.

— Stella! Where do you think you're going?

She ignores him, striding away, her arms punching the air like a Soviet guard at the gates of the Kremlin. Marlon tugs at Graham's trousers and whispers.

— Sir, that's Tommy Baker. He's suspended for headbutting Lumpy Blake in the big school. Not looking good, sir.

One of the Greek chorus shouts,

— Stick one on him, Tommy, lad.

Flicking his ciggie in a high, smouldering arc towards Graham, Tommy swaggers on. He's tall and broad. His eyes have a let-the-fun-begin sparkle. He stands side on, with his hands raised in a classic martial arts pose. Graham notices a nick through one eyebrow and a safety pin dangling from his right earlobe. His knuckles display the words 'Hate' and 'Love'. They revolve as he moves his hands in a slow, winding movement, signalling he's about to chop, jab or grab his opponent.

— So, Elvis, what was you fuckin' saying about caves?

Janine stands up.

— Tommy, leave sir alone.

He does not shift his gaze from Graham.

— Shut yer mouth, little girl. Me and lads is having a fucking laugh.

Graham tries to sound calm.

— Do you mind not using the 'F' word in front of my class?

— Oh, fuck, sorry. Sorry, boss. Fuck, sorry, kids. Really fucking sorry.

He shifts a tonal gear from sarcastic to threatening.

— You're a knobhead, teach. Like the fuckin' rest of 'em.

Tommy stabs a finger at Graham's face and his head jolts backward. The crown falls to the ground. There is a scream from Ghazala. In the distance Graham sees the low, spread-winged sprint of Laurence the Demented Duck rushing towards them. He is flanked by the geese, Liz and Richard, like two Vulcan bombers in formation with a Spitfire.

Sally-Anne takes charge.

— Shoes off! Lie on your backs!

The whole class pulls their shoes off and roll on their backs, feet in the air. Andrew shouts at Graham, who stands bewildered by what's going on.

— Sir, take your shoes off and lie on your back!

Abbi whips off her shoes and jumps on to her chair. Andrew insists.

— Do it, sir. Do it!

Laurence confronts his quarry: the only shoe-clad human in the vicinity. His demonic quacking accompanies fearsome snapping at Tommy's Achilles heel. Tommy spins and kicks but to no avail. The duck has a profound hatred of shoes and anyone wearing them. Brian and the rest of the Greek chorus flee the stage and vault the wall to safety while Laurence's preoccupation with Tommy gives the class and Graham a chance to scramble to their shoeless feet and scamper to safety.

The angry geese, their necks bending like rapiers, arrive at the scene to peck and hiss at the hapless victim who is scrabbling on all fours, trying to get to the sandstone wall border.

Abbi climbs down from the elevated safety of her chair and backs away from the mayhem, shoes in hand. She checks her escape route. Her pen and notebook lie forlornly on the grass, the analysis of drama abandoned. Instead, they are in the drama of the abandonment. She runs alongside Graham, shouting,

— Not a lot of fiction in this drama, Mr Harris.

When they stop, she puts her hand on his shoulder, catching her breath. She smiles, and Graham feels his stomach lurch at her affectionate touch.

Tommy Baker's frantic retreat generates screams and giggles from the class. Stella holds the pen door open. Her grin is as wide as the Manchester Ship Canal.

Twenty Six
The Trial Begins

It's the day of the RSA exam. From the classroom window, Graham watches as Stella and her new best friend Miriam make erratic progress up the school drive towards the prefab, Stella gesticulating wildly. They stop, they start. Something is amiss. Stella buries her face in the crook of her elbow and leans into a wall like an abandoned yard brush. Miriam loops her arm around her friend, whose hunched shoulders rise and fall with her sobs.

The pair shuffle into the prefab like a nurse and shell-shocked soldier. When Stella spots Graham, she grunts, pulls away and kicks open the door to the toilets before using both hands to slam it behind her. Flakes of dark blue paint and grey plaster flutter from the wall. A protracted, grieving howl issues from inside.

— Miriam, what's going on?

— It's *well* bad, sir.

— Go on.

— You know I call for Stell on me way in? Her new mam opened the door. She looked well mean. She said, 'Stay there, you,' and marched back inside, dead angry like. I thought, "What 'ave I done?"

An anguished cry echoes from within the toilets.

— She's... she's a lying... COW!

Graham asks quietly,

— What was the row about, Miriam?

— Well, you know how she goes on about her 'real' mam?

He nods.

— So, get this, her new mam is shouting,

Miriam turns 90 degrees to act out the scene.

— 'Go and live with her, then, you ungrateful minx.'

She swivels back, taking on the Stella role.

— 'I will then. Get away from you, yer witch.'

Miriam faces her teacher.

— That's when her new mam completely lost it. Big time. She uses the 'F' word, which I'm not allowed to. I'll say 'effin'. Effin's OK, in't it, sir?

— Of course. Go on.

She pivots once more.

— 'See if your effin real mam wants you, because *she don't*, right? Cos she's not yer effin real mam, any road. You was *adopted*. So what d'yer effin say to that? Eh?'

Miriam faces Graham and stares into the distance beyond him. There's a pause. She makes eye contact once more.

— Stell goes dead quiet. Her new mam says, 'That's shut you up, hasn't it?' So, Stell grabs her Rollers scarf and slams the door. Just like what she did just now.

Graham sighs and leans back on the classroom door.

— Oh, God.

He knows that Stella, in this mood, on this day of all days, is a walking grenade with the pin loose. There'll be disruption, sabotage, revenge. He arrests this train of thought and stares at the warped toilet door, listens to the sobs from inside. His concern about the exam is doused with guilt. Here's this kid, he tells himself, her world falling apart and all you're concerned about is your pathetic little exam! Shame on you, Graham Harris.

He looks back to Miriam, who's searching his face for an answer. He shakes his head.

— Poor Stella.

— I know, sir. It were what me mam calls a right 'umdinger.

— Look, Stella needs time out. Don't bother with assembly, Miriam. Stay with her. Take her mind off things. Sharpen the pencils. You can use the electric sharpener if you like.

— Wow! Thanks, sir. I'll sort her out. Like me mam says, a friend in need is a friend indeed.

— You're a star, kidda.

Miriam heads to the toilets. She opens the door; the aroma of stale urine wafts out accompanied by a scream of "BITCH!". Miriam delays entering, her hand on the door handle. She turns to her teacher.

— It's your drama thingy today, in't it, sir? I don't *think* she'll kick off. She likes drama now.

His heart sinking, Graham heads out of the classroom. On his way to the boys' playground, he bumps into Dennis who asks,

— What's all the noise from your toilets?

— Think *Close Encounters…* of the Stella Tupper kind. I'm on my way to seek advice from earth mother Joan.

***

Joan Groom closes the registers, takes the phone off the hook. Graham relates his sorry tale – Stella's crisis at home, the emotional meltdown, his own helplessness.

— Leave it with me, Graham.

She's seen it all before: fights, fall-outs, domestics spilling into the classroom. Joan will know what to do. Blessed are school secretaries, for they are the peacemakers.

***

Taffy has cleared the hall timetable, not because he values drama; no, it's down to the presence of HMI Waverley in his kingdom. Due deference is demanded. Mr Harris's class line up outside the hall. Now inseparable, Sally-Anne and Andrew are at the front. Sally-Anne beckons to Graham. She wants to tell him something and cups her hand to his ear.

— Me and Andy overheard Mr Formby and Miss Broadstairs. Mr Formby is planning something.

— What makes you think that?

— I heard him say, 'It'll go off just after playtime, when he's in the middle of it.' Then he said, 'Don't panic. Ignore it.' I don't know what 'it' is, though. Andy *thinks* he knows.

Graham is sceptical.

— Andy, you know how you're easily alarmed. Can you save your alarming plots for the drama, OK?

Andy's about to share his theory when Graham is distracted by Abbi as she emerges from Taffy's room, laughing. HMI Waverley, dapper in a dark pinstriped suit, is followed by Taffy, who has one hand on the inspector's shoulder and is making expansive gestures with the other. He's in his best, parents' evening poshed-up gear. Abbi, hugging a folder, moves towards Graham. She's wearing a sky-blue trouser suit and a milky opal pendant. Andrew's still talking but Graham can't hear him anymore. He's too distracted.

— I'm going to check it out, sir, says Andrew. Like Dog Detective on that *Look and Read* programme.

Graham ignores him; he needs to talk to Abbi. He gestures to get her attention.

— Can I have a quick word, Miss Tomkins?

— Of course.

— In the hall, if that's OK?

Andrew gives Sally-Anne a big-eyed, knowing nod. Sally-Anne mirrors the gesture.

Inside the hall, Abbi lowers her voice.

— A problem?

— It's Stella. She's had a big row with her stepmother. It's all kicked off. I'm worried she's going to... you know... do a Stella. It just might boil over in the drama.

Abbi sounds impatient.

— Graham, treat this lesson like any other. You've got a good relationship with your class. Particularly Stella.

He should feel reassured but doesn't. Abbi sounds tetchy.

— Look, I'll mention it to HMI Waverley, just so he's aware. He might ask you about how it affected your planning. So be prepared.

Graham returns to the line. The class are gawping at the suave gent in the pinstriped suit.

Andrew whispers to Sally-Anne.

— Looks like that bloke in *The Omen*.

— Gregory Peck?

— Dunno. Hope he's not brought Damien.

Their session of pencil sharpening therapy over, Stella and Miriam join the line. Andrew gives Stella plenty of room as she passes and whispers to Sally-Anne,

— Never mind Damien! We've got Stella. She's already thumped Karl in the goolies. She's deffo on one today.

Stella props herself against the corridor window. She's still wearing her Rollers scarf. A comforter? Her jaw muscles pulsate.

HMI Waverley approaches, running his long fingers through swept back silver hair.

— Mr Harris, dear boy. How are you?

Graham shakes his hand.

— Ah, well, you know.

HMI Waverley scrutinises the crocodile of children and

seeks permission to speak to them but, before Graham has a chance to respond, he's already addressing the troops like a rarely seen general before the big push.

— Children. Headmaster tells me you're vare, vare good at drama, so I've been invited to watch you at work today.

Andrew squeezes the front of his shorts.

— Sir? I need a wee. I'm desperate.

Sally-Anne looks pensive. Graham tells him,

— Quick as you can, Andy.

He spins, shouts, 'Meep Meep!' then skips down the line until he reaches Stella at the end. They exchange words and she ties her Rollers scarf around his waist. He turns on his heels, sprints down the corridor but not towards the boys' toilets. Graham is perplexed. The class enters the hall.

Twenty Seven
The Governor's Child

Graham watches as the children file into the hall and plonk themselves down, wangling their positions like a sack of apples dumped in a water barrel bobbing and bumping against each other. They step into the world of fiction, unconscious of the experiences they bring with them. Like Chinti's desperate escape from armed soldiers burning down his house in Sri Lanka; like Stella's unexplained abandonment; the razor slashes of racism that have scarred Marlon, Ghazala, Khalid and Miriam; Aiden's daily diet of bullying served up by his sadistic father... Where they are now, in a drama lesson in a school hall, does not have the consequences of the real world. They can sew their harsh experiences into the tapestry of the story they create without fear of exposure, humiliation or judgement.

They settle in front of a raised platform on which stands a board and easel. On the board is a simple chalk sketch in white, blue and green showing a valley, snow-capped mountains, hillsides littered with pine trees, a road meandering above a remote village of wooden huts.

Graham sits on the edge of the platform, close to the class.

— Remind me of what we decided about this picture yesterday.

Voices ring out like bids across an auction room.

— It's a lonely village in the mountains. We all live there.

— The road is from the city and goes through the valley.

— We don't go to the city. We don't like it.

— We're country people, sir. Like, farmers and that.

— We work hard. When we get home, we're knackered.

Sally-Anne spins around and glowers.

— You can't say that, Khalid! Sir's got visitors.

Khalid pulls an 'Oh my God' face.

Graham quickly moves the conversation on, introducing the role he'll take.

— Here's the things you need to know. At the beginning of the story, I'm the chief villager, Xie. When I'm Xie, I'll carry this.

He holds up a wooden staff with a goat's horn head.

— You're hard-working villagers. You toil in the fields. Your life is tough and the weather cruel. Snow and rain and hail. In the story, Ghazala is going to be a young woman from the city. We'll meet her later. You'll be able to ask her questions. She's shy, so I want you to be kind to her. Is that OK?

More head nodding, thumbs up and mumblings of 'Yes, sir'.

— Now, I know the beginning of this story, but I don't know how it finishes. *You* will tell me how it ends. I'm going to need your ideas. OK?

This is how it begins. Through swirling, darting snowflakes, villagers draw their shawls about their necks, tighten sackcloth aprons and tug sheepskin hats over their ears. The falling temperature chases the failing light. In the centre of the village is a well, surrounded by a low wall.

Chief villager Xie climbs on to it and raises his hands to quieten the chatter.

— Fellow villagers, come in close. I won't keep you long.

The villagers move closer, rubbing hands, hugging themselves, stamping their feet. Xie continues.

— I know it's cold, and you long to be around a fire, but there's something you need to know. I've just come down from mending the wall on the road from the city. As I was preparing to return, I saw a young girl struggling against the high wind. I called out, asked her where she was going. She said, 'Over the mountains.' I could see she was exhausted and told her she would die if she tried to do that. It's freezing, the wind is strong and there's sure to be a blizzard tonight. When I asked her, she told me her name was Maria.

Xie pauses and draws his hand over his face. He struggles to speak and stares into the well. Gathering his composure, he continues, although sadness is threaded through every word.

— Worse, she was carrying a baby. I couldn't let her continue, so I invited her to stay with my family tonight. She agreed, on condition I bring her a token of trust. Something that would show her I meant no harm.

Miriam makes an offer.

— I'll fetch some warm milk. She'll feel safer with two of us bringing her down.

Then Marlon.

— Take my stick. She mustn't fall.

— Thank you, villagers. You're welcome to meet our guest when we return. Now, to your homes. Get warm.

The crowd breaks up. There are mutterings. Some have no doubt Maria needs shelter. Others voice their dissent.

— We don't know her.

— Best keep your distance. She might be sick.

Karl says,

— Wouldn't 'av her in my hut. No way.

***

Ghazala, in the role of Maria, stands with head bowed. She squeezes the bundle that is her baby, wrapped in a gold-flecked beige shawl. She's barefoot. The class form two lines, an alley of villagers for her to walk down.

Aaron is the first to speak.

— She's tired.

More thoughts are cast before her, like palm leaves in a Bible pageant at Easter. She moves slowly, self-consciously. Avoiding eye contact and with a fearful expression, she walks through the thoughts of the onlookers.

— How sad.

— Poor girl.

Karl shouts wilfully,

— She's a spy!

Sue strokes her back as she passes. Barry stammers his way to his feelings.

— Un-un-ha-ha-happy. W-w-worried.

Rob's deep, rough voice shifts the tone.

— She'll be trouble. We don't want problems with foreigners.

Maria moves the baby to her shoulder. The hall is so quiet you can hear her feet sticky-padding across the wooden floor.

Miriam approaches and rests both hands on Maria's shoulders. They face each other.

— I'll send some straw to your hut, for the cot. And food – some bread, cheese.

Simon slides his hands into his pockets.

— Better put me spends somewhere safe.

Stella turns to the whole class.

— Where's the baby's dad? she snorts. He won't be around, will he? He's done a runner. That's what they all do.

Mark whispers to Chinti who wobbles his head. Aiden takes a breath as if to speak but nothing emerges, save the sound of the embarrassed blowing out of cheeks.

Stella's thoughts turn to Maria. Her voice is softer.

— She's a good mum, looking after her baby, doing her best, right?

Pauline takes Maria's hand, squeezes it and walks alongside her as if they were mother and child. Sally-Anne has moved to the end of the alleyway to meet Maria. She puts an arm around her, addresses the whole class.

— We're all she has.

Karl's aside to Rob is heard by all.

— Wouldn't trust her an inch.

Stella, incensed, takes a step towards him but chief villager Xie won't allow it, stretching his arm to hold her back.

— He makes you feel angry, doesn't he? In our village, all must be allowed to speak. We must see where the story takes us.

Graham comes out of role and sets up the next scene.

— The chief villager's family sit around a small wooden table for a simple meal of bread, mushroom soup and cheese. Maria eats greedily. She wets the lips of the baby with water, then mashes bread with milk, dipping in her little finger for the baby to suck. Bowls of tea are passed around the hut. Villagers drift in, greeting Xie with a nod or a doffed cap or a mumbled salutation.

While the class are lost in the world they've created, Graham remembers Andrew is still missing. He looks across to Sally-Anne and mouths his name. She dips her head towards the hall door. Graham turns to see Andrew slip in. He looks awkward and is no longer wearing Stella's scarf. Graham watches as he squeezes into the group and speaks to Stella in behind the hand whispers, to which Stella responds by clenching her fists, signifying victory, not anger.

Sally-Anne continues to question the young woman.

— What's your name?

— Maria, she whispers.

Karl jumps in, his tone hostile.

— Can't hear her. Tell her to speak up.

Marlon turns on him.

— She's frightened, dumbhead! She said 'Maria'. OK?

Karl waits until he looks away then pulls a face at him, screwing up his nose and shaking his head. Marlon asks,

— And your baby, what's she called?

— It's a boy. Michael.

Marlon reassures Maria.

— I know you're scared. You don't have to be frightened of us.

He gestures towards Karl.

— Don't mind Karl. That's just him. He's a smart arse.

Khalid intervenes.

— No arse, please. If you can't 'ave knackered, you deffo can't have arse.

Maria pulls the shawl tighter. Questions are tossed like kindling on to a fresh fire, each one throwing more light into the room.

— Are you from the city?

— Yes, Xialon.

— What's it like there? We heard it's dangerous.

Maria doesn't answer. She flinches, lowers her eyes. Karl says,

— She's hiding summat. I dunno what, but summat.

Janine kneels in front of her, rests her hands on Maria's lap.

— Are you frightened?

Maria nods rapidly. Rob says,

— Why were you trying to get across the mountains so late at night?

— There's trouble in the city. We're trying to get away.

Rob, to everyone,

— It's all coming out now.

Maria looks at him; her jaw muscles flex. Her tone is sharp.

— There's fighting. It's no place for a baby.

— What fighting?

— Rebels have killed the governor.

Chinti glowers.

— Who fight?

She shakes her head. Chinti turns to Mark.

— She fright of rebel.

Stella rises from her knees to stand over Maria. It's an inquisitive posture.

— Where's Michael's dad? Has he gone off with someone else?

Maria starts rocking the baby and turns to look directly at Stella.

— His dad's dead. Soldiers killed him.

A wave of concern spreads through the class.

— Where was you trying to get to? asks Aaron.

— My sister's. Across the mountains.

Rob reaches out to touch her shawl.

— Shawl's a bit posh, innit? Looks like gold thread.

She says nothing, but Simon does.

— Nice one, Robbo. It's a well smart shawl. All them gold bits in it. She's deffo a spy or summat.

Sally-Anne also looks suspicious.

— The shawl's expensive, Maria. Are you the governor's wife?

— No.

— How come you've got a posh shawl, then?

She says nothing, then shakes her head.

— That's not your baby, is it? says Janine.

Maria hugs the bundle and swallows hard.

— I'm all he has.

Miriam's voice is gentle.

— Do you look after this baby?

Karl interrupts, loudly drowning out Maria's reply.

— She's well worried. You can tell. Look at her. The way she frowns, like. She's acting, making it up.

— Why would she do that? asks Mark incredulously.

Karl expands his theory.

— She's lying to get food, right. There's a tramp what sits outside the bookies on Palatine Road. My dad says he's there to trap them that's won a few bob on the gee-gees. He tries to make 'em feel sorry for him. Then you see him buying booze at Tesco's. I don't trust her.

Sally-Anne disagrees.

— She's too smartly dressed for a tramp, and she hasn't got any bags. Tramps have bags, loads of them.

Miriam agrees.

— She's no tramp. She's in trouble, and we need to help. Let her rest. She's got a long way to travel tomorrow.

Maria lifts her head and smiles at Miriam. She mouths, 'Thank you.'

Twenty Eight
The Chalk Circle

Xie wearily mounts the low wall of the well and addresses the villagers.

Maria and the child are well rested. I've been up to the pass to check if it's possible for them to continue their journey and I'm pleased to say it is. However, upon my return, I saw two soldiers on horseback heading this way from the city. I was seen and one's followed me. We must decide what to do. He'll be here very soon.

Mutterings of 'Told yer', 'Said no good would come of it' and 'Hand her over now' can be heard above the chatter. Miriam's frustration spills out as she pleads for Maria and the baby to be hidden before the soldier arrives.

— They'll take her and the baby.

She looks to Stella for support. She knows her voice carries weight.

— We'll hide her in the barn 'til the soldiers have gone.

Marlon and Miriam lift two benches and place a PE mat over them. They hold the mat up as Maria crawls under it with the baby. As he leaves, Xie urges everyone to return to their huts.

— Everything must look normal. Go about your business. I'll take the horses to the lower field, out of their sight. Otherwise, they may seize them, and we can't afford to lose our horses.

Laid out tidily on a blue plastic chair at the side of the hall are a black beret and a green army jacket. The jacket's sleeve is ripped and one epaulette hangs buttonless. Graham shifts role from village chief to soldier, placing the beret on his head and pulling one side so that it sits at an angle. As he hauls the jacket on, he marches into the village square shouting,

— Who's in charge around here?

In dribs and drabs, unhurried, villagers emerge from their huts.

Stella is blunt,

— What do you want?

— My name is Yen. Sergeant Yen of the Revolutionary Guard. I've come from the city. I'm looking for a girl with a baby.

Miriam and Janine exchange looks. Stella shrugs,

— No one comes here, mate. We keep ourselves to ourselves. You're wasting your time.

The soldier regards her suspiciously.

— There's trouble in the city. For too long we've put up with an evil, cheating governor. He gets rich, yet we have nothing to eat. Those who complain are taken away. Enough is enough. The governor's rule has ended. We've killed him. The glorious revolution has given us back our freedom. Our leader, Kin Yen, and the Revolutionary Guard have seized power. But we won't be truly free until we find the governor's son. We believe his nursemaid has taken him. Her name is Maria. She came this way.

A voice from among the bystanders pipes up.

— Yeah, we've seen her.

All heads turn to Karl. Miriam covers her mouth with her hand. Stella clenches her fists. The soldier approaches Karl.

— Where is she?

Stella takes the soldier by the elbow and moves him away from the crowd. Her voice is low.

— He's winding you up, Sergeant.

Lorraine joins them.

— Yes, we saw the girl, but what Karl didn't say was we sent her away. We were suspicious. She had a gold shawl. Summat wasn't right. We sent her packing. She were dead keen to get across the mountains. She'll not make it. More snow last night.

— I must find them. Dead or alive. My comrade, Han, waits on the pass. We're on horseback. We'll catch them up.

He starts to move away but then stops and turns back to the crowd, pointing a finger at them. There is menace in his voice.

— You'd better not be lying. If we can't find them, we'll be back. Be warned.

The sergeant strides away. Chief Xie returns.

— What happened?

A huddle forms around the chief. Villagers call out, voices overlap.

— That were dead close. Karl nearly blew it, but Stella were clever and led the soldier away from him.

— Lorraine was right cool and got rid of him.

A muffled voice comes from the hiding place under the PE mat. Chinti and Mark rush over to release Maria, who then sits on the ground rocking the baby as the villagers gather round her.

— So you lied to him, Lorraine? says Xie.

— If you're in danger, sometimes you have to lie. To keep safe. Like when we did that 'stranger danger' thing. To keep safe, you need to tell a big porkie. Say your dad's around the corner, even when he isn't.

— Well done.

Sally-Anne issues a reality check.

— He won't find her and he'll be back, y'know.

Chinti waves his hand to get Xie's attention.

— They burn village.

— He's right, says Xie. We're in danger. We're all in it now.

Miriam kneels beside Maria and places an arm across her shoulder. She addresses the class.

— I'm not letting them hurt the baby or this girl. She didn't lie to us. OK, she didn't tell us everything, but she's frightened.

— She's a proper mam, says Stella. She cares for the baby. Even if she's not her real mam.

The words 'her real mam' hangs in the air until Sally-Anne breaks the silence.

— Why don't we dress her as one of us? Put the baby in a cot. They don't know what he looks like, do they?

— You'll have to burn their clothes, says Marlon. Get rid of the evidence, like in Columbo. Especially the gold shawl.

Andrew spots a problem.

— You can't, Marlon. Clothes don't burn good. After we burned me grandad's overalls on our bonfire guy, he found the scraps in the ashes. When he saw his Austin Allegro pocket badge he flipped his lid. Me dad had to take him for a pint just to make up for it.

— He's right, says Karl. The soldiers might see the smoke and think, 'Eh, up? What's goin' on?'

Barry has an idea.

— Bu-bu-but yer ker-ker-could hide the sh-sh-shawl in the war-war-water bucket.

Janine agrees.

— Yeah, in the well. Brill, Bazza. Wrap the shawl and the uniform round summat 'eavy. Dump it in the well.

The villagers quickly move into action. Maria is taken to Sally-Anne's hut, re-emerging dressed as a peasant and carrying the embroidered shawl which she hands to Barry. The governor's child is now swaddled in Lorraine's cardigan. Barry takes off his shoes and folds the gold shawl around one of them, kicking the other under a bench. He knots the corners of the shawl, takes off his belt and loops it round the damning evidence. He calls to Karl and Stella to help him pull the vaulting box to the centre of the hall. They ease off the lid and Barry uses his belt to lower the shawl into the improvised well. There's a commotion as the soldier re-enters the village. Barry freezes.

— You've lied to me! he cries. She *is* here. And I'll search every hut in this village until I find her.

— If you don't believe us, 'ave a butcher's, says Stella defiantly. She's not with us, pal.

Her confident bluster draws admiring looks from the others. Sergeant Yen approaches her.

— You better be right, missy.

He moves from hut to hut lifting blankets, throwing back bedclothes. His voice is abrasive.

— Move that cupboard! Empty those drawers!

The class recognise an angry adult. The bad-tempered parent, teacher, older brother or sister. None more so than little Aiden. Sergeant Yen moves towards the hut where Maria clutches the child, the class bunch around him, trying to slow his progress. He stops, changes direction and enters the hut where Kathy holds her twins. He bends over them, examines each bundle in turn.

— Be warned: if I don't find the boy, I'll be back for those two.

Kathy swivels, turning her back on him. He moves back towards Maria, throwing back sheets, moving furniture, shouting instructions.

— Lift that bed!

He berates their lack of urgency.

— Now!

Only Aiden responds.

— Open the cupboard!

Aiden, expressionless, emotionless, complies. He recognises a dangerous man. Don't disagree. Do what he says. Keep safe. The soldier paces up and down with increasing rancour. Chinti edges his way to the back of the group. Mark follows, staying close to his friend. Is this prodding a buried memory? Is it too emotionally adjacent? Too near the heat? The soldier moves from Maria's hut. He faces Barry who lowers his hands to conceal the evidence. The soldier stares at him then turns back to the others and screams in frustration.

— The child *is here*. You're hiding him!

Barry's grip loosens and he drops the gold shawl. As he tries to recover, he slips and grabs the sides of the well. The soldier turns slowly towards him, his eyes narrowed suspiciously.

— Wind that bucket up.

Barry doesn't move. The soldier screams.

— Do it!

Barry pulls up the garment and places it on the wall of the well. Sergeant Yen throws it to the ground. The class gape as the shawl with gold strands is strewn across the floor.

— So, what's this? he says darkly.

He makes a slow, threatening sweep of their faces and points to the embroidery, the gold strands.

— The governor's family markings. WHERE IS THE CHILD?

Silence.

— So, you won't tell me?

Stella at the front of the dumbfounded crowd spits out her words.

— No, we won't. You'll get nowt from us.

Yen's tone is unexpectedly reasonable, but the words are chilling.

— Then you leave me no choice. I'll bring my comrade down from the road and, one by one, we'll kill every child in this village... until you tell us which is the one they call Michael.

He points at Kathy, still holding her twins.

— We'll begin with them.

Lorraine and Pauline wrap themselves protectively around her and the cardigan twins. From the back of the crowd, a voice pipes up. It's Chinti's.

— You kill children; you kill your brother.

— What do you mean? says the soldier.

Chinti pushes his way through from the back of the class and stands before the soldier, fixing him with his gaze. His small face is marble, expressionless. He pushes the bridge of his wire gold-rimmed glasses.

— Many come from city. Escape war. Your mum, she come here with baby.

Where this is going, no one knows.

— What do you know about my mother? says Yen.

— She want cross mountain.

Another prod of his glasses. Yen's look of arrogance shifts to puzzlement. Chinti continues.

— We find her, on top road. We bring her back. She very ill woman. She ask us to take baby. Keep baby safe.

Sally-Anne moves to stand by him and his story.

— What Chint says is right. I've got your mum's family photograph.

She fumbles in her blouse pocket.

— She gave it to me. It shows you with your mum. Your name is Dys Yen, isn't it?

She pulls out a note, a creased piece of paper. In another world it's the milk numbers. The sergeant grabs the photograph. Sally-Anne points.

— See, here, you with your mum. Taken at your house before the troubles. Turn it over. There, on the back: Dys Yen, Din Yen and Biba Yen.

The soldier looks away, walks to a space. He massages his brow, trying to make sense of what the villagers are saying. Sally-Anne explains.

— We brought her here. She knew she was dying. She asked us to care for her baby, your brother.

Chinti rides on Sally-Anne's embellishment of his idea. His speech is fast, excited.

— She give us baby.

Miriam joins in.

— Look at the picture. Properly! You're there with your mum.

Putting his hand to his mouth, Sergeant Yen asks,

— How did you know it was me?

— It were Chint, says Mark. He never forgets a face. He's got a photo memory. Knows all his tables just by givin' them the once over. It's a gift.

The sergeant turns to Sally-Anne.

— My mother… is dead?

She nods.

— She was tired. The journey, the cold night. We tried to save her. It was no good. Her last wish was for us to promise to keep her baby safe.

Chinti tugs at the soldier's jacket.

— I know you. I know what you do.

Sergeant Yen places both his hands over his face.

— Where's my brother now?

— But you want to kill the children, don't yer? says Stella. Only you don't know which one's your brother?

— If you hurt us… you hurt you, says Chinti.

Stella sneers at Yen dismissively.

— So jog off, soldier, before the rest of your gang arrive and kill yer brother by mistake. Your mam wouldn't thank you for that, would she?

Sergeant Yen turns. He pauses.

— Then I'll go. I'll tell the soldiers the village is clear. You'll see no more of me.

— Go, bad man, go! shouts Chinti.

The class regard him with a mixture of admiration and fascination.

Sergeant Yen walks to the side of the hall, takes off his beret and his jacket. When he returns, he's Mr Harris. The class burst into prolonged cheering and applause. HMI Waverley is blowing his nose. He stuffs his hanky back into his breast pocket and makes a steeple with his fingers. He studies the texture of the wooden floor.

Taffy's at the door. He holds the school hand bell.

— Everything all right, Mr Harris?

HMI Waverley walks over and places a hand on Graham's shoulder.

— More than all right, Mr Jenkins. Very good. What a fantastic class. Mr Harris, you must be proud.

The children gather around Chinti in a warm huddle. Graham claps his hands and addresses the class.

— Well done, all of you. Now, let's tidy up the hall and get back to the classroom before the bell.

Taffy holds up the hand bell.

— Bit of a problem with the school bell so I'm using this. Ten minutes OK?

As the hall is tidied, Ghazala comes up to Graham.

— I've not seen Chinti like that in drama before, sir. He was well top.

Taffy addresses the guests.

— Miss Tomkins and HMI Waverley, I've set aside the school library for you to complete your deliberations. Mrs Groom has put a tray of tea and biscuits in there for you. Mr Harris, show our guests where to go, please.

Graham is watching Andrew chatting with Sally-Anne. She gesticulates and he slaps his hand to his mouth then sprints out of the hall.

Twenty Nine
The Crocodile and the Wildebeest

As Abbi and the inspector gather their belongings, Graham is tempted to ask for some feedback but bites his lip. Exam protocol says 'No'. There's still a 2000 word 'reflective analysis of the lesson' and, until that's done, the examination isn't over. But he's desperate for some indication as to how it went. A look. A nod and a wink. A knowing smile. Anything.

There were positives. Stella didn't kick off. In fact, she was a star. And Chinti's 'Go, bad man' was a moment of real theatre. What a class they are. They've come so far since the *Coronation Street* debacle.

Opening the hall door, Graham invites his examiners to follow him to the peace and quiet of the school library. They walk purposefully down a corridor filled with a soundscape of chanted tables, eruptions of laughter, a shrill rendering of 'The Lord of the Dance'.

— Look, dear boy, says the HMI, I don't think Abbi will mind me congratulating you and your wonderful class on a truly inspiring lesson.

Abbi nods vigorously. Ahead of them, at the far end of the corridor, Andrew is standing on tiptoes on a library display table removing Stella's Bay City Rollers scarf which had been wrapped around the fire alarm bell. From the shadows of the class cloakroom opposite, Syd Formby emerges and grabs the boy. Still hanging on to the scarf, Andrew slides off the table, bringing with him a clatter of books and the yellow tablecloth.

— Gerroff me, sir, he shouts.

— I'll bloody thrash you! says Formby.

Like a baby wildebeest snatched by a crocodile, Andrew hangs onto the scarf as if it were his mother's tail. The stretched scarf unravels from the alarm bell and springs free. The predator drags his prey back into the shadows of the infant cloakroom, Abbi exclaims,

— What the hell's going on?

As one, they break into a run and, as they turn into the cloakroom, they find Syd gripping Andrew by the arm, his right hand raised, ready to strike. Syd turns towards them and freezes. He scowls, red faced, eyes bulging. Andrew scrambles out of his grasp and hides behind Graham, trembling. Syd blusters.

— You're not going to credit it. This little bugger had deliberately wrapped a scarf around the school alarm bell. Can you believe it? I was just about to take him to the head. He tried to get away. I mean, what if there'd been a fire? Might've been lethal.

Andrew pipes up indignantly.

— No, sir! It were Mr Formby! He were gonna set off the alarm. He wanted to ruin our lesson 'cos it were your exam. I 'eard 'im talking to Miss Broadstairs about it. I tried to tell you, sir, but you was busy looking at Miss Tomkins.

Abbi glances at Graham who looks away, embarrassed. Syd moves towards Andrew.

— You liar. You little toad.

Abbi intervenes.

— I'd like to hear what the boy has to say, Mr Waverley.

— So would I, Miss Tomkins. If you don't mind, Mr Formby?

— Ridiculous, mutters Syd.

Andrew stays close to Graham, fixing his gaze on Syd. He adopts his Rumpole at the Crown Court stance and presents the evidence.

— Sir, I told Taff – Mr Jenkins – the bell were broken. He got the hand bell and sent me round classes to tell 'em. That's why I were late for the lesson. Like I say, me and Sally-Anne knew Mr Formby had a plan, 'cos we earwigged 'im telling Miss Broadstairs.

Syd can't help himself.

— The boy's a delinquent. You know his father's been to prison?

— Mr Formby, says the HMI firmly, please return to your class. I can only assume they are at this moment unsupervised.

— They're quite capable of working independently, Inspector. My class is not made up of ne'er-do-wells like this miscreant.

Abbi shakes her head in disgust.

— Who's Miss Creant, sir? inquires Andrew.

The inspector continues,

— You're in enough trouble, Mr Formby. I suggest you contact your union representative sooner rather than later.

— I'm not in a bloody union! says Syd indignantly before backtracking with a hurried 'Scuse my French.

— Whether you choose to be in a union is up to you. However, you might want to look up the phrase 'in loco parentis' and its legal implications.

Syd brushes his lapels with the back of his hand, tugs his shirt cuffs into view and refastens the bottom button of his jacket. Chin raised, he strides down the corridor towards his abandoned class. The inspector turns to Mr Harris.

— My boy, will you relieve Mr Jenkins of supervising your class and tell him I wish to speak to him immediately. Miss Tomkins, please accompany me to Mr Jenkins' office and take notes. It'll be good experience for you.

***

Andrew and his teacher have a chance to talk on their way to the back field.

— What happened, Andrew?

— Like I said. Me and Sally-Anne knew summat were up. We overheard Formby talkin' to Miss Broadstairs. Then you said I get too easily 'alarmed' and it clicked. I knew he were going to set off the school bell to spoil the lesson.

— To spoil the lesson?

— Like he spoiled the kidney assembly. Like he ruined our music lessons. Like he made out that smacking in the ants play were supposed to happen.

They stop at the cloakroom doors that lead out on to the back field. Graham holds the door open for Andrew.

— So, what did you do?

— I wrapped Stella's scarf round the bell. I told Mr Jenkins the bell were broke. It were a fib but it were one of those staying safe fibs. Like in the drama. Mr Jenkins said he'd use the hand bell if there were a fire.

— Why did you rush off at the end of the drama?

—I had to get the scarf back before Formby caught on. But he were waitin' for us. Caught me in the act, like. Then you and your dad turned up and saved me from a belting.

— Andrew, Inspector Waverley is not my dad.

***

Taffy summons Graham to his office at five o'clock. The great and the good have retreated to HQ, Crown Square, Manchester. As Graham passes Taffy's office window, he can see him up his library ladder replacing *The Edwardian Bee Keeper* and its alcoholic contents. Graham knocks.

— Come in and shut the door behind you, lad.

Graham lowers himself on to the comfy settee. It's further down than it looks and his landing is undignified.

— Steady, boy. Anyone'd think you'd visited my sherry store.

He waves the *Edwardian Bee Keeper*.

— Well, Graham, as with most activities you're involved in, there've been highs and lows today.

— All highs, I thought, Mr Jenkins.

Taffy's expression shifts to sombre as he regards his youngest teacher from the top of the library ladder.

— All highs, eh? Well, not from where I'm standing, lad. As headteacher, I have the overview. The big picture, as it were.

Gingerly, he descends to ground level and sits behind his desk.

— The thing is, boy, HMI had some strong words about an unfortunate incident involving Mr Formby. You were present, I understand?

— I certainly was, Mr Jenkins.

— HMI reassured me that, as far as he was concerned, no further action should be taken and I agreed to deal with it internally. To that end, I've spoken to Syd and made it abundantly clear that this kind of thing will not be tolerated in the future.

His tone becomes less formal.

— Thing is, Graham lad, I accept Syd is a bit free with his hands but, as I've said, I've laid it on the line with 'im. There's to be no more of this. And I think he's shocked enough to take it on board. Quite ruffled his feathers. Anyway, I'd appreciate it if you didn't mention what happened to other members of staff. Best kept in house, if you know what I mean.

Graham's dumbfounded. That's it? No further action? Keep it under wraps? He raises his gaze to the ceiling then closes his eyes. Taffy continues,

— Thing is, boy, yes, Syd isn't great with the slower bods. But you know as well as I that he's bloody top notch with the bright ones. He works 'ard and does the kind of things that interests them. Building radios, writing stories, reading classics for children. All that high-falutin stuff. And then, God love 'im, e's top notch with the music. He's got a good working relationship with Miss Broadstairs. And there's not many who can claim that! The choir, for God's sake. Wonderful! As well you know, Union Street is renowned across the city for its music.

Graham can control himself no longer. He springs up, brimming with fury.

— So, that's it? A teacher who smacks kids gets a bit of a ticking off from the head?

Taffy is startled. He pushes back on his desk; his captain's chair slides in quick reverse.

— Don't you raise your voice at me, Mr Harris! Remember your place.

It's too late. All the frustration, anger and humiliation spill out.

— I haven't even mentioned the personal threats, the intimidation, the... BULLYING OF STAFF!

— I know nothing about threats to staff. What are you talking about?

— Well, *I* certainly do. I've been at the sharp end of it.

Taffy's voice shifts up an octave.

—Personal threats? Intimidation? Why haven't you come to see me about any of this?

— Well, your current position re Formby's behaviour may be a big clue. What's the point? He gets away with anything he does.

— That's ludicrous! My understanding is, and I can't reveal my sources, but I understand things have been pretty tense between the two of you for quite some time. Apparently, he calls you Trotsky. Is that right? And you allow your children refer to him as 'Beat 'Em and Thrash 'Em, Formby'. Is that not the case? And your class make derogatory gestures at the mention of Miss Broadstairs' name. Am I right?

Graham cannot deny these things. Taffy is now also on his feet. The two of them stand eyeball to eyeball, sweat, spit and nose drippings hit the polished yellow beech desk, Taffy drops his aitches like marbles from Aiden's holey pockets.

— Your problem is, my boy, you 'ave turned an 'appy and 'armonious school into a Sicilian village of personal vendettas. A nest of vipers, which is not good for the staff or the image of the school, right? It's all about the two of you trying to undermine each other. Pushing each other to move on, resign. Well, I'm not 'avin it, understand? *I* decide who stays and who goes and I'm pretty clear *when* this trouble started.

— Oh. So, it started when *I* arrived.

— If the cap fits, Mr 'arris.

— So, Mr Jenkins, *you* haven't got a problem with a teacher who physically threatens and punishes children? Because I do. You have no problem with a streaming system, based on Miss Broadstairs' homemade tests? Because I do. No problem with classes selected on the basis of who's difficult to manage, who wears the most pristine blouses or has the sharpest creases in his trousers. Start Right Children... Persil White. With the emphasis on the WHITE.

— I think you'd better leave, Mr 'arris.

— D'you know what, Mr Jenkins, so do I. I don't think I fit in this elitist, cardboard cut-out of a prep school. It's good timing, I'll move on just as my class moves to secondary school. We'll bugger off together. Find somewhere with mixed ability teaching, teachers who don't thrash children. Somewhere where the stench of discrimination doesn't fill the staffroom. Where staff with different ideas are not beaten into submission. Away from an institution ruled by a clique. A dry, out-dated, curriculum...

The door to Joan's office is flung open. The school secretary stands frowning, her eyes moving rapidly from one to the other, her arms folded and her coat on.

— Will you two stop this at once! You're behaving like a pair of six-year-olds. No, no: worse! I will not leave this room until you both behave like grown-ups.

Taffy's clock ticks in the silence.

— I'm waiting.

Taffy sits down. His voice is calmer.

— Graham, lad, sit down and listen to me. Let's sort this out like grown-ups.

Graham flops on to the settee. Joan blows out a breath of air before saying,

— Thank you. Now, may I go home in the knowledge that you two will discuss whatever it is you have to discuss like two professional adults?

Taffy pulls a red handkerchief out of his jacket breast pocket, wipes his sweat-beaded brow and blows his nose.

— Go home, Mrs Groom. You're quite right. I do apologise.

— I'll put the kettle on and make a cup of tea, Mr Jenkins. *Then* I'll go home.

She pulls the door to and the awkward silence returns. Graham sits with his head in his hands. He's so angry. He's blown it, of course. Word will get around. That's primary schools. He won't get a new job in Manchester. Still, there's always Oldham, Rochdale, even Stockport. Taffy takes off his bifocals and fogs the lenses before rubbing them clean with his hanky between thumb and forefinger. His voice is weary.

— Do you know when I first came into teaching? Before you were born, lad. The kids couldn't even move out of class until they'd attained 'a standard'. Standard one, standard two. Great lumpen 11-year-olds, hulks of children still in the first standard class with the tiddlers. Humiliating? You can't imagine it. And as for teachers as bullies... they were armed with canes. Vicious. Sadistic. OK, you're right, we've still got the leftovers. But, you know, things have changed. There was 50 in a class, not 30.

He sits back. Contemplates the young, headstrong idealist perched on the settee. Was that him 35 years ago?

— You'd better go. Have a think. Let me know if you intend to resign by the end of the week. I'd like you to stay. But you'll have to work alongside folk like Syd and Miss Broadstairs. You bring fresh ways of working, new ideas. You challenge the old guard. Including me. Especially me! The kids like you but, by God, you'd better come off your high horse. Get realistic. Start to compromise. Change doesn't happen overnight. It's slow, hard and often painful.

Graham stands, grinding his teeth. As he opens the door, Taffy calls after him,

— By the way, in case you think nothing changes, I've agreed with Inspector Waverley about bringing in mixed ability classes next year. We're going to introduce some standardised tests to give a fair distribution of academic achievement. You see, things do change. Close the door behind you, Mr Harris.

Thirty

The Hanging Tree

The children have gone home. Two piles of unmarked books await Graham's attention, but he's not in the mood. He'll head off to the Dog and Duck for a swift half, a bag of pork scratchings and some spiritual guidance from his trusted counsellor, Don Middleton.

What a day it's been, starting off in the depths of Stella's despair, rising to the heights of 4H's dramatic brilliance, then plummeting into bitter disagreement with Taffy and ending with acrimony and resignation. It all got too personal.

Abbi had told him not to get into confrontations, to let the children and his teaching do the talking. The kids did their bit. They demonstrated their ability in the drama exam. They challenged the school's streaming system. Now all that good work had been undone by his row with Taffy. Maybe he should have reported Syd's behaviour to the head earlier. But would it have done any good? Would Taffy have been any less inclined to cover up Syd's crimes?

His mind wanders back to his days at the car factory and a simpler world of work. You clocked on, a car rolled past every one and half minutes, and eight hours later you clocked off.

He digs into his jacket pocket and pulls out his teacher's union diary. As he scribbles a phone number on a scrap of paper, the classroom door bursts open.

Aiden stands breathless, gasping, red-eyed, unblinking. He flops forward at the waist, hands on knees, and drags in a gulp of air.

— Aiden? What's up?

— I were gettin' a mop and bucket for Mr Miggleton. This big man came out of the cloakroom and he grabbed me and he said 'Find Mr Harris and tell him Tug's sorted it'. He made me say it again. 'Tug's sorted it'.

Aiden's face crumples.

— Sir, sir you gotta come quick. Mr Formby's been hung.

— What do you mean *hung*?

— Well, he's not dead. He's... wriggling.

— Where is he?

Aiden is in the grip of unspeakable fear. He emits a long moan, then spins and dashes out of the classroom door. Graham races after him, shouting,

— *WHERE?*

By the time he catches up, Aiden's halfway across the playground, panting as he talks.

— In the cloakroom.

As they reach the double doors of the main building, Aiden stops.

— The big man said don't be frightened. But I am, sir.

Graham squats in front of him and reaches for his hand.

— OK, this is what we'll do. Keep hold of my hand. I'll lead the way; you show me where Mr Formby is.

They edge their way down the corridor, past empty classrooms to the boys' cloakroom. There are muffled noises from behind the glass panelled door. Aiden whispers,

— In there, sir.

He lets go of Graham's hand and backs away.

— Well done, Aidey. Now go find Mr Middleton. Tell him what's happened and where I am.

Aiden's bottom lip starts to tremble.

— Don't worry, little man. Mr Middleton and I will sort it out. Now run as fast as you can.

The lad jumps up and scampers off in the direction of Don's lair. Graham peers through the opaque glass panels of the cloakroom door. He can see a distorted shadow on the other side, crucifix shaped, not moving. Drawing a calm-down breath, he pushes hard at the door. He's expecting to see a dangling body, slowly rotating, a noose around its neck. What he actually sees is Syd Formby hooked by his jacket on to the top row of coat pegs. With his upper arms horizontal and his forearms perpendicular, his hands swing like twin pendulums. His mouth is sealed with gaffer tape. Syd's eyes dart from side to side. There's a note sticking out of the breast pocket of his blazer. Graham snatches it. The handwriting is Tug's.

> *Bomber. As promised, popped up the East Lancs Road to visit Herr Goering. Had a shufty round his pad. Found some S.S. uniforms in the wardrobe and some mucky snaps in a shoebox under his bed. He looked surprised to see me when he got home, so I took him for a jolly in the van to calm him down. Chatted about unacceptable work practices. Demonstrated a few to help him. He agrees it's time he found employment elsewhere. Told him I'd keep the snaps until he got a new job.*
> *Yours Tug.*
> *P.S. Your sound effects tape is in his jacket pocket.*

Graham recovers the C90 cassette and sits in front of Syd, on a bench underneath another row of coat hooks. He folds his arms, puts a finger to his lips and adopts a solemn tone.

— I have to admit that while my friend's methods of dealing with racist bullies are unusual, they do seem to be effective.

Graham waves the cassette tape in front of Syd who gurgles his displeasure.

— Syd, I like to read my class a story at the end of a day. I think finishing off with a story helps them feel good about coming in the next day. They're a captive audience. You're also a captive audience. But, in your case, I want to tell you a story to *stop* you coming in tomorrow. You might recognise some of the characters in this story. First off, there's yours truly, the Cowardly Lion. Then there's you, the Scarecrow. So, let the Cowardly Lion tell the Scarecrow, with no brain, a story.

Syd gurgles once more. Graham leans forward, his hands clasped together, elbows on knees.

— The Cowardly Lion used to work in a car factory and one cold November nightshift, the heating went off. Trying to fit aluminium grills to Vauxhall Vivas with screws and grommets no bigger that your little fingernail became impossible. The workforce was not happy. The Wizard in the Emerald City promised it would be fixed, but an hour later the heating was still off. The Cowardly Lion didn't have the nerve to do anything about it on his own. But when he was standing in the car park with 11,000 workmates, guess what? He found his nerve. He raised his hand and they all downed tools. Very soon the heating went back on and everyone went back to work. Happy ending.

Syd seems perplexed. Graham produces a small red pocket diary.

— In here, there's a phone number. It's a contact number for Cowardly Lions. Those who haven't got the nerve. It puts me in touch with the union's nerve centre. If I only had the nerve, eh? So, tomorrow, at the end of the day, story time again. I'm going to ring my union regional office and tell them a story. A true story. All about you. The scarecrow who hasn't got a brain.

Graham starts to hum 'If I only had the nerve' from the Wizard of Oz. He moves to Syd and catches the corner of the grey gaffer tape covering his mouth. He rips it off his face, singing in his best Bronx accent,

— If I only had the *noive*.

— You're dead, Trotsky.

Graham waves the audio-cassette under Syd's nose.

— Exhibit one, your honour. Child being physically abused by the accused. Oh, plus some interesting photos, your honour. The prisoner dressed up in his favourite uniform.

— Bastard!

Don walks in, hands stuffed in the pouch of his overalls. A glowing pipe of tobacco juts from the corner of his mouth. He takes it out, blows a cloud of smoke and points the mouthpiece at Syd.

— Have you interviewed the prisoner, Bomber?

— No need.

He hands Tug's note to Don who reads it.

— Your chum's a useful lad to know, isn't he? Top job, well done.

— Where's Aiden?

— Don't worry; he's safe. Feeding the school terrapins.

— Thing is, Don, how do you deal with a vicious, abusive, racist colleague? Ignore his threats of violence and report him to the authorities? Knowing the only consequence will be a few strong words from the boss? What's the point?

— You report him, of course. But, like you say, if you're not supported, if you haven't any faith in the powers that be… Remember, 1938? That man waving a sheet of paper? Peace in our time? No, sometimes the only thing that works is to confront them. Is Tug's direct action the most effective way? In my experience, if all else fails, yes.

— I agree but I've decided to take some action myself. I'm bringing in the union.

— Fair enough, Bomber. Good move.

Don turns to face Syd, nodding with satisfaction at his predicament. He moves in nose to nose. His voice is low, his saliva speckling Syd's cheeks.

— Tell you what I'm going to do with you, you Nazi shit. I'm going to hand in a sick note, forged on your behalf. It'll say you're unable to return to school before the end of term. Give you a chance to get your resignation in the post and look for employment elsewhere. Maybe one of those tin-pot private schools you love so much. By the way, don't even think of applying anywhere around here. Word gets around. The caretakers' union is a tight and exclusive club. Right, Bomber, lad. Let's get him down.

They grab Syd under his armpits and haul him off the coat hooks. He stumbles and looks unsteady. Don concludes his instructions to Syd.

— You can call in during the summer holidays to collect your stuff from the classroom. There'll be no children or staff around.

Syd looks at the two of them. Then, under his breath,

— Bastards.

He repositions his jacket, brushes down the sleeves and staggers to the door. Don moves to the window.

— There he goes. The rat!

Graham puts out his hand.

— Thanks, Don.

They shake and Don slaps Graham on the shoulder.

— No, well done you… and your chum!

— Yeah. Tug to the rescue. How about we meet up for a

drink at the Dog and Duck later? About eight?

— Good idea. You can give me the lowdown on this Tug. Sounds like my sort of chap.

He picks up the strips of gaffer tape strewn around the floor.

— Better get back to Aiden. I'm taking him home and I promised we'd call at Mrs Milligan's sweet shop on the way. Think he deserves a treat, the little hero. His dad will have gone to work. Usually have a cuppa with Mum. It all helps keep him safe.

Don hitches up his overalls and leaves. Graham can hear him whistling 'Colonel Bogey' as he marches down the corridor. Graham heads in the opposite direction singing, 'If I only had the nerve'.

Thirty One
The Long Goodbye

The class busy themselves with colouring in, free reading and the close study of comics. An elite task force of Miriam, Sally-Anne, Andrew and Ghazala is engaged in the most prestigious end-of-term activity, extracting the staples from the display board. 'Top job, that one, sir.'

Syd's on the sick following his humiliating experience in the boys' cloakroom. The doctor described it as 'debility' but 'culpability' would have been more accurate. Don's plan to ensure Syd never sets foot in Union Street again has worked.

Graham sits at his desk reading a note from Joan Groom. It's attached to a farewell card.

'Could you sign the attached card (today please!). As you will have heard, Mr Formby will start at Derra Bauke Music School in Surrey in September. Please put your contribution to his farewell present in the tin. Miss Broadstairs has suggested a recording of Richard Strauss's 'Tod und Verklarung' and 'Till Eulenspiegels Lustige Strieche'. (She knows best)

Joan

Graham opens the card and pauses, his pen circling in the air above the 'Good lucks' and 'Best wishes' in a variety of ink colours and nib widths. Finally, he scrawls,

Good luck with your new career.
I am sure the private sector will give you the chance to
do what you do best.
Love Trotsky X

Graham puts an old two-shilling piece he's been trying to get rid of into the tin.

— Ghazala, could you take this card and tin to Mrs Groom, please? Tell her Mr Harris says everyone's signed it so it's ready to be posted.

He reaches for the lined paper that lies on his desk and returns to preparing his speech, 'Farewell my drama guinea pigs'. It's his attempt to compose a humorous and affectionate goodbye message to his class. Something he'll read out loud, to mark the moment of their departure. A fond adieu, au revoir, see yer, sir.

As tomorrow is the last day of the summer term, Sally-Anne is organising a holiday rota for the care of the new guinea pig, Hamlet. She determines that Jordan Mansell, who joins Graham's class next year, will be the one to bring it back on the first day of the new term.

Janine's exemption from the rota was prompted by the unexpected death of her dog, Bullseye, the guinea pig murdering Staffy.

— I don't want nuffink more to do with pets, she said.

On the day the class buried Hilda, Bullseye had choked to death.

— That day were a double blow to me heart: Bullseye *and* Hilda.

The autopsy put it down to a meal of small sharp mammal bones and wax wrapping paper, the kind used for sliced loaves. Graham said nothing but the phrase 'just desserts' crossed his mind.

***

The class is clearing away at the end of the day. Graham's finished their reports and needs to get them to Taffy for his signature.

— You don't need me to remind you that tomorrow is your last day at Union Street Junior School.

There are cheers and, to the tune of One Man Went to Mow, an enthusiastic chorus of:

One more day to go,
One more day of sorrow.
One more day in this old dump
And we'll be free tomorrow.

Graham raises his hands to quieten the singing.

— Quite so. On the fifth of September, you'll be starting at big school.

Graham feels a wave of sadness as he speaks. Miriam rubs her palms together frenetically.

— I'm excited and scared at the same time, sir. All those new people.

Andrew can't resist.

— You've no need, Miriam. Just start singing; nobody will go near you.

Sally-Anne whispers, 'Careful, Andy,' as Miriam twists in her seat to eyeball him.

— Have you ever woken up with a crowd around you, Wiseyman?

— What you on about?

— Just watch my fist.

Graham breaks it up.

— Thank you, Miriam. Thank you, Andrew. Can you two try to get on? For one day?

Miriam sticks her tongue out at her nemesis, then returns her gaze to Graham, her lips pursed, arms folded.

— As I was saying, tomorrow is the last day of term so you may bring in games to play.

More cheers.

— And when I say games, I mean quiet games. Chess, ludo, Monopoly or Scrabble. Colouring books, comics, annuals, that kind of thing. Any questions?

— Sir, can I bring in Buckaroo?

The very opposite of what Graham wanted. Chinti raises his hand.

— What Buckaroo, Mr Hurries?

— Buckaroo is a game designed to give your teacher a heart attack.

Kathy interrupts brightly.

— It's a top game, Chint. You've got this mule, right? You press its tail, then you hook stuff on its back. A saddle or rope or summat. When there's too much, it flips its back legs and chucks all the pieces up in the air...

Graham interrupts, less brightly,

— And all over the classroom!

— So, can we bring in Buckaroo?

Graham leans his head back and closes his eyes. Before he can pronounce on the matter, Marlon interrupts.

— And Operation, sir?

Graham grimaces. It *is* their last day.

— Yes, he sighs, I suppose so.

More cheers.

— OK, now line up at the door for home time.

And, for the penultimate time, Graham sends them streaming out and down the school drive. Running, dawdling, skipping. Each daily ritual now has a poignancy, a reminder that he has to let go.

***

It's two-thirty on the last day of school. Graham has survived the spills and thrills of Buckaroo and Operation. Buckaroo was terminated by Stella when a horseshoe landed in her yoghurt. The battery ran down on Operation, ending the nerve-shredding buzz that signals every failure to remove a funny bone or broken heart.

Aiden is red-eyed after lunch, and Graham calls him up to see what the problem is. The boy stands close to his teacher's chair, so small that he can rest his elbows on Graham's desk, head in his hands.

— Aidey, what's up, mate? Have you been crying?

His little voice squeaks his reply.

— I don't want to go to the big school, sir.

— Aiden, it'll be great. There are art rooms, a gym and a drama studio. Loads of stuff we haven't got here.

Worry ripples his forehead.

— They stick your 'ead down the toilet on the first day.

— Who told you that?

— Karl's bruvver.

Graham is annoyed at the re-emergence of this myth. He addresses the class.

— Can you stop whatever you're doing and listen, please? There's a rumour going around that, on the first day at the big school, you get your head stuck down the toilet...

Karl confirms it.

— Yeah, our kid said that. They won't do it to me.

Stella shouts out.

— Or me.

Aaron pipes up.

— Who's gonna try it with you, Karlo? Your brother's cock of lower school.

Karl fires an index finger at Aaron then transforms it into a thumbs up, accompanied by a smug smile.

This isn't helping Aiden, and Graham's determined to put a stop to it.

— It's a rumour, right? It goes around every year to frighten you.

Stella says, belligerently,

— Don't frighten me.

— Well, it frightens some kids, Stella.

She looks pointedly at Aiden.

— That's 'cos he's a wuss.

— Stella, some kids get upset more easily. Is there anyone else who's a bit nervous about going up to the big school?

Ghazala and Barry raise their hands.

— You wouldn't call Ghazala and Barry wusses, would you, Stella?

— Yeah, I would.

Sally-Anne smacks her forehead in irritation. Marlon turns to Stella, but his volume is set for the class to hear.

— Stell, we have to stick together at the big school, right? That's how we've done stuff this year, isn't it? Like trips out and top dramas, it's 'cos we've stuck together. We got Mr Harris his drama exam, 'cos we stuck together. Sir calls us Team 4H. Right? That's what we've got to do next year at the big school. Watch out for each other, yeah?

Graham sits back, impressed by Marlon's speech. They think collectively... well, most of them. Stella has the last word.

— Yeah, OK. But Aidey's still a wuss.

Aiden returns to his desk. Ghazala reaches out and places her hand on his shoulder, gives him a squeeze, a smile and a cute nose scrunch.

Graham puts the last of the school reports in a buff envelope, leans back in his chair and takes a final scan of the class with whom he has shared a year of his and their lives. Mark is bin-grovelling to rescue the Buckaroo horseshoe from Stella's yoghurt carton. Lorraine is pulling the last of the staples from the pinboards and Ghazala is wiping the revolving blackboard with a damp cloth. All so relaxed, they've become an extended family, close and supportive. Graham's going to miss them. But there are things to look forward to: the summer of love with Abbi, a camping trip to the Gower peninsula and then off to Stratford to see a play starring some bloke called Ian McKellen. Graham is adding the final words to his farewell speech when the door opens and Joan Groom leans in.

— A word with yourself and Stella Tupper, if I might, Mr Harris?

Stella pulls a quizzical face. Graham waits for her to make her way up the aisle between the desks and follows her out. At the end of the corridor stands a tall woman in a bright yellow and green paisley dress. She holds the hand of a little boy who looks about six or seven.

— Mam!

Stella runs towards the woman. She wraps her arms around her waist and buries her head in her bosom.

— She's coming home with me, sir. If that's all right?

Joan begins,

— It's Stella's...

She pauses.

— Her real mummy, Mr Harris.

There is a pyramid of hugging and affection. Two children and their mum. Graham's voice trembles; he's on the point of tears.

— That's wonderful, Stella.

He turns away to hide his emotion. Stella calls after him,

— You can call me Stell, sir.

He looks back. She gives him a stiff, splayed-hand wave and a huge smile.

***

It's five to four. Graham needs to escape Taffy's office and relieve Agatha Day who has reluctantly agreed to keep an eye on 4H.

The boss is in full flow, sharing his thoughts regarding Syd's appointment to a private music academy.

— E's better suited to posh bods, lad.

A picture flashes through Graham's mind of a budding Jacqueline Du Pré walloping Syd with a cello bow. Taffy prattles on.

— Funny how things turn out, boy. There's you, finished your probationary year, letters after your name... What letters are they, by the way?

— RSA Diploma in Drama Education, Mr Jenkins.

Graham glances once more at the clock. He's starting to panic.

— I must make a move. I've got a farewell speech...

— Diploma in drama, eh! Well, there's lovely, bach.

Three minutes to four. Graham holds up his hands.

— Right. I'd better...

— One thing before you go. Now you're a fully-fledged teacher, I've decided to offer you a promotion. Scale two for boys' games! Icing on the cake, eh?

Graham tries not to appear ungrateful as he edges towards the door. He's almost bowing.

— Gosh. Well, yes, I'd love to... perhaps we can talk once I've dismissed my...

He puts his hand in his pocket and fingers his speech. He must get back; it's their final farewell.

Taffy starts to ramble, again.

— When teachers give up their free time for practices and matches, it should be recognised. Finishing bottom of the league is irrelevant. Inclusive, that's our new motto, isn't it?

Graham reaches the door and feels for the handle. He presses it down and edges towards the gap. Mrs Groom's voice booms out from her office.

— Mr Jenkins! A word.

— Better go, lad. She who must be obeyed calls. You're keeping me from my duties.

Graham sprints in the direction of his classroom. Dennis is heading towards him looking as if he wants to speak. Graham shouts,

— Can't stop!

He reaches the prefab and slides into the classroom, skidding to a halt. Agatha Day stands next to his desk. He looks around the room. They've gone! Agatha looks up from rooting in her bag.

— Oh, there you are. I sent 'em home, Graham.

A lump rises in Graham's throat. His disappointment is profound.

— Oh, but I haven't… I was going to give a little…

She isn't listening.

— That Sally-Anne was busy-bodying as usual. Hanging around for you. I told her to get off home.

She slips her handbag over her shoulder and lifts two carrier bags full of fruit and vegetables, Findus Crispy Pancakes and a red tin of Smash with, allegedly, a new, improved recipe.

— 'Ave a good holiday. See you in September.

She sweeps out before he can establish how long it is since the children left. The room is full of their absence. Outside, shrill laughter, shouting, the high-pitched calling of names. The sounds gradually diminish and finally dwindle to nothing.

Graham looks down at his desk. Sally-Anne has swept over it like a whirlwind, her final administrative mission as adjutant to Bomber Harris. She's on the move, a new posting, a comprehensive shift in career. Another battle in the war against chaos calls for her endeavours: she'll have new teachers to manage, more untidiness to order.

A slip of paper juts out of the register with the words 'Mr G Harris' in Sally-Anne's neat, rounded hand, in royal-blue fountain-pen ink.

It's her final set of instructions:

I've locked the fire door and put the key in your top drawer. Right side.

Hamlet's cage has been cleaned out and his 'doings' binned. Miriam has taken him and his cage. His summer holiday rota is:

Miriam (two weeks)

Sean (two weeks, Miriam is camping at Rhyl)

Jordan Mansell (last two weeks of the holiday)

Jordan will bring him in September. He is an experienced guinea pig carer. He looked after Mrs Topham's Pomagne over Easter. (It died but it wasn't his fault.)

Thank you for an unusual year.

Happy dramas.

Sally-Anne

P.S. Don't worry about Aiden at the big school. Me, Stella and Marlon will keep an eye on him for you.

That's it, then. The drama guinea pigs have gone on holiday, but they won't be returning. Graham is shocked to feel a tear slide down his nose. It plops on to Sally-Anne's note. 'Happy' bleeds blue and seeps into 'dramas'. He feels cheated. Scrabbling in his pocket he pulls out a scrunched up piece of paper – his

'Goodbye to Drama Guinea Pigs' speech. He surveys the emp , tables and empty chairs. He'll give it anyway.

— Class 4H, there are a couple of things I'd like to say before you leave the room which has been our home for nearly a year. First, a big thank you from me. We've had great times. Remember Aiden and the first manned flight of a bladder? The Redcoat who gatecrashed our maths lesson and took you to fight the Scots at Culloden Fields? Karl getting drunk in the Rover's Return and Stella releasing Laurence the duck and the geese? Our coach trip to York, where we made Aiden the new mayor of Hamelin? Ghazala when she was Maria with the baby? And brave Chinti, who took on the soldier and told him what he thought? Great moments and great dramas. Thank you for being so patient, especially when I got things wrong. Thank you for helping me pass my exam so I can do it all again next year and get better. And one day, when I'm retired and sitting in the Dog and Duck playing dominoes, you'll come up to me and say, 'Hiya, sir,' and 'I'll buy you a drink' and we'll say 'Cheers!' and 'Here's to all the happy dramas we had together.'

There's silence. No quips from Andrew. No reminders from Sally-Anne. No singing from Miriam. No painful struggle to get the words out of Barry.

The sound of clapping from the open door behind Graham interrupts his reverie. It's Abbi. She beams a warm, understanding smile at him.

He blushes.

— I was just... they'd gone... before I had a chance to...

She lifts her hand to stop him.

— Hey! Their rushing off is the highest compliment they could pay you. Believe me. You've given them the self-confidence to move on. What more fabulous gift than that? You should be relieved. The last thing you want is them hanging on, too frightened to face the future. They'll support each other. That's

.ght them. They're a can-do bunch, and one
ⱼnise the power of collective endeavour.

.e, she's right. Graham's the one hanging on to
ᵤy are released. They won't forget this year and neither
.r Harris. Abbi holds out her hand.

— Well, shall we go and have that celebratory drink? You're
not expecting Tug, are you?

Acknowledgements

I owe everything to my partner Vivien. This book would have never been written without her love and support.

I had the privilege to work with some extraordinary drama tutors during my teaching career. Their theory and practice are embedded in this story. I will be forever grateful to my good friend and higher education colleague, Nigel Toye. His first-class teaching skills, wise words and drama ideas inspired many of the moments in this book. We shared a fantastic drama teacher and mentor, Kathy Joyce, who developed and nurtured our practice. My eternal gratitude goes to Denise Evans, who not only read early drafts of the manuscript but also shared her considerable drama teaching experience as a primary school practitioner in Manchester and as a tutor at the University of Cumbria and Manchester Metropolitan University.

The novel's idea was seeded on Tuesday, the 12th of July 1977. A Redcoat soldier marched across the playground of the first school I taught at in Manchester. This signalled the arrival of the M6 Theatre in Education Team, Nick Maloney, Sue Johnston, Dave Swapp, Mike Kay and Mary Cunningham. Their Programme, 'The Year of the Sheep', changed my life and the way I taught. Thirty-five years later, I sat in the Guardian Offices on York Way, London, for a writing Masterclass under the guidance of Michèle Roberts. She shared her approach to

. fiction and her understanding of drama as a
⸝proach.

⸝up of writers included Marc Lee and Helen Cullen;
.ained their advice and support years after our initial
m͟ ⸝g. Marc brought all his skills to become the best editor
I could have wished for and a trusted friend. Alongside their
incisive feedback came encouragement from Natalie, David C.
Deborah, and David L.

Having found the power and comaraderie of writers' groups,
I dragged Mr Harris around on 'writing improvement' trips
to Villa Pia, Italy, Kendal, County Clare, Eire and any group
of writers that would let me in. At Villa Pia, Steve and Kay
built a wonderful writing haven with advice from extraordinary
tutors, including Blake Morrison and Mark McCrum. The
atmosphere was convivial, and the shared sessions were of the
highest quality. So, thanks to all those fellow toilers in the
vineyard of literary ideas. You made it fun and challenging.

In county Clare, Ireland, Nial Williams and his partner
Christine Breen ran a course of outstanding hospitality, intensity
and writing quality. Nial brought about significant changes
to the manuscript and made the humour more accessible.
Emma Flint, with Samuel, Mary and Clare, were inspirational
colleagues on that adventure.

There comes a time when a writer needs the honest opinions
of the 'well read', and Steve, Gill and Faye of the Holme Park
crew were open and positive in their feedback. Many thanks
to them for their time and support. Gabriel organised a group
of Beta readers to look at issues from an ethnic minority
perspective, and this work was enhanced by Ellie's detailed
critique. So again, thanks to all those readers. Their comments
initiated essential changes to the text.

Throughout the writing and re-writing of Mr Harris,
skilled editors have helped me examine characterisation, the

arc of the story and where to cut. My sincere gratitude must go to Daniel Jefferies, Sarah Steele Janni Howker and my dear friend Joy Wood, for their editorial insight. In addition, Anna Caig raised issues around marketing and presenting the novel to the outside world. As for proofreading, Alison, thank you. Your keen eye and words of encouragement made the process gratifying and informative.

I must mention the Kendal writers who read the in-embryo attempts to get the narrative moving. Initially Capt. John, Gordon and Hannah from the Brewery Arts Centre writers' group, before the emergence of the café-loving splinter group, Dinah, Helen and Avril. We swapped work in progress and poems over coffee and warm scones. What larks!

This acknowledgement would only be complete by mentioning two critical groups of collaborators, school pupils and drama students. From 1994 to 2008, Drama students experienced dramas and tested them out for themselves. Commenting upon them and improving them.

Thanks to the primary school pupils I taught for over 35 years who provided the words, actions and, often bizarre, events that inform this tale. So, to the children of Burnage, Moston, Didsbury and Moss Side, Sunderland, Sandwell – Small Heath, Wednesbury, Tipton and West Bromwich, Blackburn, Morecambe and Lancaster, Ambleside, and not forgetting Kendal, to all those children, for all those ideas, thank you.

I cannot leave this thank you list without mentioning my dearest friend, Ron Johnson. When I asked him to read the manuscript, he remembered every detail of our former 'damp coursing' escapades from the 1970s. In so doing, he added much detail and accuracy to the Rising Damp chapter. I miss him dearly.

Finally, my son Sean and his partner Tessa have listened to my endless misgivings and unease about the novel's progress.

oth for their tolerance, patience, reassurance, persuasion. I love you both dearly, thank you.